Lilith shook in Jarod's arms. .

He looked at her. She was sta
breathing fast and ragged.

"Lilith?" He tried to turn her away from the window but failed. Gently, he ran his hand over her hair, pressed his lips against her throat. "Lilith."

Her lips strained for words, finally produced a raspy sound. "Kill me," she breathed. "Ialdaboth will have you all, through me, if you don't."

"There's a way to save you," he said, "and we both know what that is."

"If I take you now, I'll kill you."

"No, you won't."

Her eyes had widened, desperate and wild. "I will. I need it so much."

"Then take it." Clenching his teeth, he broke the scabs on his wrist and held the wound to her lips. The blood reddened her mouth and her pupils contracted. . . .

She turned away from the window, grabbed him, and sank her teeth into his throat.

Her fangs stung sinking in, tiny scalpels puncturing skin and vein. His hands went up involuntarily, but when he grasped her arms, he couldn't push her away. She was immovable. Her mouth pulled at his throat, drawing mouthful after mouthful of blood. The pain, though, had stopped, leaving behind only the rhythm. It matched his heartbeat. She shifted, and he felt her body against his, her breasts pressing softly against his chest, her hands spread on his back.

Let go, he thought. *That's enough. I can't take anymore.*

I can't, her answer came. *I can't stop.*

He would have called for help if he could, but his voice stopped in his throat behind her penetrating teeth. His heartbeat filled his head, pounding, pounding . . . how long until it stopped?

To Doug

Other Books by Katriena Knights

Vampire Apocalypse Book One: Revelations
Time and Time Again
The Haunting of Rory Campbell

Vampire Apocalypse Book Two: Apotheosis

***

Katriena Knights

ImaJinn
Books

VAMPIRE APOCALYPSE BOOK TWO: APOTHEOSIS
Published by ImaJinn Books, a division of ImaJinn

Copyright ©2003 by Katriena Knights
Printed and bound in the United States of America. All rights reserved. No part of this book may be reproduced in any form or by any means (electronic, mechanical, photocopying, recording, or otherwise) without prior written permission of both the copyright holder and the above publisher of this book, except by a reviewer, who may quote brief passages in a review. For information, address: ImaJinn Books, a division of ImaJinn, P.O. Box 545, Canon City, CO 81215-0545; or call toll free 1-877-625-3592.

ISBN: 1-893896-69-2

10 9 8 7 6 5 4 3 2 1

PUBLISHER'S NOTE:
This book is a work of fiction. Names, characters, places and incidents are products of the author's imagination or are used fictitiously. Any resemblance to actual events or locales or persons, living or dead, is entirely coincidental.

Books are available at quantity discounts when used to promote products or services. For information please write to: Marketing Division, ImaJinn Books, P.O. Box 545 Canon City, CO 81215-0545, or call toll free 1-877-625-3592.

Cover design by Rickey R. Mallory

ImaJinn Books, a division of ImaJinn
P.O. Box 545, Canon City, CO 81215-0545
Toll Free: 1-877-625-3592
http://www.imajinnbooks.com

Prologue

From Lucien's personal journals

To Whom It May Concern:

I leave this document behind in the hopes that no one but myself will ever read it. For if this is found and I am not here, then I am most likely dead, and all has been lost.

Enough with the melodramatics. On with the story.

Let's start with me. I was born twelve thousand years ago, give or take a century, in a cave in the Carpathian Mountains, the offspring of a virgin girl and the demon to whom she was offered in an effort to placate the angry gods. I had three half-brothers, each born to different mothers. We are not vampires, but we birthed that entire race through exchange of blood. May I take this moment to apologize on behalf of the four of us? After all, the gods, unplacated by our births, continued to be angry, and the vampire race has not yet been much of a boon to the planet.

They might be, though, someday. That's where the rest of the story comes in.

Four and a half thousand years ago, I died. More or less. It was the Flood, the big Black Sea flood the Sumerians wrote about. The Hebrews did, too, if I remember right. There was torrential water and mud, and I didn't get out in time.

Neither did my half-brother, Aanu. We drowned and were lost in the mud for a century or two. And we dreamed.

Eventually, we clawed our way out. When we compared notes, we discovered we'd dreamed the same dreams. Or overlapping dreams, something of that nature. In any case, when we started writing them down, they fit together. So we compiled them and gave them a fancy name—*The Book of Changing Blood*.

We weren't sure what they all meant. Prophecies, maybe. But over four thousand years passed before they started coming true.

Okay, here's the part where you need to start paying attention. Because if the unthinkable happens and we have lost and Ialdaboth has won, the only way to salvage anything might be to reconstruct the sequence of events. Otherwise there will be no shoveling us back out of the darkness.

It started with an old Indian shaman—some variety of Sioux, I think, but I'm not sure—and some herbs given to his tribe by an unnamed vampire back in the mists of time. His people safeguarded the herbs until, one day, the vampire Julian washed up on the banks of their favorite fishing river. With the aid of these herbs, Julian abstained from human blood for over two centuries.

Abstaining changed him. He became less sensitive to daylight and able to consume some forms of solid food. His transformation was kicked into high gear when he fed from two other vampires, then from the Senior of the New York City vampire enclave. Normally, this should have killed him—instead it killed them. I never knew the Senior's name. It's not important. He was old. Very old. Old as dirt, even, but not quite as old as me.

The interaction of the different blood within Julian's body changed him yet again. But he needed one more catalyst, which he found in the blood of one Lorelei Fletcher, coincidentally or, actually, probably not— the woman he met and fell ass-over-fangs in love with.

When he took her blood, he became something else. Something no longer a vampire. He no longer fed on blood but on human energy. I do that, as well, but when I take energy, it depletes the person from whom I feed. Julian's feeding amplifies the energy of the fed-upon. It's a strange and rather miraculous process, with implications which have yet to be fully explored.

There's a Dr. Greene here with us, in the enclave, who's experimenting with different blood combinations, isolating catalysts, things like that. He was able to use Julian's blood, combined with blood from another vampire named Nicholas, to cure cancer. That should give you some idea of where all this could be headed.

Much of this, I've discovered, is outlined in the *Book of Changing Blood*, or what remains of it. Because a good deal of it was destroyed by my two brothers, Ialdaboth and Ruha, and their followers, who believe vampires should not change, that we and our Blood-Born progeny are demons and will always be demons, and we should just deal with it. I don't believe that is true. I don't believe the vampire race was created to drag the world into hell. I believe we and our Children have the potential to save the world, or at least part of it.

So some of our work has involved reconstructing the *Book*. And the rest has been figuring out what the hell is going on as the shit hits the fan around us. For instance, Julian got Lorelei pregnant. We have no idea what that's going to mean. Vampires are sterile—but he's not so much a vampire anymore, is he? So we're waiting to see what happens, waiting to see what kind of progeny she produces. Then there are the Children—vampires who were Changed before they reached puberty. Julian has Dr. Greene working on a way to return their mortality. If it works for them, could it work for other vampires?

The biggest obstacle right now, though, is Ialdaboth. He's determined to stop us, and if you find this place in ruins, with my bones decorating the office and slaughtered vampires strewn about in the halls, he's done just that. He tried to finish off Julian, kidnapping Lorelei as bait, but his former minion Lilith got in his way and stopped it. She was dead for about five minutes until Julian got to her. Ialdaboth blasted the living hell out of her, and Julian brought her back to life. Brought her *back to life*. I can't stress that enough. We're not sure where her loyalties lie, but we are sure that Ialdaboth will try again. And if he does, we have to stop him.

Have to. Because if we don't, everything we've found is lost, I am dead, and you are reading this.

Let's just hope to God no one ever reads this.

Julian's Journal

We strive for a world in which there are choices. The choice to be vampire or mortal. The choice to be a child—to live the life that was taken.

Does immortality become a gift I can bestow, without the curse of vampirism? Can I also give mortality to those who desire it?

What is my vision for the community of vampires? Not only those whose enclave I now guide, but all of them, everywhere, throughout the world.

Do we become a force for good, or do we become a catalyst for evil?

My touch, my blood, can perform miracles, can give life where there was none, can restore mortality where there was only the curse of undeath.

What have I become? What has Lorelei become? And what of the child she carries? Children—twins. Will they be human or vampire? Or something else altogether?

Then there is the matter of Ialdaboth. We defeated him once, Lucien and I, but only temporarily. I have doubts about whether we can do it again. We need more. More power, more knowledge.

I should know more than I do. The Senior knew things I do not, but I can't access all his memories. I should be able to, but there are barriers. Perhaps I have to go through all of the Senior's life, his time, his powers, and his loves, to find what I need.

I don't look forward to the process. There are places in there I really don't want to go. So I fill my time with other concerns, gathering what information I can.

Lilith must know something. She was with Ialdaboth's enclave for a long time. Could she be the key? I wonder whenever I visit her, watching her as she lies in her hospital bed, a pale, beautiful thing. She looks as if she is made of white wax, or marble. What knowledge lies behind those quiescent eyes?

Lilith

. . . likewise joy shall be in heaven over one sinner that repenteth, more than over ninety and nine just persons, which need no repentance.

Luke 15:7

It is impossible for those who were once enlightened . . . if they shall fall away, to renew them again into repentance.

Hebrews 6:4-6

If they want to come, let them come. I'm not turning anyone away.

Email—Julian to Lucien

Blessed be the Children of the Dark, for they may return to the Light, and thus be saved.

The Book of Changing Blood

One

Lilith hurt everywhere, deep, pervasive pain that filled every inch of her. She could barely move without it shifting, growing and receding and always moving, as if some bizarre form of life had taken root just beneath her skin.

She supposed she shouldn't complain, though. Not that long ago, she'd been dead.

It was hard to judge the passage of time, but she thought it had been about three days since Julian, Lucien, and Lorelei had brought her here. Her sworn enemies, up until that time. Until Julian had brought her back to life.

Here, in this part of the vampire Underground, there was no real day or night, but the pull of the daytime Sleep still claimed her at appropriate intervals. Here they fed her on harvested blood and kept her carefully alive in spite of the role she'd recently played in Lorelei's kidnapping.

If she'd returned to her own people, she would be dead by now. Instead she'd passed into the realm of the enemy and remained alive.

She blinked at the pale green ceiling of what she supposed could most accurately be called a hospital room. It still amazed her that they were leaving her alone. She could have yanked out her IV and slipped away, feeling her way—somehow—out of the convoluted turnings of the corridors and tunnels of the Underground. But she had no desire to go anywhere. Once or twice Julian had come in and said hello to her, held up his end of a short, inane conversation while his dark eyes had studied her with discomfiting intensity. Lucien had done the same, though he hadn't bothered to talk. He'd just looked at her. She had no doubt that they both could read every thought that meandered through her head. So they knew where she stood. They knew she was, at least for the moment, conflicted enough to be considered safe.

The door to her room squeaked, and she looked up to see Dr. Greene enter. He came every day at about this time to check on her.

He smiled. "Good evening. How are you doing?"

He took her chart from the table by the door and looked at it. She wondered why. He couldn't have that many patients, not here. Surely he could remember what her problems were.

"Like shit," she answered.

He nodded soberly. "I've been running some cultures in the lab. My prediction is that the pain will start to decrease in about twelve hours."

"That's a relief."

He checked her IV drip, where rich, garnet blood had begun to enter her system minutes after she'd returned from the Sleep. "Are you hungry at all?"

"No. Not really."

"It's not quite the same, is it?"

"No. Not quite."

Her system's dissatisfaction with the stale blood was secondary, though, to the consuming pain. Still, the doctor's understanding surprised her. He was a mortal, after all, full of live, pulsing blood. He would have made a damned fine breakfast.

Seemingly unconcerned by his status as possible food item, the doctor checked her IV again, adjusted the timer, looked at the machine that blinked with her vital signs. "You'll be all right."

"Yeah." She doubted that. She'd made some very dangerous enemies by protecting Lorelei and her unborn child. Ialdaboth wanted her dead. Sooner or later, she knew he would get what he wanted.

Dr. Jarod Greene closed the door behind him and leaned on it, gathering his thoughts. Lilith was improving rapidly. No surprise there. Vampires healed with predictable rapidity when given half a chance. That Lilith had been technically dead for a time didn't seem to have affected her recovery rate.

Yes, physically, she was recovering nicely. But he was still concerned about her mental and emotional states. Especially since he knew Julian and Lucien would be all over her with questions as soon as he declared her healthy.

And so went his dilemma as a doctor. The information Julian wanted from Lilith was important, but Jarod didn't want to risk her health. Nor did he want to endanger Julian's plans to move against Ialdaboth's forces. He had to make the right call, and he wasn't sure yet what that was.

In any case, Julian was expecting him—again—right now. These daily meetings were starting to get tedious.

As usual, Julian and Lucien were waiting for him in his office.

Jarod had asked them repeatedly not to touch anything in there—he had a number of projects and experiments underway. Still, as he entered, Lucien snatched his hands away from a shelf and hid them behind his back. Julian gave Lucien a wry look.

"You can talk to her tomorrow," said Jarod. He hoped giving them an answer up front might gain him some privacy.

No such luck.

Julian settled onto the edge of the desk. "What's your opinion of her?"

"My opinion?" Jarod shrugged. "I think she'll be well enough for you to talk to her in twelve hours."

"I mean as a person."

He rarely got any but medical questions from his patients. He liked it that way. It made everything less personal and helped him forget he was the go-to medical guy for a colony of vampires.

"She's not a person," he said, not really thinking. "She's a vampire."

His lack of tact registered when Julian narrowed his eyes, his mouth compressing.

"All right then," Julian said, his tone clipped. "What do you think of her as a *vampire*?"

"I'm not sure what you're getting at."

"He wants to know if you think she can be trusted," Lucien put in.

"Look, guys. I'm a doctor. I'm not a psychiatrist or a counselor or even a very good judge of character. I look at blood cells all day."

"You've spent more time with her than any of the rest of us," Julian countered.

Jarod lifted his hands in a gesture of helplessness. "She's . . . confused. I think she's afraid you might kill her."

"Do you think she would go back to Ialdaboth?"

"I don't know. He doesn't seem like the kind of guy who would forgive and forget, based on what you've told me."

"But she hasn't said anything to you about him?"

"We don't really chat."

Silence fell. Julian and Lucien regarded each other, seeming to pass messages through their eyes.

"I think we can trust her," Lucien finally said.

Julian didn't look happy, but he nodded. "We may have to." He slid off the desk and headed for the door.

"Trust her with what?" Jarod asked.

Julian looked at him, and Jarod saw the age in his eyes, age tempered with long-standing pain. "With the future," he said. "With everything."

With nothing remaining to be said, he and Lucien left.

Jarod tried to settle down to some serious work. He'd been toiling on a project for Julian for the past week, and some aspects of his experimentation were finally coming together.

He'd lived in the vampire Underground for nearly ten years, and he had to admit, he'd never seen the kind of weirdness he'd seen since last Halloween. Julian's blood cells coming back to life, Nicholas's convoluted cancer cure, Lorelei's unprecedented pregnancy, Julian's latest project to save the Children, and now Lilith. Oh, and Lucien, but everything about that guy was weird. Jarod longed for the good old days, when he just sat in his lab inventing blood replacements, like Vivian's plasma drinks.

Which reminded him—he hadn't picked up her empties yet this week.

Looking again at the cultures from the two Children he was working with, he made a few notes, then put his notebooks away. The walk to Vivian's would do him good.

It was a long walk, and a weird one for those not used to it. Vivian's house was technically above ground, but it somehow adjoined the Underground. He was the only mortal he knew of who could make the trip unaccompanied. It had taken him five years to acquire the skill, and he still didn't understand how it worked. The doors and corridors and hallways changed every time, but he somehow always knew the way.

Ten years among vampires could change a man.

He picked up the collection of empty bottles next to Vivian's refrigerator and settled them into the canvas bag he'd crafted for the purpose. The house was quiet with approaching daylight. Time was when he could spend a few hours by himself during the day, before grabbing some sleep. These days Julian and Lucien popped in at any hour of the day or night. Maybe they didn't need sleep, but he did. Luckily, they generally honored the "Do Not Disturb" sign he'd made for his bedroom door.

As he returned to the hospital wing, he thought about Lilith. He wondered exactly what Julian had in mind for her, though he suspected. With her knowledge of the enemy—the Dark Children, Lucien called them—she could be an invaluable asset.

In the lab, he set the bottles in the sanitizer, then went again to Lilith's room. She lay still as a corpse in the daylight Sleep, her straight, white hair spread against the pink pillowcase. Vampires didn't breathe in the Sleep, and she looked eerily dead.

Though he hadn't talked with her a great deal, he'd gotten the impression she was deeply conflicted. As if she couldn't decide which side she should be on and wasn't prepared to make the choice. But she was afraid, as well, and seemed less afraid when he was with her.

He would have to come back an hour or two before sunset to hook up her IV blood drip. No point in letting her wake up hungry. But he didn't have to worry about her until nightfall. In the meantime, he could head off to bed.

Still, he stood, looking at her, at her silent face, like marble statuary. Her features were gracefully put together, the clean lines striking in their frame of platinum hair.

He was, he decided, fairly sure he could trust her.

Leaving her to her recuperative quasi-coma, he turned off the light and headed for his room.

Two

Lilith hadn't believed it possible, but the pain was gone in the morning. Disconcerted, she blinked at the ceiling. For the past three days she'd drifted out of the Sleep on a tide of aching agony—now she was just drifting. She closed her eyes and savored the sensation, smiling. When her breakfast began to flow into her veins from the IV drip, she wriggled and purred like a cat. At the moment, this was a good place to be.

Uneasiness returned, though, when Dr. Greene made his usual stop. Not so much because his presence disturbed her, but because he himself seemed ill at ease.

"Good morning," he said, picking up her chart.

"What's wrong?"

He quirked an eyebrow at her. "Nothing. Why?"

"Something's up."

He flipped a page on the chart, then dropped it back on the cabinet. "I told Julian and Lucien they could talk to you today."

Lilith knew he meant more than just a casual chat or the weird, one-sided sessions she'd already had with them. Cautiously, she sat up, mindful of the needle in her arm. "What do you think they want?" She couldn't help the fear. She'd spent too long in Ialdaboth's enclave, where interrogation meant torture and any questioning of the hierarchy led to dismemberment or death.

"What do *you* think they want?"

Of course she knew. "I'm not sure what to tell them."

He met her gaze directly, his green eyes kind behind round wire-rims. "They're good people." He grinned. "To the extent that they're people at all."

She nodded soberly. "I think you're right."

A few hours later, she sat in Dr. Greene's office, rubbing her arm where the IV needle had been. It itched, the punctured skin and the vein beneath healing rapidly. The doctor had given her a plasma drink, as well. It had tasted strange but had settled her hunger nearly as well as the IV. And there was something satisfying about the feel of warm liquid moving down her throat, even if it wasn't red.

Dr. Greene sat behind his desk, watching her as she sank into the big couch.

"I'll stay if you want me to," he said.

"Yes." The thought relieved her more than it should have. "Yes, please."

He nodded. In his silence, which had an awkward feel to it, she looked around the room. There were several arrangements of blood in test tubes, Petri dishes, measuring devices she didn't recognize.

"What is all this?"

"Various projects having to do with the changes in Julian's blood and what happens when his blood combines with other blood. Like when we healed Dina."

She wasn't sure what he was talking about beyond understanding that there was something strange about Julian.

"My main project right now has to do with the Children," he went on.

"The Children?"

"There are several here. They were treated fairly well under the previous Senior, and Julian has improved things even more. But he wants to find out if we can make them mortal again."

"Really?" Such a thing would never have occurred to her.

"Yes. What was done to them was—and is—wrong, and he wants to try to fix it." The doctor shook his head. "There's a boy here who's been ten for five hundred years. It's just not right."

She'd never thought of it that way before. There were pre-pubescent vampires among Ialdaboth's followers, but not many. Few made it through the rigorous probation and training period he enforced for all his followers. Those who did make it were often slaughtered by adult vampires as soon as they became autonomous hunters. The Children were smaller, weaker, vulnerable.

The door opened and Julian came in, with Lucien behind him. The arrangement puzzled Lilith, as well. Julian was clearly the Senior, but she could tell by looking at him that he was younger than Lucien, less powerful. Lucien, on the other hand, possessed the same aura of power Ialdaboth had. He wielded it differently, though, seemed more comfortable with it. Yet he deferred to Julian.

In her world, the world of the Dark Children, such a situation would not have been possible. Ialdaboth would have slaughtered Julian at the first sign of abnormal power. That Lucien had not done so would seem, according to Ialdaboth's rules, to be a sign of weakness. Lilith wasn't so sure.

They sat in the big chairs that occupied the doctor's office, making themselves comfortable.

"How are you feeling today?" Julian asked.

"Much better, thank you."

"Dr. Greene said he thought you might be up to answering some questions. Are you?"

"I believe so."

"Is there a reason the doctor's still here?" Lucien put in.

"I'm staying," said Dr. Greene. "I'm her doctor, and I need to be on hand in case any kind of situation develops during your interrogation."

Julian laughed. "It's not going to be an interrogation. I left my thumb screws in my other pants."

Lucien went directly to the point. "Lilith, do you want him to stay?"

"Yes." She was prepared to argue if she had to.

"Fine. Then let's get on with it. We need your help."

Lilith nodded. "Go on."

Julian took over. "Before your arrival, we put plans in motion to send a spy into Ialdaboth's territory."

"Bad idea," said Lilith.

"Possibly. But it needed to be done. With you here, we now have another option. If you're willing to tell us everything you can about our enemies, it would be very helpful."

She looked at Dr. Greene, who regarded her steadily from his seat behind the desk. His expression gave her no clue as to what her answer should be.

"What if I don't?" she asked. "What would you do to me?"

"You would be allowed to stay among us," Julian said. The answer surprised her. "No harm would come to you."

"Unless it came from Ialdaboth," Lucien added, "when he takes over the place because you didn't help us." His tone was wry, but not angry.

No doubt about it—these two were crazy. They should have tied her to a pole and beaten her until she told them what they wanted to know. Or better yet—

"Why don't you just read it all out of my mind?"

Lucien smiled. Julian looked sheepish.

"We have, a little," Lucien said, sounding not at all repentant. "We need more, though, and what we need is inaccessible without your cooperation."

Ridiculous. It would be so simple for them to force their way into her mind and take what they wanted. They were weak, unwilling to do what was necessary to defeat the Dark Children. If she set herself up properly in this place, she could kill them all before Ialdaboth arrived, gain his favor through the blood of his enemies, and sit at his right hand when he took over the whole of the vampire world and began the wholesale slaughter and enslavement of humanity. . . .

She closed her eyes, quashing the thoughts. That was the way she'd been trained to think, over two hundred fifty years of initiation, training, brainwashing, whatever you wanted to call it. Her brain, her body, both wanted to follow the old patterns. Only her heart was prepared to change.

Fighting the echoes of Ialdaboth's voice in her head, she slowly opened her eyes.

"I'll do whatever I can for you."

"Good." Julian stood. "Take some time, then. Collect your thoughts. We'll meet again at midnight."

She watched Julian and Lucien leave, still not sure she was right to trust them.

"Are you sure you're okay with this?" Dr. Greene asked.

She jumped—she'd almost forgotten he was there. "Ialdaboth would kill me in a heartbeat. Julian's offering me a second chance. It makes sense."

"Do you think you'll be all right? If you need more recovery time, say the word and I'll be sure you get it."

He was so sincere, Lilith thought. No one had ever been concerned about her well-being. Of course, he was a doctor, so it was his job, but it felt like more than that. More personal. She smiled gently at him, and he smiled back, his green eyes warm.

"Thank you," she said. "I want to do this, though, and as soon as possible." She felt good. Like all her pieces were back where they belonged. "I'll be fine."

He shrugged. "Do you want me with you, then? Just in case? Or for moral support?"

"Yes. Yes, that would be nice."

Jarod wasn't sure what had prompted him to offer to be with Lilith during her questioning. Physically he knew she was fine. Emotionally she seemed to be holding up remarkably well. In short, she didn't need him.

Why had she agreed, then? For the same reason he'd offered? A deep-seated gut feeling, an inexplicable impulse? It was hard to say.

She was nice to talk to, though. He didn't get to spend much time simply talking to anyone. Though their conversations had been far from normal, at least they'd involved some kind of social interaction.

That was it. He was lonely. And she was conflicted. A match made in heaven.

Whatever Jarod's motives, at midnight he was sitting in Julian's office while Julian and Lucien interrogated Lilith.

Perhaps "interrogated" was too strong a word. That was how he'd thought of it, but they merely asked a series of questions, and she answered them as best she could.

"How many are in the main Enclave?"

"I'm not sure. Perhaps five hundred."

Julian's question was asked gently, and Lilith's answer was soft and carefully considered.

"Damn," said Lucien. "Where is the largest colony? Scotland or New Zealand?"

"Those are the same colony. They stay in Scotland in the winter and New Zealand for the summer. Or, actually, the winter again. To take advantage of the long nights. The largest colony is in Eastern Europe. Near the Carpathians."

Julian snorted. "Transylvania."

"In that vicinity, yes."

"Why? Just for the highest possible level of ridiculousness?"

Lilith shook her head. "There's a reason. Ialdaboth says he was born there."

"He was," said Lucien. "So was I. The Mother's Spine Mountains. There's a sacred cave, or there was. The four of us were born there—myself, Ialdaboth, Aanu and Ruha. But I haven't heard from either Aanu or Ruha in several thousand years."

"That's too bad," said Julian. "Didn't you travel with Aanu for a while?"

"We drowned in the Great Flood together. We wrote the *Book* when we came back."

Jarod, watching Lilith, noticed a slight change in her skin color as the shadows under her cheekbones went grayer. Her forehead creased in a frown.

"Lilith, are you all right?" he asked.

She shook her head. "I'm not sure. I remember something . . ." She looked at Lucien. "I think I might know where Aanu is."

Three

Just past dawn, Jarod sat in Lilith's room, making sure her transition to the Sleep went smoothly. There was no reason to worry, he supposed. She appeared to have healed, her vampiric systems functioning normally.

At her request, he hadn't prepared the IV. Instead, he'd laid in a supply of Vivian's drinks for her with strict instructions on when to drink them. He'd have to stop by at dusk to be sure her system had responded properly to the plasma.

She was fine. She wasn't breathing, her skin was waxy and cool, her heart silent. But there was something about her—an aura of sorts he'd learned to sense—that told him she was alive.

Still he lingered, her revelations of a few hours ago running through his head. Eastern Europe. The Carpathian Mountains. An expedition.

He thought about the day Julian had carried her into this room and put her on the bed. Jarod had sat next to her, daubing blood from her face, holding her hand, just as he held it now. He'd felt something that day he'd never felt before, something he wasn't supposed to feel. He wasn't supposed to get attached to his patients.

His thumb made lazy circles on the back of her hand. It was a comfortable sensation. He'd grown used to the feel of vampires, the differences in body temperature and skin texture. The last time he'd shaken hands with a human, the skin had felt too hot. Julian felt strange to him now, with his near-"normal" physiology. This hand, though, Lilith's pale hand with its long fingers and oval nails, felt right.

Finally he let her go and left the room, pausing in the hallway. When he started walking again he went not toward his own room but in the other direction, toward the heart of the Underground.

Julian was in his office, staring at a computer monitor. He sat with such absorbed, preternatural silence that it was hard to remember he was no longer a vampire in the strictest sense. He didn't move until Jarod cleared his throat, at which point he looked up and blinked.

"Dr. Greene," he said.

Fleetingly, Jarod wondered if Julian even knew his first name. Then he realized he wasn't sure what he wanted to tell Julian, or to ask him.

"Can I help you?" Julian said after a moment.

"How's Lorelei?"

Julian shrugged. "Fine, for the most part. Morning sickness is a bitch."

"I can give her something to help with that. She should have come to me before."

"I think she has a hard time thinking of you as an obstetrician."

"One of the downfalls of being a vampire doctor, I guess." Again, a fleeting thought he barely had time to acknowledge—why the sarcasm? Why the vague bitterness? But he barreled on, not prepared to psychoanalyze himself. "I think you're going to need a doctor on this expedition of yours."

"I don't know who could go. We need you here."

"Not so much right now. I can't do much more with Vivian or Nicholas. We found out what we needed to know, but it will be a minimum of fifty years, by my estimation, before the experiments produce a reliable cure for cancer."

"What about the Children?"

"There are issues beyond the physical. Those need to be addressed before we do anything else with them."

"But are you close to being able to help them?"

"Very close."

"Then what about Lorelei?"

"She'd probably be better off—and more comfortable—if she found a more conventional OB/Gyn. It's really not my area of expertise, anyway."

Julian looked at the monitor again, then tapped the Enter key. "So why do you think we'll need a doctor in the lovely and amusing state of Transylvania?"

That was the question, wasn't it? Jarod wasn't sure he had a good answer. "Lilith's been through a great deal of trauma. I'd be uncomfortable sending her off on a journey of this magnitude in her current condition without an attending physician."

Julian nodded soberly. "She doesn't seem to think that's necessary."

"With all due respect, I'm the doctor, not Lilith."

The corner of Julian's mouth twitched. "Any other reasons?"

How about I'd like to get the hell away from this place for a while? How about I'd like to be, just once, somewhere that doesn't reek of vampires?

"If her suspicions regarding Aanu are correct, there's no way to know what condition he'll be in when we find him. You may need my help."

"I'm not going."

Jarod blinked in surprise. "I assumed you were."

"So did I, at first. But I don't want to leave Lorelei alone for that amount of time. It makes more sense to send Lucien, while I hold down the fort."

Jarod nodded. "So I'm talking to the wrong guy?"

"Yes, indeed you are." Julian smiled. "I'll talk to Lucien."

"All right. Thank you."

He returned to his room to sleep, and was awakened six hours later by a knock on the door. Bleary, he looked at the clock. It was almost one p.m. Daylight. He was hungry. The knock sounded again.

"Yeah, whatever!" He fumbled his way out of bed and to the door. Behind it stood Lucien.

"We leave tonight at sunset. Be ready."

It occurred to Jarod, belatedly, that it might not be the wisest thing to be the only mortal among a group of vampires, particularly right after dusk, regardless of what he knew about his personal genetic makeup. Julian had assured him that everyone had eaten, one way or another, but a couple of them still looked hungry to him.

It was a small group. Lucien would lead the expedition, with Lilith navigating. Another vampire, Sasha, had also joined the group. Apparently she spoke fluent Romanian. She looked abominably young. One of the Children, he supposed. He'd spent a good amount of time looking at their blood but not much thinking of them as actual beings, Changed before full maturity. Julian's project to restore them to mortality had seemed ridiculous when he'd proposed it. Now it seemed actually possible. Looking at Sasha's too-young face and ancient eyes, he hoped his hypotheses proved valid.

Then there was William, the last member of their entourage and the least likely, as he really had little to offer the expedition. Julian and the accountant had never gotten along, although Jarod wasn't sure why. Maybe Julian just wanted William out of the way for a while.

Julian briefed them on where they were going and why, how they would get there and how long it would take. Jarod, who knew most of the plan already, paid less attention to Julian and more to Lilith.

She seemed tired, a little too pale. She'd drunk the plasma drinks as he'd instructed, but he wondered if she needed more. He'd have to catch her on the way to the airport, see if there was anything he could do to help.

When Julian finished speaking, she headed for the door, behind Lucien. Jarod started to follow, but Julian caught his shoulder.

"A minute?" Julian said.

"Of course." He turned to face the not-quite-vampire and suddenly noticed the tension around his mouth, the gray hue behind surprisingly human skin. "What's wrong?"

"My head," he said. "I need something for the pain."

The pain must be beyond human comprehension for Julian to ask for painkillers. "Do you know what caused it?"

"I had to access the Senior's memories to set up this trip. I had to sustain the connection for several hours. It always gives me a headache. This time is worse than usual."

Jarod took a moment to process what Julian just said. "You have access to the Senior's memories?"

"Yes. Apparently I absorbed them with his blood when I killed him." He squinted, as if against the light, and Jarod could see a vein bulging in his temple.

"Does William know this?"

Julian shook his head, his lips thinning. "No."

"He should. He thinks you hate him. Hell, everybody thinks you hate him."

"You're right. But I'm not ready to deal with that yet."

Jarod begged to differ. Julian should have addressed the issue a long time ago. William certainly had a right to know that Julian carried the Senior's memories of their century-long relationship. But now wasn't the time to discuss it.

"There's a variety of painkillers in my drug cabinets," he said. "They're all clearly marked. I'd guess you'll need some of the really heavy-duty stuff to even make a dent. But be careful with it—you're not a vampire anymore."

Julian nodded. "Thank you."

"And get topside for Lorelei. Find as many different kinds of ginger as you can. Tea, crystallized, raw, fresh, ginger candy. One of those should help her."

"I'll do that."

"All right. I suppose I should get going."

"They won't leave without you."

He met up with the rest of the group in the hallway, and they went on together. He fell in next to William, but within a matter of a few steps, realized Lilith was pacing him.

"Is Julian all right?" she mumbled. "He looked ill."

"He's fine," Jarod answered, then realized she'd asked out of more than polite curiosity. There was fear in her eyes. "Nothing serious."

She studied his face a moment, as if looking for a lie. "Good."

They left the Underground in a seedy part of town—all the exits were in bad parts of town—to find a stretch limo waiting. The human driver ushered them into it and took their bags. Lilith eyed him closely, and he gave her an uncomfortable smile.

"He's not on the menu," Jarod told her.

"Neither are you, more's the pity." She raked him from head to foot, then flashed a predatory grin as she got into the limo.

Her look caught him off guard.

"Doesn't it make you nervous?" she asked as they settled into the seat. "Having all these vampires around?"

"Sometimes," he admitted.

Sasha cocked a brow at him. "It shouldn't. Your blood reeks."

Jarod nodded. "I've been told that."

Lilith seemed surprised at the comment. "Doesn't smell too far off to me."

"I wouldn't try it if I were you," Sasha cautioned.

Jarod watched the exchange with interest, especially when Lilith turned her attention to him, sizing him up like a box of chocolates.

"Why?" she said. "Would it piss somebody off?"

"Yeah. And it might kill you, too."

Lilith frowned at Jarod. "Is this true?"

Jarod shrugged, amused at her reaction. "Maybe. I haven't quite figured out the chemical reactions yet. I did find a genetic marker, common to the vampires here, that exists in my blood."

"You're serious?"

"I'm a doctor. I'm always serious."

She bent toward him, her nose almost touching his throat. She sniffed delicately, then touched her tongue to his skin, right on top of his pulse.

He wondered fleetingly if she was going to bite him right there in front of the rest of the group. They had become the center of everyone's attention. Strangely, though, he wasn't embarrassed. Nor was he particularly frightened. Instead, he was quickly becoming aroused.

Her tongue trembled there, right against his pulse. It occurred to him that, in all his ten years in the Underground, he'd never been aroused by a vampire. Maybe because none of them liked the smell of his blood. He wondered what her mouth would taste like if he just turned his head and kissed her. His mind conjured a picture of stroking her tongue with his. . . .

"Either eat him or eat him, if you get my meaning," Lucien said laconically.

Delicately, Lilith moved away, and Jarod shifted in his seat, hoping no one looked too closely at the changed contours of his lap.

Lucien went on. "If you eat him, Julian won't be pleased. The doctor has several projects at home that I know Julian's counting on."

Lilith's gaze was still on him. "And if I eat him?"

"None of us really wants to see that." He tapped the glass behind him and gestured to the driver.

"I do," said Sasha.

Jarod gave her a dark look. He almost told her that was no way for a teenager to talk before he remembered she wasn't a teenager. There was no telling how old she really was.

The limo slowed and turned. "Look sharp," Lucien said. "We're almost at the airport."

They debarked near a runway on the outer edges of JFK Airport. Jarod could see the lights of the airport proper some distance away. A hundred or so feet from the car sat the huge, bulk of an SST.

"Since when do vampires own supersonic jets?" he said to Lucien, the question mostly rhetorical. "Besides, I thought they retired the Concorde."

"Retired but not destroyed," Lucien answered. "We don't own it, but when you have to get to Eastern Europe before sunrise, you make things happen."

"No wonder Julian had a headache."

A man approached them across the tarmac, pointing a flashlight in their general direction. "Are you Lucien?"

Lucien stepped forward. "I am."

"I'm Buck." The man put out a hand for Lucien to shake. "I'm the pilot." He looked warily at the vampire's face. "This is everybody?"

"This is it."

Sasha leaned toward Jarod. "*His* blood smells quite tasty."

Jarod turned to see her lecherous smile. So did Lucien. Jarod gave her a tolerant smile, but Lucien looked grim.

"No one touches the human helpers." His voice was cold and brittle. "Anyone who does, answers to me. And I'll ask for your life."

Sasha looked chagrined. "Jeez, it was just a joke."

"Not a funny one."

She was stuck at sixteen, and it showed, Jarod thought. He wondered what she would say if he offered her the possibility of returning to mortality.

Buck looked decidedly uncomfortable. He shook his head. "Damn. I'll never get used to you people."

He led them toward portable stairs that had been pushed against the plane. Lucien followed directly behind him, his imposing presence enough to keep the rest of them in line. Even Jarod felt as if he'd done something wrong, and he had no desire whatsoever to exsanguinate the pilot.

The plane was big, a full-sized Concorde. Jarod headed for the middle rows, choosing a seat near the wing. There was certainly plenty of room. They could sit far enough away from each other that they'd barely be within shouting distance. Which was fine with him. A little isolation sounded good right now.

Seconds later, Lilith plopped down in the seat next to him.

"Do you mind?" she asked.

"That depends. Are you going to lick me again?"

She grinned. "You'd like that, wouldn't you?"

"Not so much." He looked out the window at the distant lights and the empty, black tarmac. "Look, I was planning to grab some sleep."

"You're kidding, right? With all these vampires around?"

"Lucien won't be sleeping. He'll keep an eye out for me. Besides, you heard what Sasha said. They don't like they way I smell."

"I didn't get that. Why?"

"Because, somehow or another, all the vampires here are related to Lucien, and so am I."

Her eyebrows rose. "How could you be related to Lucien?"

"The four First Demons had biological children as well as Blood Children. Their blood carries specific genetic markers. Lucien's and Ialdaboth's are far more common than the other two. Particularly Aanu, as he's been missing—"

"So I'm not part of the family?" she broke in, afraid he might go on in the same didactic way all night—he seemed the type who could.

"That would be my guess. You're more likely related to Ialdaboth, or the fourth First Demon. His name was Ruha, but I don't know if he still uses it."

Lilith looked distant. "Of course he does. Those two liked the demon names."

"As did you, apparently."

She blinked coolly. "Lilith wasn't always a demon. Neither was I."

"You were never a demon," he said gently. "Not like Ialdaboth."

Her face relaxed, and she smiled a little. "You can say that because you didn't know me before."

He shrugged, not sure how to answer.

"You just sleep," she said. "I'll make sure nobody bothers you."

"Not even you?"

"Not even me."

Lilith peered past the sleeping Dr. Greene to look at the sweep of night sky, the wing of the plane silhouetted against it. Then she looked down the aisle, where she could see Lucien's hand dangling off the edge of the armrest.

All the passengers had settled into silence. The pilot, of course, was all locked up in the cockpit. Literally. Anti-terrorist measures worked equally well against vampires.

She looked again at the doctor, still surprised he could sleep so easily. But he was right—his blood smelled strange. She hadn't noticed it at first. But his skin had tasted odd, and now she could sense the vague, tangy odor. She wouldn't want to risk taking a whole meal from him. The effects might very well be deadly—even before Lucien or Julian killed her for doing it.

Still, in spite of the smell and the danger, his blood called her. Not so strongly she couldn't ignore it, but constantly. She wondered why. She hadn't felt it in the Underground. Maybe because she'd been hooked up to the IV, receiving whole blood. The plasma drinks weren't as satisfying.

She was experiencing another new reaction to the doctor, too. He aroused her. Just looking at him lying there, sleeping with his glasses still on, she felt her body responding. She hadn't responded sexually to a human in a very long time. Usually she only wanted their blood.

That urge was harder to resist. Shifting in the seat, she leaned toward him, sniffing the spot under his ear, above his pulse, near where she'd licked him before. It was her favorite place to smell on any potential sex partner. Even vampire males carried a certain, vaguely different odor there that she enjoyed.

The doctor's was particularly nice. Almost sweet, but a masculine sweetness. She touched the spot with her lips. Then, not entirely sure why she did it, she lowered her mouth to his and kissed him.

She knew the moment he woke because his lips opened under hers and one hand rose to cup the back of her neck. He pressed her close, his tongue pushing against hers, his body hardening under her. She answered his sudden passion, enjoying the heat of his mouth, the small pulses there, the taste of him.

Finally, she drew away. "Dr. Greene," she said, "what's your first name?"

"Jarod," he answered. "Why are you kissing me?"

"I'm not at the moment." She looked down at his lap, just to see what had transpired there. He definitely had responded positively to her advances. She reached to trace the line of his arousal, but he grabbed her hand.

"No," he said. "Not here."

"Why not? Haven't you always wanted to join the Mile High Club?"

"Not really." He pushed her back a little, studying her face. "Why is this happening?"

"I don't know."

"Probably a doctor-patient, father-figure rescuer, transference thing."

"I take it you're not a psychologist?"

"No, nor do I play one on TV. But my point is that we need to be careful. I don't want to hurt you, and I don't want you to hurt me, either, particularly since you have sharp, pointy teeth."

"No quick flings in your world?"

"Occasionally. But I'm not sure I'm up for that. Not with you."

"I'm hurt."

"No, you're not."

"You're right. I'm not." She smiled and traced her finger down his nose. "So shall we see what happens? If our . . . mutual attraction . . . wears off in a few days, we'll just pretend it never happened. And if it doesn't . . ."

"If it doesn't, then we'll talk. Or something."

"I vote for the 'something.'" Disappointed, but not angry, she sat up. "When do we land?"

He looked at his watch. "About an hour."

The SST landed in Paris, where they boarded a private jet. The jet was sun-tight, all the windows welded shut and painted black.

"From the Italian enclave," Lucien told Jarod as they took their seats near the front of the plane. "They use it to shuttle to other parts of Europe from time to time."

"Do they have any information on Ialdaboth's enclave?" Jarod asked.

"Enough to know they don't want to get involved at this stage."

His expression gave Jarod no clue as to how he felt about that.

Taking a seat next to him, Lilith said, "Smart decision. They're too close geographically."

Lucien half-turned in his seat across the aisle from them to look at her. "What do you know about the Italian enclave?" he asked.

She looked away. "Only how many of them we've killed over the past three hundred years or so."

Lucien nodded. Jarod looked at his watch. At this time of year, at this latitude, they should reach Bucharest before sunrise, with a comfortable margin. He looked at Lilith, who was rubbing her forehead. "Are you all right?"

"Headache," she said.

He put an arm over her shoulders, and she looked at him in surprise. He gave her a half smile. Watching her rub her forehead, he wondered what she looked like naked. Somehow, even though he was her doctor, he'd managed not to discover the answer to that question.

In Bucharest, the human pilot of the jet escorted them to a house near the airport. Lilith, still fighting a headache, watched as the pilot spoke in Italian to Lucien, who nodded and passed him a handful of Euros.

"We stay here," said Lucien. "It's sun-tight and shielded from the locals."

"Human or vampire locals?" Sasha asked.

"Both," said Lucien.

Jarod laughed. "A vampire safe house."

"Something like that."

Lilith hoped it was true. It was unavoidable, of course, that they would end up far too close to enemy territory, but now that they were actually here the idea made her nervous.

"Will they be able to sense you?" Jarod asked her.

"I don't know." She winced at the sound of her own voice.

Jarod, ever the doctor, looked concerned. "Headache still?"

"More than that."

"Tell me."

"Later."

That Ialdaboth might sense her had occurred to her, of course, and she wondered about the wisdom of their mission. She should have drawn maps for Lucien and Julian and stayed in New York, where she felt at least partially safe. Here she was too close to old memories, old ways of thinking. She could almost hear Ialdaboth breathing behind her. She couldn't exactly sense him, but she couldn't swear that he couldn't sense her. If he could, they might be dead by morning.

"He doesn't know we're here," Lucien announced abruptly, and Lilith realized he'd addressed her.

"Stay out of my head," she snapped, without thinking, then flinched, anticipating punishment.

But Lucien only smiled. "I'm not in your head. You're projecting. You might want to stop."

"How can he not know we're here?" she countered.

"I know things he doesn't. You'd never get him to admit it, but there are things to be learned on the path I chose. If you remain a demon, you close yourself off to a great deal."

"He would say the same about your path. That you closed yourself off."

Lucien nodded. "He would be right. But right now, what I know trumps what he knows."

The others, Lilith noted, had followed the conversation with interest, and William voiced the question she guessed was on everyone's mind. "So we're safe here?"

"Until nightfall tomorrow," said Lucien. "Lilith, William and Sasha, you need to pick out sleeping quarters. Dr. Greene, I saw you sleeping on the first leg of the flight. Are you up to keeping me company?"

The doctor nodded. Lilith looked at him, and he smiled encouragement. Reluctantly, she followed the other two vampires up the stairs, to the second story bedrooms.

There were four rooms, and so no arguments. She sat on the bed in her room and put her head in her hands.

Daylight approached. She still had some time, but not much. And inside her head it seemed a thousand voices battled for her attention. All voices from her past, all demanding her soul. It belonged to them. She had stolen it. Blasphemed, by joining her fate with that of those who had denied their fate, who refused to accept their demonic nature. The Damned Ones. The Children of the Lie.

The voices screamed and whispered, cajoled and demanded. She pressed her fists against her temples and screamed.

Four

"So, was this house supplied by the Italian convocation, too, or—"
Jarod broke off as the scream shredded the air. *Lilith*, he thought,
freezing for a shocked split-second before tearing up the stairs, with
Lucien on his heels.

But when he shoved open Lilith's door, Lucien was already there,
sitting next to her on the bed, holding her wrists as she struggled against
him, clawing the air, clawing toward her face, her eyes.

Jarod stood transfixed, staring. Lilith's screams hadn't stopped,
but tore at him as if her hands and her long nails were slicing into his
belly. Behind him, vaguely, he heard William and Sasha come in to
stand and stare with him.

Lucien was getting nowhere. Lilith fought him with every breath,
howling and spitting into his face. Jarod knew, as surely as he knew his
own blood type, that their mission was teetering on the edge of disaster.

A moment later, with equal certainty, he knew what to do about it.

He crossed the room fast and pressed his wrist hard against Lilith's
mouth.

She bit down, hard, and he went almost to his knees with the pain.
Lucien grabbed him, propping him up. "I hope you know what you're
doing."

"Me, too— Ah, shit—" He clutched Lucien's shirt with his free
hand, twisting the cloth in his fist until, abruptly, the pain disappeared.
Lilith's mouth clutched at him, suckling, and he could feel the blood
draining out of him, as if she were pulling it out of his heart.

"If she takes too much, you're a dead man," Lucien muttered in
his ear.

Suddenly, Lilith let him go, falling back against the pillows, a thread
of blood tracing its way down her cheek. Lucien grasped Jarod's wrist
just below the wound, squeezing hard, but the flow had already become sluggish. Within moments, it stopped, congealing around the twin
wounds.

Jarod wrenched free from Lucien's grasp and turned his attention
to Lilith. She was still breathing too fast, and when he peeled back an

eyelid he saw black, dilated pupils. She slapped at his hand.

"Stop it."

"Are you all right?" he asked, reaching for her other eye.

She looked at him, obligingly showing him the other dilated pupil. Both were gradually contracting to a more normal size. "No. But I'm better. The voices have stopped." Her gaze shifted to his bloodied wrist. "How did you know?"

"I'm a hematologist," he said.

"That's a stupid answer."

"It's the best one I've got."

She shifted on the blankets, slowly, as if her body were too heavy to move. "I'm so tired."

He bent close to her. "Just go." His lips brushed her cheek. "Rest. We'll see you at dusk."

With that, nearly an hour too soon, she shifted into silence, her breath gone, her face still. With his thumb, he wiped blood from her mouth, then straightened.

For a moment, he'd forgotten he wasn't alone with her. But when he turned, it was to face Lucien's far too serious expression, and behind him William's surprise and Sasha's smirk. Jarod's face went hot. Lucien assessed him, then turned to the others.

"Get out of here," he said. They obeyed, heading toward their own rooms. "So what the hell was all that about?" he went on when the others were gone.

"She's been acting weird ever since we got here," he replied. "I think she's too close. They have some kind of hold on her."

"And the blood?"

"Not just any blood. Human blood from your biological line. And I doubt it's a permanent solution."

Lucien waved him toward the door. "That would suck for you. No pun intended."

A half-hour later Jarod sat stretched out on the couch, sipping milk. Whoever had supplied the safe house had known they would need human food. He'd found bread and a package of pastrami, and he'd polished off two sandwiches. His body was starving for protein.

Lucien had watched in silence, apparently not in need of nourishment himself. At first Jarod had found being stared at disconcerting, then realized Lucien wasn't really paying any attention to him. Half the time, he sat with his eyes closed and his head cocked to one side, as if listening. The rest of the time he stared absently into space, and Jarod came to realize that the eyes that occasionally seemed to point in his general direction weren't actually focusing on him. Once he made a face at him, just to see what would happen. Lucien gave no indication he'd noticed.

Yet as soon as he set down the empty glass, Lucien said, "Do you think she'll need blood again in the morning?"

"It wouldn't surprise me."

"So how does it help?"

"My blood's related to yours, somehow, on a genetic level."

Lucien nodded reflectively. "Natural reproduction."

"That would be my guess." Since Lucien and the other First Demons were fertile, they could have left any number of descendants scattered throughout the world. The blood ties wouldn't be as strong as those between blood-made vampires, and the offspring weren't immortal, or even vampires in any sense, but the echoes were still there, even after twelve thousand years of dilution.

"Something like the way Lorelei's genetic marker came to be."

"Yes, but that was some kind of cross-breeding between your blood and either Ialdaboth or Ruha—" He broke off, realizing he was boring himself. "It's not important, though. What's important is that we figure out what to do about Lilith."

"I think we're going to have to get her out of here."

"But you need her."

"I don't know that I'll need her once we find this cave. And I might be as likely to find it as she is." Lucien shook his head. "I'm not sure what to do, frankly."

This admission surprised Jarod. He'd though Lucien had a well-laid plan, with all contingencies considered. Then he realized the proto-vampire was looking directly at him, eyebrows raised in expectation. Jarod blinked. *He* was supposed to come up with a plan?

"Not necessarily a plan," said Lucien. "Just some advice would be good."

"Don't do that," Jarod muttered.

"I'm sorry. I thought you said it out loud."

"No, I didn't." He scrubbed his forehead with both hands. "The information she can supply is vital. But her links to Ialdaboth and the others may endanger our mission. My blood—somehow—reduces that danger by muting the bonds. But I can only spare so much blood."

"Are you prepared to die for the cause?"

"Not really. Besides, if she bleeds me dry, what do you do the next time she goes loopy?"

Lucien nodded. "And we have no lab facilities here to see if there's another way to neutralize whatever's in her blood that ties her to Ialdaboth."

"His blood is what's in her blood. I'd guess she's a first- or second-generation blood-child of his."

Jarod saw Lucien's eyes go distant again, looking straight through him to a point on the back wall. He resisted the urge to turn around to see if he could figure out what Lucien was looking at.

"We need to keep her here as long as we can," Lucien finally said. "I'm not sure where to find the cave, but I think between the two of us we could suss it out. Plus we might need her, if we run into a situation where we need to get by Ialdaboth's guards, or pass through some part of his convocation's sanctuaries."

Jarod shrugged, looking at the bite marks on his wrist. Some bruising had spread around them, but the edges were white and clean. "I'll give her what I can."

Lilith dreamed. Deep in the daytime Sleep, she saw Ialdaboth's face.

What makes you think you can leave us so easily? What makes you think our control over you is gone simply because you ran away?

She was helpless to avoid the echoes of his voice, but somehow she knew he was bluffing, or at least half-bluffing. He couldn't reach her, not quite, not with Lucien close by and Jarod's blood in her veins.

Remember what you were. Remember what I made you.

She didn't want to remember, but she did, anyway, in a sudden flash, a condensed version of her hundred years of initiation, the murders, killings of humans and vampires, senseless and retributive.

If they knew. If they only knew exactly what you are. . . .

The voice, perhaps, was Ialdaboth's. But it might also have been her own.

In spite of his nap on the plane, Jarod drifted off before noon. It was a spotty sleep, though, leaving him aware of Lucien's movement around the room. Lucien didn't sleep, apparently, but he spent a ridiculous amount of time walking in circles.

Just past noon, Jarod bolted awake. His mouth tasted like metal, and some vague dream-shadow twinged at the back of his memory. Whatever it was, it had been nasty. He rarely remembered his dreams, and in this case he was glad.

When he rolled off the couch, Lucien was nowhere in the room, so he headed into the kitchen to look for more pastrami. He was abominably hungry. He wondered if the food and the sleep had been enough to replenish his blood in case Lilith needed it this evening. He needed more meat, some green leafies. Iron, folic acid, B12. Drugs for anemia. Anything. Otherwise she might just kill him, which would not be a good thing.

Footsteps on the stairs announced Lucien's return. Drinking directly from the jug of milk, Jarod met him at the kitchen door.

"Something's up with Lilith," Lucien volunteered, "but I don't know what."

Alarmed, Jarod lowered the milk jug. "Is she all right?"

"She's fine. She's dreaming."

"That's unusual, isn't it?"

"Unusual but not unheard of. I was afraid someone might be tracking her, but the links don't seem that strong."

Not for the first time, Jarod wondered how Lucien could come to such conclusions—exactly what abilities he had that made it possible for him to evaluate a sleeping vampire's dreams. Or read a human hematologist's mind, for that matter.

Lucien was looking through him again, his attention apparently focused on the opposite wall. "We're going tonight," he said. His focus returned to Jarod. "I wanted to give it a couple of nights, to scope things out, but this is just too dangerous. I don't want them tracking Lilith, and I don't want Lilith bleeding you to death. We need you. So we go tonight."

Jarod nodded and finished off the gallon of milk. "Can I get out of here for a while before sundown? I need more food."

Late in the afternoon, fortified by a large meal acquired in the village, he slipped silently into the safe house. Lucien was downstairs on the couch, flat on his back, staring at the ceiling. He didn't seem to be aware of Jarod's presence. Somehow, though, Jarod knew that if he'd been one of Ialdaboth's crew, or anyone else who posed a danger to the occupants of the small house, Lucien would have been up in a flash, killing people.

Unsure whether noise could disturb Lucien's meditation or trance or whatever it was, Jarod tiptoed past him and slipped up the stairs to Lilith's bedroom.

She lay stretched out on her back, exactly as he'd left her at sunrise. He touched her face. The texture and temperature of her skin felt normal. Something trembled in the room, though— one of those odd sensations he occasionally picked up in the presence of vampires. It reminded him strangely of the dreams he'd had earlier in the day.

He sat in a chair next to her bed, absently rubbing his wrist. It had ached dully off and on throughout the day. The thought of her teeth piercing him there again left him with an odd mixture of arousal and revulsion. The wound hurt enough that he didn't want to think about its being opened again, but his body anticipated the intimacy of the process.

Whatever you do, don't let them bleed you, his great-grandfather had told him a few years before he'd died, passing the mantle of vampire doctor to his great-grandson. *You never want to get that close to them.*

Too late. Even before Lilith's arrival, Jared admitted, he'd found he was becoming more attached to the new inhabitants of the Underground than he'd ever been before Julian had arrived. He and the Senior had gotten along well enough, but the Senior had been merely a vampire, plodding along, holding his small enclave together and trying in various ways to live a mostly moral life. The whole system had been imperfect, and to Jarod it had seemed stagnant, as if it were a clock wound centuries before, now slowly running down.

But Julian had wound the clock spring tight, bringing fresh possibilities and hope to the New York enclave. To every vampire on earth, in fact, if they were willing to accept what Julian had to offer. The possibility of returning to mortality or of entering a different, non-destructive form of immortality. Even of bringing others that same gift. It was all there, Jarod thought, or at least the seeds of it, in his laboratory. There was no guessing what the next few years of experimentation might uncover.

Great-grandpa Greene could never have imagined what his great-grandson would fall into by carrying on the family legacy. Jarod's mouth twisted in a wry smile. He'd certainly had no inkling when he took over. He still wasn't sure he had a clear picture of what the next several months were likely to bring.

On the bed, Lilith stirred. Jarod straightened in the chair, watching her face. If she woke needing him, he wanted to be ready. He only hoped Lucien was paying enough attention, in case she needed too much blood and he needed Lucien's help controlling her.

She moved restlessly for a few minutes, her eyes moving under her lids as if she were in dream sleep. In the back of her throat, her voice made small sounds of distress. Then, abruptly, she opened her eyes and stared at him.

Her expression remained blank for several minutes. Disconcerted, Jarod nevertheless stayed still within her blinkless stare. Finally she moved her head, barely, and closed her eyes. When she opened them again she was obviously awake and aware.

"What are you doing here?" she said, sitting up.

He held out a bottle of plasma drink. "Breakfast?"

She smiled wanly and took the bottle. "I hate this stuff."

"Everybody says that."

"You could at least make it blood-flavored." She screwed off the lid and sipped at it, making a delicate face.

"I tried that. It seemed to trigger hunger in the vampires who tried it, so instead of satisfying them, it sent them out onto the streets in a rampage."

She took a deeper drink. "That could be a problem."

"Yes."

Silence fell as she finished the bottle, drinking slowly at first, then chugging the last half. When it was empty, she set it on the nightstand and reached toward him, wiggling her fingers. "More."

He handed her another bottle, which she chugged, then a third. When that one was gone she wiped her mouth with the back of her hand. "It tastes better after the first one."

Nodding, he took the empty bottle from her and set it next to the others. "How do you feel?"

"All right."

"You don't feel . . . him?"

"Not so much at the moment." She pushed a hand through her hair, straightening the long, platinum tresses. "I had bad dreams, though."

"I know."

She gave him a puzzled frown, then nodded. "Lucien."

"Yes, but I think I might have overheard some of them, too. While I was asleep."

"That's bizarre."

"Yes, it is."

"Do you think the blood bonded us?"

He shrugged. "Probably." He rose from the chair and sat next to her on the bed, touching her face, turning it so he could look into her eyes. Her pupils looked a little too wide, but maybe that was his imagination. "Lucien wants to go to the cave tonight. Do you feel up to it?"

"I don't know. The closer we get—" She broke off and looked away. A shadow of pain passed over her face.

He clenched his teeth against a stab of pain through his wrist. "We'll deal with that when the time comes."

"I don't want to hurt you."

"We'll figure out something." He stood, holding a hand out to her. "Come on. Let's go see what Lucien's up to."

She smiled and took his hand, sliding off the bed. "He's probably in some kind of a telepathic trance, arranging transportation."

"It wouldn't surprise me."

Lucien was arranging transportation, but apparently the telepathic trance option was out for the evening, because he was talking on a cell phone.

"A helicopter would be best. Yes, not too far from Bacâu. As soon as possible." He caught sight of Jarod and Lilith and waved them forward.

Jarod heard footsteps on the stairs behind him—William and Sasha had joined them.

"Perfect," said Lucien. "We'll be there in an hour."

Five

The helicopter touched down on a mostly level spot on a mountainside in the Carpathians, not far from the city of Bacâu. By the time it settled its landing skids against the rock, Lilith's head felt as if it were going to explode. Fighting the pain, she let Jarod help her out of the helicopter, then concentrated on her surroundings, trying to orient herself.

"We're in the right vicinity, correct?" Lucien asked her. He tossed a couple of blankets over his shoulder. They'd brought them on the assumption Aanu would be infirm or need help.

She nodded. "It should be down the mountain and just a bit to the south."

"That's about what I was guessing." He gestured to Sasha, who spoke to the helicopter pilot in Romanian. The man nodded. Lucien pulled a handful of bills out of his pocket and gave them to the pilot. "That should keep him here until daybreak," he muttered to the others. "Let's go."

They proceeded single file down the mountain, Lucien and Lilith trading the lead position. He seemed to know where they were going as well as she did, making her wonder why she'd had to come at all. But, after about forty-five minutes, Lucien stopped.

"I've lost it. You take over."

Lilith drew a long breath. "Let's rest a minute." She put her hands on her knees and lowered her head, drawing in the cold air. It made her whole body hurt.

"Are you all right?" Jarod, of course. He bent next to her, trying to see her face.

"Not really."

"What is it?"

"Headache."

He seemed on the verge of speaking, but stopped. Smiling wryly, she said, "Yeah, blood would probably help, but I'm not quite that desperate yet."

"We're awfully close to them here," Lucien put in. "I don't think we should wait until you're that desperate."

Lilith looked up, into Jarod's eyes as he crouched next to her. Past the glint of his glasses' lenses, she saw calm. He held up an arm—not the one she'd bitten yesterday. "Take it if you need it."

How could he be so accepting? It angered her. He didn't understand what she had been—what she still was. She didn't deserve his trust, or his blood.

But if she wanted to avoid causing all their deaths, she would have to accept the blood. While the others waited, she took his wrist and drank.

She had more control over it this time, and was able to stop after less than a minute. Withdrawing her teeth, she licked the wounds gently to seal them. She couldn't look at Jarod as she did it, or at anyone else, for that matter. The touch of her tongue against his skin made her prickle with desire, and suddenly she felt as though she were having sex with him in front of an audience. She gave him one last, utilitarian lick and let him go without looking at him.

The wash of his blood into her system had cooled her headache almost immediately. She wished she knew how close Ialdaboth and the others actually were. Certainly there would be guards by the cave. Would they be able to sense her approach?

She exchanged a look with Lucien. The big demon just nodded. Wondering how much of her thought process he'd overheard, she took the lead, winding her way along the path, down the mountain, toward the cave she knew lay below.

Two hours later, they lay together, all four of them, on the ledge above the cave. A lone vampire stood guard, a young-looking man with dark hair, a high forehead and broody eyebrows. He didn't look very focused on his task. Undoubtedly, Ialdaboth's convocation didn't expect to see intruders.

"This is it," said Lucien.

"Yes," said Lilith, then realized he wasn't asking her. There was a strange light in his eyes, joyous but fierce.

"It all started here—where I was born."

"You remember that?" she asked.

"Hell, I can't remember yesterday." He shifted, leaning farther out over the ledge. "But I remember these mountains. And I have a mental picture of what I think must have been the birthing caves. We're going to have to go in the front way. I can shift through the walls once I'm inside, but I don't want to risk it from up here. There's too much rock under us."

Lilith nodded. She'd seen Ialdaboth shift directly into the cave from about this point on the hill, but he'd known exactly where he was going. "Good choice," she said.

"I'm glad you approve." She winced at the sarcasm in his tone, but he smiled to soften it. "Lilith, you and William head back up to the chopper. Sasha, you distract the guard while Jarod and I go in."

Lilith gaped. "What? You're kicking me out?"

Her hiss came out a bit too loud, and below them the guard suddenly stilled. All four observers froze—until he relaxed again.

When Lucien spoke again, his voice was barely audible. "I can't risk your getting any closer. We can take it from here. You go back. No more chances."

She looked at William, who shrugged apologetically.

"Fine," she finally said.

William turned, retracing their path up the mountain. Lilith reluctantly followed.

"You ready?" Lucien said.

Jarod drew a deep, steadying breath. "Ready as I'll ever be."

At Lucien's signal, Sasha crept down the incline to their left until she disappeared into the darkness. A few minutes later she reappeared, slipping up behind the guard.

Jarod couldn't hear what she said, but he doubted it mattered. She had pulled down the neckline of her already barely-there top, exposing her shoulders and the tops of her ample breasts. The guard, being male, found this quite intriguing.

"Not exactly what I had in mind," Lucien muttered.

Jarod stifled a laugh. From his vantage point above them, he could see even more of Sasha than he suspected the guard could, standing in front of her.

She draped an arm over the guard's shoulders, practically putting her breast into his face. She gave him a sultry smile, then cracked him over the head with a rock.

"Absolutely not what I had in mind," said Lucien. "Let's go."

He put an arm around Jarod, and a moment later they were both standing in front of the cave opening.

Jarod knelt next to the guard's prone body. "He's alive."

"Of course he is." Sasha seemed offended. "I had no intention of killing him. Look how pretty he is."

"He's a bad guy," Lucien said. "We don't care if he's pretty."

"I do. Can we take him home?"

"I'll think about it. C'mon, Dr. Greene." Lucien headed into the mountain.

Jarod flipped on his flashlight and followed. He barely kept pace as Lucien picked up speed through the main corridor. Obviously Lucien had picked up a scent or, maybe, tapped into one of his elusive memories. They followed the corridor down twists and turns and a series of switchbacks, until it hit a dead end.

Lucien put his hands against the rock wall and closed his eyes. "This is it."

"Then let's get it over with and get the hell out of here." Jarod felt cold but not on his skin. He was used to the presence and smell of vampires, but this was different. The age of the place seemed to press down on him, and he suddenly wondered how long people had been using these caves. Since well before Lucien's birth, he imagined, and that had been twelve thousand years ago. It wasn't the millennia of occupation he was feeling, though. Blackness lurked around the edges of the place, like shadows left by evil.

"Are you ready?" Lucien said.

"I guess."

"Then let's go."

He felt Lucien's hand on his elbow again, and in the next instant, they'd blinked to the other side of the wall. He had less than a second to register details hit by the beam of his flashlight—a small cave, bright paintings on the walls, a stone table lurking altar-like in the middle of the room . . . a pile of bones lying on it.

And that was as far as he got before he went to his knees, gasping with the realization that there was no air whatsoever in the room. He groped toward Lucien, managing to grab his sleeve as he went down.

"Shit," said Lucien, somehow, and they blipped out.

Back in the corridor, Jarod put his face in his hands and breathed. "What the hell—"

"That was Aanu." Lucien's voice was thin.

Jarod sat up, his breathing still labored. "The bones? Then we're too late."

"No. We have to get him out."

"Lucien, he's a pile of bones."

"Doesn't matter."

Apparently the lack of air had gone to Lucien's head. Jarod fought for patience. "He's dead, Lucien. We're too late." He pushed himself to his feet. "We should go before we get caught."

Lucien was looking at the wall. "Stay here. I'll be right back."

"Lucien, no—"

The Demon cut him off with a glare from cool, ancient blue eyes.

His patience rapidly evaporating, Jarod repeated firmly, "He's dead."

"Remind me to tell you sometime about the Great Flood. Or the volcano," Lucien said. "I've been dead, too. Couple of times." He touched the wall and disappeared.

Jarod sagged against the wall and rubbed his forehead. The few seconds of oxygen deprivation had given him a headache. Or maybe listening to Lucien had done it. Whatever the case, he'd reached his limit. He needed a break.

Lucien reappeared, carrying the blankets, folded and bunched into a makeshift bag. Judging by the bulges, Jarod assumed the bones were inside.

"Let's go," Lucien said.

Outside the cave, Sasha had trussed up the guard with ropes from her backpack and was kneeling next to him, her fingers on his forehead.

"We're going," Lucien told her.

"We're bringing him," Sasha said.

"Don't give me any shit, girl. I said we're going."

Jarod had never seen Lucien so agitated.

Sasha just glared back at him. "They'll kill him if we leave him here."

"Why should I care about that? He's one of them."

"So was Lilith," Jarod put in gently. "I know it's bad timing, but if there's a chance to save any of them. . . ."

Lucien rolled his eyes. "Pansy-assed idiots, both of you." He waved them toward him.

Sasha pulled the guard half into her lap, then reached to take the hand Jarod offered her. He felt Lucien's hand on his shoulder, and they blinked up the mountain, back to the helicopter.

Lilith, like William, lacked the ability to teleport, but they still made good time. Even so, she had barely crawled back into the helicopter, her head pounding so badly she could hardly see, when Lucien and the others appeared only yards away. They half-ran to the helicopter and climbed in awkwardly, carrying a large bag and an unconscious vampire Lilith was pretty sure she recognized.

"Oh, joy," William muttered. "They brought company."

"Rafael," Lilith said.

Lucien looked at her. "You know him?"

"He's Brigitte's. I'd forgotten she likes to keep him here, out of trouble."

"Do we take him?"

Sasha started to protest, but Lucien silenced her with a gesture. Lilith considered, studying Rafael's quiet face. "Yes. He was Brigitte's—he'll know things."

Lucien nodded decisively. "Then let's go." He tapped the pilot on the shoulder, and they rose into the air, heading toward Bucharest.

They had just touched down when a spear of pain stabbed through Lilith's head. "He's here," she managed, as flashes of red and black filled her vision. "He's waiting for us."

Lucien stiffened, his head lifting, hands clenching on the bag of Aanu's bones. She was almost certain he sniffed the air and crinkled his nose at whatever he smelled.

"Shit," said William.

Lilith glanced at the accountant and saw raw fear in his eyes.

"All of you, stay in the chopper," said Lucien, shoving the bag toward Jarod. "Be ready to run for the plane." He turned to the pilot. "Can you fly that plane?"

The pilot nodded. "Sure."

"Then you be ready, too." He climbed out of the helicopter, leaving the rest of them to plaster themselves against the windows.

Lilith tried to, but her legs faltered under her. Jarod caught her before she hit the floor and helped her to the window. She looked out and trembled as he held her. "My God, no," she whispered. "Don't do it, Lucien."

Jarod heard Lilith's warning, but he doubted anyone else had. In any case, Lucien seemed to have made up his mind already. He was striding purposefully across the field toward the plane, which stood only a handful of yards away. Between him and the plane stood a lone figure. A man.

Not a man, Jarod realized. Not a vampire, either. One of Lucien's kind. A First Demon.

"Ialdaboth?" he asked, and Lilith nodded.

Jarod had heard, second- and third-hand, about the confrontation between Lucien and Ialdaboth that had led to Lilith's arrival in the New

York Underground. It had sounded decidedly unpleasant. Lucien had emerged victorious, but barely. If Lucien couldn't pull it off again, they were all dead.

Ialdaboth straightened, squaring his shoulders, as Lucien approached. He seemed ready to talk, perhaps to launch into some preliminary ritual, but Lucien gave him no chance. He lifted his hands and Ialdaboth flew backwards, nearly slamming into the plane.

"What was that?" Jarod said. He'd seen nothing pass between the two men, and they certainly hadn't made physical contact. But Lilith, still shaking in his arms, didn't answer.

He looked at her. She was staring out the window, pupils dilated, her breathing fast and ragged. Outside, Lucien advanced on Ialdaboth, fists raised in front of him. Jarod knew he could do nothing to help Lucien, so he focused instead on Lilith.

Carefully, he shook her, but she continued to stare out the window as if ensorcelled. "Lilith?" No response. He pushed at her shoulders, trying to turn her away from the window.

"He's got her," William said. "There's no way she'll ever be able to break free. You should let her go. Or better yet, kill her. She's too much of a danger."

"Shut up, William," Jarod snapped. "Why the hell are you here, anyway?"

The accountant shrugged. "I really have no idea." He returned his attention to the preternatural wrestling match on the landing field.

Gently, Jarod ran his hand over Lilith's hair. "Lilith." Nothing. He pressed his lips against her throat. "Lilith."

Her lips strained for words, finally produced a raspy sound. He lowered his ear to her mouth.

"William's right," she breathed. "Kill me. He'll have you all, through me."

"No. This connection you have could be important. We just have to figure out how to use it to our advantage." His reassurance was more than unbridled optimism, more than whispered hope born of his affection for her. It was, he was almost completely certain, based on scientific fact.

At least he hoped it was.

"There's a way to save you," he said, "and we both know what that is."

"If I take you now, I'll kill you."

"No, you won't."

Her eyes had widened, desperate and wild, like a trapped animal. "I will. I need it so much. . . ."

"Then take it."

Vaguely, he realized both Sasha and William were looking at him now, instead of out the window at Lucien. The pilot, too, had taken an inordinate interest in what should have been a private conversation.

There was no help for it. Voyeuristic onlookers or not, he wasn't going to let Lilith fall to her fate. Clenching his teeth, he broke the scabs on his wrist and held the wound to her lips. The blood reddened her mouth and her pupils contracted, just a little. . . .

She turned away from the window, grabbed him, and sank her teeth into his throat.

Her fangs stung sinking in, tiny scalpels puncturing skin and vein. His hands went up involuntarily, but when he grasped her arms, he could neither push her away nor pull her closer. She was immovable. He opened his mouth to speak but nothing came out.

Vaguely, he heard Sasha say, "What should we do?"

William answered, "Nothing, yet. He's the doctor—I assume he knows what he's doing."

Well, partially right. He thought he knew what he was doing, but with vampires you could never be a hundred percent sure.

Then William said, "Holy shit, Lucien's knocking the living hell out of this guy," and Jarod felt all eyes turn back toward the landing field.

Lilith's mouth pulled at his throat, drawing mouthful after mouthful of blood. The pain, though, had stopped, leaving behind only the rhythm. It matched his heartbeat. She shifted, and he felt her body against his, her breasts pressing softly against his chest, her hands spread on his back.

Let go, he thought. *That's enough. I can't take anymore.*

I can't, her answer came. *I can't stop.*

He would have called for help if he could, but his voice stopped in his throat behind her penetrating teeth. His heartbeat filled his head, pounding, pounding . . . how long until it stopped?

Then, abruptly, Lucien's voice broke through his trance. "Grab the bones, Doc . . . *shit* . . . Lilith, let him go!"

She responded not at all. Jarod pushed weakly with his hands on her arms, but to no effect.

Then, suddenly, she was off him, sprawling on the floor of the helicopter, blood dripping from her mouth. Jarod went to his knees, gasping, pressing his hand against the wound at his throat. Blood seeped between his fingers. Lucien's hand tore his away, then pressed against the wound. Heat filled Jarod's veins, and the pain faded.

He looked up at Lucien and flinched. One side of the proto-vampire's face was sheeted in blood. White bone showed through a wide gash across his forehead. His clothing was ripped and blood-drenched.

"You'll be okay," said Lucien. "I hope."

And you? Jarod thought. Though Lucien was on his feet, he looked as if he'd been thrashed within an inch of his life.

In clipped, economical tones, he said, "William, grab the bones. I'll take Lilith."

Only then did Jarod realize that Lilith still lay motionless on the floor, her eyes closed. "Is she all right?"

"You're the doctor," said Lucien, pushing him toward the door. "How the hell should I know?"

Jarod could smell his blood now, an odd, earthy reek unlike human blood. "Is there anything I can do for you?" he asked, hesitant.

Lucien bent to lift Lilith's limp body into his arms. "Just get the hell out of my way."

William grabbed the bag of bones, and Jarod was left with no choice but to trail after the rest as they ran for the plane. He pressed a hand against his neck. The blood there felt thick and sticky, and he could tell the wound had partially closed.

Ialdaboth's body lay crumpled not far from the plane, blood all over his face and shirt. Without thinking, Jarod reacted, stopping to check the Demon's pulse. He found none under the thick mess of blood.

"He's dead," said Lucien, "at least for the moment. We need to get the hell out of here."

Jarod, reminding himself that his Hippocratic oath had no provisions for creatures who could be dead one minute and alive the next, climbed into the plane in time to see Lucien stagger down the aisle, set Lilith gently in a seat, then collapse.

Jarod rushed to his side. "Lucien!" He couldn't see the other man's face very well through its coating of blood, but Lucien's eyes were open.

"Give me . . . a minute," he managed.

Jarod automatically felt for a pulse; it was there, but faint. Unfortunately, he wasn't sure how strong it was under normal circumstances.

"Are you all right?" he ventured.

"Better than the other guy," Lucien grunted. He straightened a little in the seat. "Lucky Ialdaboth depleted himself kidnapping Lorelei and trespassing in the Underground, or I'd have gotten my ass kicked." He touched the side of his face and looked at the blood that came back on his fingers. "I mean, worse than this. He'll be down for the count. I just need a nap. For about a year and a half." He pushed to his feet and walked unsteadily to his seat.

Wishing he could do more for him, Jarod turned his attention to Lilith. She half-lay, still limp and unconscious, in the seat where Lucien had left her. He could do nothing for her, either. So he sat down, across the aisle from Lilith, and felt helpless. His wrists and throat ached.

To think, the fate of the world rested on this bedraggled lot. This could not possibly be a good thing.

Jarod managed to stay awake for the flight from Bucharest to Paris, but the minute he took a seat on the still-waiting SST, he fell headlong into sleep. He did have time to wonder how Lilith was, but the thought lasted only a moment.

At first, his sleep was deep, dark, and bottomless. Then dreams rose out of it.

He was with Lilith, holding her close, her heart and his beating in synchrony, the sound like a separate entity between them. He bent his head to kiss her gently, but the kiss became passionate almost immediately. She clutched at him, her mouth frantic on his.

You have to save me. The words rose from the place where her breasts pressed against his chest, from the rhythm of their joined heartbeats. *Save me from him.*

I will.

She pulled back and looked at him, eyes drenched with despair. *You can't. You don't know what I am.*

Then she opened her mouth and blackness poured out of it, a thick, ugly river of terror and filth. She was choking on it, dying, but she couldn't stop the flow—

Jarod jerked awake to see Lucien standing over him.

"I was just about to wake you up," Lucien said.

He was still carrying the bag of bones. He'd cleaned himself up, washed off the blood, but the gashes were still there, wide parallel lines like claw marks across his right cheek, as well as the deep forehead wound. His hands were shaking. Jarod wondered if stitches would do the Demon any good.

"How's Lilith?" he asked.

Lucien shook his head. "Hard to tell right now. You'll have to check her when we get back. How are you?"

"Still breathing. You?"

Lucien snorted. "I'll live. That's a given. Come on—let's go."

Jarod followed Lucien out of the plane. It came as a shock to see that it was full morning. The others were nowhere to be seen.

"Where—" Jarod started, and Lucien pointed. Three large wooden crates were being rolled out of the plane's baggage compartment and loaded into a waiting truck by three men wearing airport security uniforms. Jarod wondered how much the humans knew.

"They'll be fine. We had everything ready, just in case."

"Good thing we did."

Lucien nodded. "I'd planned on coming back at night. I'd hoped we would have more time. But 'expect the best, prepare for the worst,' that's what I always say."

"You've said that for twelve thousand years?"

Lucien shrugged. "I don't know. Maybe five. Ten tops." He pointed at the truck. "Let's go. The sooner we get home, the sooner we can get Lilith straightened out. Not to mention Aanu."

Jarod had no idea what he could do to "straighten out" someone who'd been reduced to a bag of bleached bones. Sighing he followed Lucien to the truck.

Six

He worried most about Lilith, perhaps because he was certain he could help her in some way, even if he didn't know exactly how. Aanu's bones seemed hopeless, irrelevant. And his own condition, after the bloodletting on the helicopter, was more immediate than either of the others.

Still, he ignored the overwhelming exhaustion and forced himself to keep his eyes open as Lucien transported him from a warehouse near the outskirts of New York City to the hallway outside Lilith's bedroom.

"I'll be back with Lilith," Lucien said, then disappeared.

He reappeared only seconds later, kneeling next to the crate that held Lilith's sleeping body. Effortlessly, he pushed it over the threshold into the bedroom, leaving it next to the bed.

"You're going to leave her in there?" Jarod asked.

Lucien shrugged. "Doesn't make much difference. She'll get out when she wakes up."

Jarod chewed the inside of his cheek, considering. Just as Lucien was almost out the door, he said, "No. I want her out of the box and on the bed."

Lucien stopped, looking back with his eyebrows raised. Only then did Jarod realize he'd basically issued an order.

"May I ask why?" Lucien asked mildly.

"Her condition concerns me. I want to hook up an IV before she wakes up."

"You think it'll help?"

"If I can figure out what the hell I'm doing and what the hell's wrong with her, yes, I think it'll help."

Lucien nodded. "Fair enough."

He peeled the top off the crate, popping the nails as easily as if they were thumbtacks. Then, gently, he lifted Lilith, settled her onto the bed.

"Thank you," Jarod said.

Lucien nodded. "I'm going to get Sasha and William." He pointed at the makeshift blanket-bag on the floor—Aanu's bones. He was trembling again, but he drew his hand back quickly, making it clear he wanted to hide his state. "Take care of Aanu," he said.

He disappeared before Jarod could ask what the hell he was supposed to do with "Aanu." Sighing, he knelt next to the bag and opened the sagging mouth to look inside. . . .

"Oh, my God."

As quickly as possible, he hauled the bag down the hallway to one of his better-equipped hospital rooms. There, he emptied the contents onto the bed. It came out in a clump. Connective tissue had begun to regenerate between the bones, attaching them to each other again. Unfortunately, they'd been piled together in a mish-mash in the make-shift bag.

Carefully, Jarod began to separate the jumbled remains. Small, square bones—he couldn't tell if they were metatarsals or metacarpals—had fused to one arm's ulna. The other end of the ulna was connected to the mandible, protruding from the chin. Vertebrae studded a clavicle like a necklace, glued to it with fresh, pink tissue.

"What a mess," he muttered, and grabbed a scalpel.

A few minutes later, when Lucien found him, he had separated about half of the incorrectly reconnected bones and set them aside, careful to keep them a few inches away from each other.

"So you figured it out?" Lucien said.

Jarod glanced at the proto-vampire. He was leaning in the doorway, his expression uncomfortably smug. "More or less," Jarod muttered.

He gently separated a collection of phalanges—which actually seemed to be in the right order—and set them down next to the other hand bones he'd already sorted. He hadn't yet separated them into left and right hands. "Was this regeneration triggered by the exposure to air?"

"Yes. That's why there was no air in the cave. I should have realized there wouldn't be before I dragged you in there."

Jarod barely registered the almost-apology. "At a guess, I'd say the more oxygen the better, to regenerate the cells."

"Probably."

He slipped a tibia free from a mass of bones and tissue at the bottom of the bag, where the bones had settled and become severely confused. "I need a hyperbaric chamber. Can you get me one?"

"How much?"

"Fifty grand, at least."

"Buy it. I'll make sure the funds are there."

Two hours later, the bones were arranged in careful order on the bed. The entire time he'd been working, Jarod had been thinking about what might happen over the next few days, as Aanu's healing progressed. Would he regrow his brain, with all the knowledge it had previously held? How could a sophisticated consciousness possibly regenerate from bones that had been bleached dry for countless hundreds—even thousands—of years?

It boggled Jarod's mind. Gave him a headache, even. And he couldn't afford to waste time on speculation. There was still Lilith to think of.

He left Aanu to his own devices and went to tend to his other patient. The hyperbaric chamber wouldn't arrive until sunset tomorrow, by which time he figured he could rustle up enough vampire help to get it set up and running.

Lilith seemed well enough, as far as he could judge while she was still in her daytime Sleep. He looked at his watch. Still a few hours until dusk. Time enough to do what he wanted to do.

He'd given her IVs before, to assuage her hunger, blood ready to pump into her veins as soon as the sun set. He set up equipment to do the same thing tonight, with one small change.

He had plenty of blood in storage—part of a supply he kept current by channeling several pints a week from a half-dozen local blood banks—but as one of a very few humans living in a colony of vampires, Jarod considered it prudent to keep a supply of his own blood fresh and ready, in case one of the natives got overenthusiastic. He checked his supplies, and set two pints of it aside for Lilith's morning meal.

Whatever was wrong with Lilith, whatever Ialdaboth had done to her to keep her loyal, his own blood seemed to alleviate the effect. Perhaps it would need to be fresh to work, but this was definitely worth trying. Maybe his stored blood could counter her symptoms long enough for him to rest and for his hemoglobin levels to return to normal. In the meantime, he still had enough left to give himself a transfusion if necessary.

With his work finished, exhaustion finally caught up with him. He could barely keep his eyes open as he made a few, final notes in Lilith's file. He scribbled his initials under them and laid the file aside, then sat next to Lilith on the bed. Gently, he ran a strand of her pale hair through his fingers.

"We'll get this to work," he said. "Don't worry."

Her still, waxy face remained unmoving. He smiled and kissed her lips, surprised to find they held a vague warmth. Then, with no energy left to carry him down the hallway to his own room, he stretched out next to her and fell asleep.

Night came, but Lilith did not awaken. Her sleep rose from the depths to tremble on the verge of wakefulness, but she couldn't swim those last few inches to the surface. She was vaguely aware of the presence of night, of blood flowing into her veins from the needle in the bend of her elbow, and of a warm weight next to her on the bed. But she couldn't open her eyes, couldn't move. Couldn't wake up. Not quite.

Who was in bed with her? Who did she know who was stupid enough to lie next to a vampire at dusk? The answer came to her immediately—Jarod.

And it was his blood moving into her veins. She recognized the difference, a flavor of sorts, as it began to pump through her. Then she lost the thread that had drawn her nearly to consciousness, and sank once more into Sleep.

To her surprise, she could feel him there, too. A vague sense of his presence that became gradually clearer. He slept, as well, and their minds seemed to call to each other on that plane, bound by shared blood.

Lilith.

You shouldn't have brought me back. She couldn't help the despair—it bubbled up unbidden from some deep place within.

Why?

You don't know what I am.

Show me.

If I do . . . If I do you'll never love me.

Show me.

The despair thickened and darkened around her, and suddenly she felt Ialdaboth's presence within it. It was part of the conditioning, that despair, part of what had made her so totally his, until Lorelei's interference had made it possible for her to question. It would, undoubtedly, not be the last obstacle.

But in another way, it was real. If Jarod knew who she had been, what she had done, how could he possibly accept her? How could he look at her again with desire, as he had on the plane?

That's my problem. His presence radiated gentleness. *Show me.*

There were no secrets here. She let it all go.

She had been born Catherine Gibson in 1760, in the Virginia Colony. By the time the Revolutionary War started, she had very little to depend upon but herself. Following the armies from battle to battle, giving soldiers pleasure where she could, she eked out a barely acceptable existence.

Then she'd met the vampire. She couldn't even remember his name, wasn't sure he'd ever told her. He'd been among the soldiers, taking blood where he could, often from injured soldiers on the battlefield, where their deaths would be unremarkable. Even then, misguided as she was, she'd recognized the smell of evil. She'd decided it didn't matter.

He'd offered her gold for sex, which seemed like a good exchange. But the sex had become brutal, and he'd Turned her in the process, unasked but not entirely unwilling.

Not the rest. This much alone was too much.

Some part of her, distant, felt Jarod moving beside her. He was still asleep, caught in unconsciousness with her, but he put his arm around her.

There, in the darkness, where they were both together, he said, *Tell me. You feed on my blood. I have a right to know.*

The vampire had liked her. She had been a bitter woman, stripped of every comfort. Her mother had been a prostitute, her father a thief who'd eventually beaten the mother of his child to death.

"Would you kill him?" the vampire had asked her. "Would you kill your father, and anyone else who might belong to your family? Do you know if you have brothers or sisters?"

"Do I care?" she'd replied bitterly. "If they are spawn of his flesh, they deserve to die."

As I deserve to die. I deserved it then and I deserve it even more now.

Hush. Jarod's presence comforted her, then urged her to go on.

The vampire had told her there would be a great reward for her, a place for her in a community of vampires where she would be loved and accepted. All she had to do was kill her father. She had done it, and reveled too much in the killing. He'd had a wife she'd happily slaughtered, too.

And the vampire took her to Ialdaboth.

A hundred years of initiation. A hundred years of brainwashing, of committing the most hideous acts, killing humans, children, other vampires. Whatever I was told, without question. It's a testing period, and I passed.

Pictures passed through her mind, memories of atrocities she'd committed. Since her rejection of Ialdaboth she'd tried to push them away, into places where she couldn't find them, wouldn't have to feel them, but there they were. Clear as day and bright as blood. They spun themselves out in vivid color for her mind's eye to see.

And for Jarod to see, as well.

Inside, she wept. Whether she would awaken to find tears on her face, she didn't know, but here in this place of strange consciousness, her body shuddered and spasmed with horrible weeping.

Do you see? You can never leave me, because of what you've done. Ialdaboth's voice. Not his actual presence, but his voice, ingrained in her mind with the hundred years of indoctrination and, after that, the hundred years of loyal service. *No one there can ever truly accept you. They all know you can't really change.*

Despair clung to her like tar, dragged her down. She could sink with it, into the deep void, and never come back. It would be so easy. . . .

Let her go! Jarod's voice, his thought-voice, shocking her out of the black despair by its intensity. *Just let her the hell go!*

It's not really him, Lilith responded automatically. *It's just his voice, left behind in my head. . . .*

And suddenly she was awake, staring up at the ceiling of her bedroom in the Underground. Next to her, Jarod also gasped awake, his arms clutching at her, pulling her close. She pressed her face into his chest. Here, in the world of light and consciousness, there were no tears.

Seven

"It can't be that easy. He can't be gone." She watched Jarod's hands moving down her arm, his gentle fingers as he pulled the IV needle free. He was Dr. Greene now, the touch quiet but impersonal. He curled the tips of his fingers into the bend of her elbow, feeling the vague pulse there as she spoke.

He turned his attention to her face, lifting one of her eyelids to peer at her pupils. "Your blood carries markers from Ialdaboth, because one of his children Changed you. I think the collision between that blood and mine, which carries markers from Lucien, canceled out some aspect of the brainwashing."

"How?"

He looked into her other eye. "Beats the hell out of me. Most of this vampire shit makes no damned sense."

She laughed a little. He touched the pulse at her throat. It felt more like a caress, and there was warmth in his eyes.

"It isn't over," he said. "It'll be a process, and you just got it underway."

"A battle." She should have known that. Ialdaboth wouldn't give her up without a fight. A fight she'd brought right to the Underground's door.

"Julian should have killed me," she said. "It would have been safer."

He cupped her cheek, looking into her eyes with concern. "If Julian wants you here, then there's a reason. Trust him." He bent toward her, brushing her lips with his. "I do."

He made sure she was comfortable, then left her. Her heart lurched as she watched him walk out the door. Why was he so good to her? There was such warmth in his eyes when he looked at her. It was too much to hope that he might actually care about her, especially after what he'd seen, what she'd shown him. He was just concerned for her, as her doctor.

She had to leave. If she stayed here, she would endanger everyone. Perhaps Jarod most of all, because he was so often close to her. What happened to her didn't matter, so long as this place was protected.

Sitting up in the bed, she swung her legs out from under the covers, touched her feet to the floor. She could still feel the brush of his lips against hers, their gentle warmth. She regretted that she would never get a chance to explore their mutual attraction any further.

Maybe she should leave him a note. But, in the end, she decided against it.

Getting out of the Underground proved more complicated than she'd expected. When she'd infiltrated the place before, she'd had Ialdaboth's abilities on her side. Now she had only her own. While formidable, they paled next to her erstwhile master's.

So she wandered the corridors, following the flow of strange, vampiric magic, going toward the places where the magic waned and the smell of vampires was fainter. And, finally, she found an exit and let herself out into the dark New York City night.

She allowed herself one look back, one pang of regret, but no tears.

* * *

Jarod was looking forward to seeing Lilith the next evening. Exhausted from lack of sleep and blood loss, he'd spent the day mostly unconscious, and had awakened with thoughts of her crowding everything else out of his mind. He was looking forward to talking to her, touching her, even if only in a diagnostic manner. Or maybe she would let him kiss her again. It seemed a fair bet.

But she was gone.

He stared blankly at the empty bed for stunned moments, unable to comprehend what he was seeing. Where could she have possibly gone?

"She left."

Julian's voice startled him. He turned abruptly.

"Where did she go?"

"Topside." Julian settled a shoulder against the doorframe. "She's trying to protect us all from the danger that is Lilith."

A stab of pain went through Jarod's wrist, and he grimaced. What was it about vampire bites, that they kept hurting, as if he were being bitten again?

"I want you to go fetch her."

Jarod blinked. "Me? Why me?"

"You might be more convincing." He smiled a little, then sobered. "She's wrong about her bond with Ialdaboth. We need her."

"Do you know where she is?"

He nodded. "I'll take you there."

She had set up temporary housing in an abandoned apartment building, in the windowless basement. The rooms above had all been boarded shut, but she didn't trust them to be sun-tight.

She didn't trust anything at this point. Skulking the streets of Newark, New Jersey, she'd had the distinct feeling someone was following her.

She'd seen a shadow out of the corner of her eye that had sent her senses tingling. Her first thought had been that Julian had noticed her missing and sent someone after her. But no vampire from the Underground would need to behave so furtively only for her sake. No, whatever the thing was she'd sensed, it had a dark feeling to it.

Could Ialdaboth have agents here?

The minute the question occurred to her, she realized how stupid it was. Of course, he did. That's why she'd left Manhattan, wasn't it? If they could trace her through her blood, they could follow her right to the depths of the Underground, regardless of any safeguard Julian had engineered. And they *could* track her; they'd proven that in Romania. Yet they hadn't been able to do it while she'd been full of Jarod's blood. . . .

The shadow she'd seen could have been anything—a mugger, a stray dog, her own imagination. It didn't matter, though. Even if her worst fears were true, she'd had to leave the Underground. Her presence there endangered the entire community.

She didn't doubt for a second that if she stayed in this dismal hellhole, they would hunt her down and kill her. Jarod's blood would only keep her safe for so long. But maybe, if all they wanted was her, her death would protect the rest of them.

A shudder ran through her as she took in her surroundings. The place, like her thoughts, was miserable. She ached from the day spent in Sleep on the concrete floor. It was cold, and she heard rats from time to time. Not necessarily a bad thing, the rats. At least she could eat them.

She might have to. Hunger twisted her gut, and she really didn't want to hunt. Not now. The thought of human blood repelled her, but it also called to her. Yet if she went outside, into the place where the shadows stalked, she might not survive long enough to feed.

Stay—go. Feed—starve. She couldn't think clearly enough to work through any of the conundrums facing her. She didn't want to kill, but she was so damned hungry. . . .

"Lilith."

She spun, staring. Jarod stood at the doorway to her new lair. He lifted a bag of rich, garnet blood.

"I brought breakfast," he said.

She started to smile, then pressed her lips together, hard. "Why are you here?"

"Julian sent me."

"Why?"

"He wants you to come back."

The flutter of hope that had leapt in her heart died. "He wants me to come back. *He* wants me to."

"Lilith . . ."

"Go away. If Julian wants me, he can come and get me himself." She turned her back to him and knelt on the floor, straightening the nest of blankets she'd slept in.

She heard Jarod take a step closer but refused to turn around.

"Lilith . . ."

The pleading in his voice made her angry. She surged to her feet, spinning to face him. He blinked, but didn't retreat. "Would you have come after me if Julian hadn't told you to?" Her voice was bitter and mocking.

"No, because I wouldn't have known where the hell to look for you." He held up the bag of blood. "At least eat something. Maybe you won't be so bitchy."

She jerked the blood from his hand, let her fangs slide free and sank them right through the plastic. If she had thought to shock or disgust him with the display, she failed. He only stood watching, impassive.

She drained the bag and threw it to the floor, irritated at his lack of reaction. Then again, he was a vampire doctor. She should have known a little blood-drinking wouldn't faze him.

"Feel any better?" he asked.

"A little. You should have brought more."

"It was all I had left of mine."

Of course. "So you came to medicate me."

"No. I came to ask you to come back."

"Why? Because Julian needs me?"

"No. Because if you don't, we may not be able to stop Ialdaboth from slaughtering us all." Her lip curled into the beginnings of a sneer before he added, "But most of all, because I need you."

Her gaze met his. She could neither deny nor resist what she saw there—pain, need, desire. Love. She swallowed, surprised at the intensity of it, more surprised at the intensity of her own reaction. Blinking, she gathered herself.

"All right," she said finally. "That's more like it."

"Good." He took her arm. "Then let's go."

They left the building together, and Lilith immediately sensed the shadows. They were closer, darker, more of them than there had been before, and she knew for certain now that they were neither stray dogs nor muggers. She clasped Jarod's arm.

"Do you see them?" she whispered.

"See who?" He matched her barely-audible tone.

"The shadows." Could it possibly be her imagination? Surely not—it was too real for that. They flitted at the corners of her eyes.

Jarod glanced from side to side without moving his head. "I don't see anything." His eyes narrowed a little, though, and Lilith was certain he was looking directly at one of the shrouded lurkers. "Vamps?" he said.

"Yes."

"I don't see them. Are they ours?"

"No." She made herself as still as she could, as still as only a vampire was capable of being. Jarod's necessary breathing sounded like a gale-force wind next to her, his heartbeat deafening. The vamps would be looking for her, though, so the tumult of his humanness shouldn't matter.

In her shroud of silence, she watched. She could see only the vague, dark shadows. They were too distant for her to make out details, and seemed to be protected by some sort of magic. But they were Ialdaboth's. She was certain of it. They would sense her, at any moment, and they would come to her and take her, murder her, murder Jarod, then go on to the Underground, to destroy the others. . . .

They moved. Shifted toward each other until they stood in a small clump. There were three or four of them—the magic distorted them enough that it was hard to tell. Lilith held herself utterly still.

And they disappeared.

"They're gone," Jarod murmured, his perception surprising her.

"Yes."

"Why did they leave?"

"I don't know. I think they were following me. Maybe your blood killed the trail."

"That would make sense." He grasped her arm as she relaxed again. "We need to tell Julian."

"It's not unexpected." Julian's calm response to the news that she'd been followed surprised Lilith.

"What if they find us?" she asked, wondering if he was truly as calm as he appeared to be, trying to match her demeanor to his. Inside, her stomach was trembling and twisted. She guessed Jarod, standing behind her, sensed her turmoil when she felt his comforting hand on her shoulder.

Julian, sitting at the desk, steepled his fingers and frowned. "I don't think they will. I've put up a few more safeguard layers. The margins of this place are so muddled by now they're practically impossible to sense unless you're one of us."

"How did that go?" Jarod asked, and Lilith heard carefully muted concern in his voice.

Julian looked at him briefly. "As well as can be expected."

She had no idea what they were talking about, but it didn't matter. Only one thing did—protecting the Underground—and she didn't trust any so-called safeguards.

"I can't stay here," she blurted out. "It's not safe. It's why I left. You have to understand that."

Jarod's hand tightened on her shoulder, as if to hold her there, to stop her from leaving again.

"You're wrong," Julian said firmly. "You have to stay here. I need you. I can use the link you have to keep track of Ialdaboth, to judge when he's likely to come after us again."

"But he can use it, too!" she said. "It will lead him here!"

"Not if we keep you . . . inoculated, so to speak." Smiling, he glanced again at Jarod. Then, his expression softening, he said to her, "I need you, Lilith. You're our secret weapon. As long as I have you, I have control over when and where I face Ialdaboth, when the time comes."

She hesitated, needing to be certain she wasn't surrendering for only selfish reasons. She felt her Jarod's fingers squeeze her shoulder yet again, gently this time. "You're sure about that?" she said.

Julian nodded. "As sure as I can be."

"But will it be safe for Jarod?"

Close behind her, Jarod put in, "As safe as we can make it."

"I'll let you two work out the details on that one," said Julian. He fluttered his fingers toward the door. "You can go."

She followed Jarod to her hospital room and sat on the bed.

"Still hungry?" he asked her, moving to stand between her knees.

"Not so much."

"Good." He traced his fingers down her cheek. "You're not in this alone, you know." His hand slid down from her face, across her collar bone, until he cupped her breast.

"Dr. Greene, I don't think that's very professional behavior."

"Do you want me to stop?"

"No."

"Then shut up." He bent to kiss her, his mouth soft and searching. She kissed him back, threads of heat singing through her body.

"When you have problems," he whispered against her lips, "you'll need me to help you."

"I'll need your blood."

"Uh-huh. So it might be a good idea to keep me close at hand."

"A very good idea." Her hands slid down his body, feeling his warmth, his heartbeat. His blood inside her seemed to call to its source, inside him.

"They say," he said softly, "that when a vampire takes your blood, she can make it like sex. Is that true?"

She smiled. "I can do more than that. I can make it *be* sex."

"Do you think you might need another dose? I mean right now?"

"It certainly couldn't hurt."

Jarod gathered Lilith close against him and kissed her, deep and long. He wondered, just for a moment, what the hell he was doing. His great-grandfather had always told him not to get too close. Yet here he was, peeling off her shirt and ravenously mouthing her breasts, about to get as close as it was possible to get. And he had no intention of letting somebody else's prejudices stop him.

What had Great-grandpa Greene been afraid of? Maybe of admitting the possibility of what Jarod now knew was true—that proto-vampire blood ran in his veins. He'd have thought the old man would have figured it out by the time his hundred and twentieth birthday rolled around.

Jarod laughed at the thought, and Lilith peered at him curiously.

"What?" she said as he kissed his way down her stomach.

"Nothing." He paused just below her navel to look up the length of her body at her face, framed by her breasts. "You're beautiful."

She watched his face disappear between her thighs and fought tears. He was a good man. Certainly, he deserved better than her ancient and damaged self. But Fate seemed to disagree. And she wasn't about to argue.

Especially not when he was working such magic on her. She'd wanted his mouth there ever since their encounter on the plane, and he was certainly living up to her expectations. She wondered how long it had been since he'd been with a woman, then decided she didn't care.

Then she couldn't think much about anything as the hot, spiraling pleasure flooded through her. She felt his smile against her skin as his tongue nudged her just a little further, a little more. . . .

Jarod watched her hit her peak, tumble over. He kept her going for a few minutes, tapping with his tongue and feeling her shudder, until suddenly she twisted under him, and he felt her teeth. Not in his throat this time, but in the hollow of his shoulder. She could sip blood there but not gorge on it. He tried to remember what major veins passed close to the spot where she'd penetrated him and how far they were from the prick of her teeth, but she shifted again, and suddenly he was penetrating her.

Instinct took over then, and he slid home, claiming her. Then he held still, feeling the tight sheath of her sex around him, the pulsing of his own blood, the beating of it as it went into her mouth. For a split second, he was certain he was going to die. It would have been a very, very happy death.

She freed her fangs and moaned under him, licking the wound as an afterthought. Eyes locked to his, she smiled. He returned her smile and slid out, then in again, deeper. Her soft gasps guiding his rhythm, he stroked until her body clenched and pulsed around him, and he followed her over the crest to completion.

For a time afterward, he just breathed. Then he settled next to her on the bed, and cradled her against him. She closed her eyes, her head on his shoulder—the unbitten one—and pushed her white-blonde hair out of her face.

"Remind me to check my hemoglobin levels before we make love again," he said, soft laughter in his voice.

She rubbed her cheek against his chest. "I think I love you," she said.

The admission surprised him. He shifted to look at her, but she wouldn't meet his gaze.

"That's good," he said. "That's very good, in fact." He put a finger under her chin, tilting her head up, making her look at him. "Because I think the feeling is mutual."

She managed a watery smile. "I don't think you know what you're taking on."

"Probably not." He kissed her on the nose. "I rarely do. It hardly matters."

"Just don't get too far away."

He nestled her closer. "Never. You can count on that."

Julian's Journal

The one who was dead will feed on life without creating death, and the life that was death will bring power. That's Lucien's piece, which is all I have at the moment.

But what the hell does it mean? And how much more do I need? There must be more pieces. Perhaps each of the four First Demons, the half-brothers born all within the same span of twenty-four hours in a cave in Romania twelve thousand years ago, carries a piece of the puzzle. I have Lucien's. I need Aanu's and Ruha's and Ialdaboth's.

Lilith thinks Rafael may have knowledge of Ialdaboth's part in this, because of his association with Brigitte. If he can give us that, we'll be halfway there.

As for the other two, that may prove more difficult.

Aanu is a pile of bones in the hospital wing. I have to wonder if his brain will actually grow back, and if it does, if he will be able to use it. What happens when you've been dead for four thousand years? What does it do to your memory? Is it possible to recover from that thorough a desecration? Can the healing abilities manifested in myself and Lucien aid his regeneration? I guess we'll find out. Though Lucien may not be a great help, given his condition. He tries to hide it, but I can tell his confrontation with Ialdaboth took its toll.

Ruha seems to be out of the picture. But he is also within me. Ruha and the Senior were lovers once, and his memories now lurk in the depths of my memory. I have sought—and failed—to find them. I have no choice but to seek again.

I will. I will find a way to save the Children, to restore their mortality. And I will find a way to kill Ialdaboth, if I have to die to do it.

And I might die. I can sense him, and his minions are already here, lurking around the margins of the Underground. I have provided what protection I can, all that is within my power. But he is strong, and he is dark, and I don't know how long I can stand against him.

Rafael

Light is sweet, and it pleases the eyes to see the sun. However many years a man may live, let him enjoy them all.
Ecclesiastes 11:7-8

In the revivification of the red cells we seem to have found a reaction between catalyst A and catalyst B, when combined in proper proportions. Frankly, the involvement of Nicholas' blood in this formula surprises me.
Email—Dr. Jarod Greene
to Julian Cavanaugh

The one who feeds from life without diminishing it—he will be the one who changes everything. Some may be inclined to call him Messiah.
The Book of Changing Blood

One

With the coming of dusk, Rafael woke and, as he did every time he slid out of the daytime Sleep, wondered if he was still a vampire.

He must be, though. Otherwise he would be craving a nice, juicy T-bone instead of a good mouthful of blood. Even now, after four years, the thought revolted him. Some days it was all he could do to eat enough to stay alive. Some days it occurred to him to wonder if he was the world's only anorexic vampire.

With those ever-present questions asked and set aside for the day, he was free to move on to other puzzlements. Like where the hell was he?

He sat up, shoving a hand through his hair. Damned hair, anyway. It would all be sticking straight up now—not that he cared. He was more concerned about getting the hell out of here. But when he tried to move the other arm, he found he couldn't past a certain point.

He looked at it and saw a needle taped into the bend of his elbow, plastic tubing leading from it to a bag of garnet blood hanging on a metal hanger like they had in hospitals. The blood had moved nearly all the way down the tube, and as he watched, it filled the tube completely. A moment later, he felt it go into his veins. Cold, and strange, but it soothed the hunger that had begun to grow. An intriguing solution. He could go for this on a permanent basis. Ialdaboth would never allow it, though. He wanted those in his enclave to take hot blood fresh from the throat of a preferably innocent victim.

Ialdaboth was a prick.

"Good morning," said a male voice, and Rafael jumped, afraid someone had just read his last thought. He'd had too many similar thoughts over the past few years, and had always been terrified some-one would overhear and have him killed. Or maybe he'd hoped some-one would overhear and have him killed. He wasn't entirely sure.

But the person who'd spoken was unfamiliar. Something about him reminded him of Ialdaboth, an aura of some kind, but the resem-blance ended there. This guy, Rafael was certain, was not a prick.

"Thank you," the big man said, stepping closer to the bed.

He was tall, with thin scars on his face and a prominent nose that looked like it had been broken two or fifteen times. He had fresh wounds on his face, too—gashes down his right cheek and a partially healed laceration across his forehead. His skin had a gray, waxy pallor. His blue eyes, though, were bright and clear.

"How are you feeling?" he asked.

Rafael didn't feel like answering the question. "Who the hell are you?"

"Lucien."

"Where am I?"

"New York City. Sort of."

Rafael took a minute to absorb that. The last thing he remembered, he'd been standing in front of a cave in Romania. Guarding the cave, technically, though he'd done a piss-poor job of it. There'd been that girl, the one with the breasts. . . .

"How long have I been unconscious?"

"About three days." The guy, Lucien, was standing next to the bed now, towering over him, arms crossed over his broad chest. "Sorry about that, but I had to keep you under for a while. We had too much shit going down to worry about what you were up to."

"You kept me under? How does that work?"

"Quite well, apparently." He gestured toward the IV tube. "That going down okay?"

"Fine." The efficiency of the method surprised him. His hunger had faded almost immediately. He was used to having to fight horrible, raging hunger as long as possible, before it drove him to feed. A few times, he'd gone days without feeding at all, finding it easier to go off in a blinding rage than to be aware of what he was doing.

"You're lucky you're here," Lucien said, a wry grin on his mouth. "You're pretty screwed up in the head."

"You're pretty damned nosy." Rafael's reaction came more from indignation than fear.

"Don't worry. You're safe here. Definitely safer than you were in Romania. So what's your name?"

"Rafael."

Lucien nodded. "Your given name, or one you picked later?"

"Does it matter?"

"No."

"Then I picked it later. I didn't care for my given name."

"Which was?"

"None of your damned business."

Lucien laughed. "That's an odd name."

Rafael was starting to get tired of this nonsense. "So do I get to leave at some point, or are you planning to kill me, or what?"

"That's up to you." Lucien looked toward the door. "Here comes the doctor."

The door opened, and another man entered. This one was a mortal—Rafael could tell from the smell. He wore a white lab coat and carried a clipboard. He had brown, slightly receding hair and wire-rimmed glasses, as well as a set of prominent, fairly fresh teeth marks on his neck.

"You're awake," he said. "Good."

"Who's been chomping on you?" Rafael said, not sure what inspired this brashness. Maybe just the knowledge that he didn't have to kill anyone today, and that no one was, apparently, planning on killing him, either.

The man grinned. "My girlfriend." He held out a hand. "I'm Dr. Greene."

"Rafael." Grudgingly, he shook the offered hand.

"Hmm. How long have you been a vampire?"

"About four years."

The doctor jotted notes in his chart. "How old were you when you were Turned?"

"Is that your business?"

Dr. Greene smiled patiently. "I'm your doctor, as of now. Vampires don't have blood pressure, not much of a heart rate most of the time, and forget about trying to figure out anything based on blood sugar levels. So, yes, it's my business."

Rafael frowned. "I was seventeen."

"Ah. That explains a lot."

Rafael wondered what, exactly, it explained, but decided he'd rather not know. "Anything else?"

"That's it for now. I'll get back to you if I have any more questions." With a polite smile, he turned his attention to the chart, setting it down on the counter by the wall and making notes.

"He's awake. Cool." A new voice had joined the fray in the small room, which was quickly becoming crowded. Rafael looked toward the door to see a pretty, buxom young woman with wide, uptilted green eyes and black hair. She smiled brightly. "Hey."

"Hey," he answered. "I know you. You're the bitch who knocked me out."

Her smile widened. "I'll do it again, too, if you keep calling me a bitch."

"You knocked me unconscious and dragged me across the ocean," he said, but he really wasn't sure he was all that upset about it.

She sauntered across the room to stand next to him. The slinky walk didn't seem to be put-on at all—rather it seemed to be her natural way of moving, as if it had something to do with the way her joints were put together.

"Tell the truth," she said. "You wanted me to."

"Maybe."

She leaned a little closer, giving him an intriguing view of her cleavage. His body responded, twitching and hardening in all the right places. He had the sex drive of a seventeen-year-old, and he wasn't afraid to use it.

Her gaze locked with his. "I'm Sasha."

"Rafael." She was definitely an older woman. At least a century older. "Thanks for not killing me."

Lucien cleared his throat. Rafael looked up to see him and the doctor watching with interest.

"Shall we leave you kids alone?" Lucien asked.

"Absolutely," said Sasha.

"Let me get that IV out," said the doctor. Rafael watched as Dr. Greene deftly pulled the IV from his arm and rolled the rack against the wall. With a small smile, the doctor gave Rafael a quick salute and departed. Lucien followed.

"Don't cause him too much damage," said Lucien to Sasha, closing the door behind him.

Rafael looked at her. "Do you have plans to damage me?"

"No, not really." She bent over him, looking into his eyes from the uncomfortable distance of two or three inches. "How do you feel?"

"Fine, I guess." He craned his neck away from her. Her green eyes had merged into a single, Cyclopsean eyeball in his vision. He found the image disturbing. "Did you know you're quite a pain in the ass?"

She leaned back, grinning. "It's what I'm best at."

"Then you don't need any more practice." He let his gaze slide down her body, resting finally on the cleavage trying to burst out of her blouse. "Are you good at anything else?"

Her smile went hot. His body followed suit, but he had other plans. Sasha bent close again, her breasts mounding against his chest, her lips fluttering millimeters from his own.

He grabbed the lamp from the bedside table and whacked her over the head with it. She slumped.

"That's for Romania, you annoying little bitch."

He crawled out from under her unconscious body, arranged her comfortably on the bed, and slipped out into the hallway.

He didn't get far. Before he'd walked three yards down the corridor, Lucien appeared in front of him. "Where do you think you're going?"

"Somewhere that girl isn't," Rafael shot back.

To his surprise, Lucien smiled. "Sorry. I thought you liked her. C'mon. I think it's time you met Julian."

The quick briefing Lucien gave him on the way to Julian's office came as a surprise.

"You mean you're not the Senior at this enclave?" Rafael asked.

"No. Julian was already established when I arrived."

"Why didn't you kill him and take over? You're, like, what, a thousand years old?"

"Twelve, but who's counting?"

Rafael stopped abruptly. "You're Ialdaboth's brother."

"Half-brother."

"Belial?"

"That's correct."

Rafael shook his head. "You should be the Senior here."

"That's not the way I work."

They walked a little further along the corridor before Lucien stopped and knocked on one of the doors. At the muffled "Come in," they entered.

Meeting Julian, Rafael almost understood. Julian was quite old—not nearly as old as Lucien, but still old—and a strange aura surrounded him. He was also, Rafael noticed when they shook hands, vaguely warm.

"Have a seat," he said. Rafael sat on the couch, Lucien settling next to him. "I need to ask you some questions," Julian went on.

"Ask away."

"First, let me apologize for the way we kidnapped you. Sasha had no permission to do what she did."

Rafael shrugged. "No problem. I was about five minutes away from getting killed over there, anyway."

Julian cocked an eyebrow. "Really. Why?"

"I'm really not a very good vampire. Much less a nasty, evil one."

"So what was keeping you alive?"

"Sex, mostly."

Lucien was laughing behind his hand. Julian gave him a cold look.

"I have a feeling this story might not be all that amusing, Lucien."

Julian's apparent concern for him caught Rafael by surprise. "I guess it depends on how you look at it," he said. He cleared his throat. He didn't really want to go into this right now, not when it had just occurred to him that he might be lucky enough never to see Brigitte again. "So what did you want to ask me?"

Julian's demeanor went abruptly businesslike. "What can you tell us about the cave you were guarding?"

"Not much. There was something important in there, that's all I know."

"They never told you the significance of that cave?" Lucien was surprised.

"I'm a four-year-old vampire flunkie who was failing initiation. Why would they tell me anything? Brigitte put me there to get me out of the way."

Julian eyed him curiously. "So you don't know anything about the bones?"

"I heard something about some bones, yeah. I don't know whose they were, though. Look, I've spent the past four years just trying to keep my ass out of trouble. I didn't ask questions, I didn't cause problems. It kept me alive. They told me to go stand in front of the cave every night for a month, so I did. I'd be there right now if that little bitch hadn't conked me over the head." He paused. "That reminds me. Somebody might want to go check on her."

"Why?" said Lucien.

"I clocked her with a lamp."

Julian rolled his eyes.

Lucien, stifling laughter, rose. "I'll go."

"We'll come with you. I want Rafael to see what was in that cave."

Rafael had to admit he was curious, but he wasn't prepared for what he saw.

Julian led him to a room in the hospital wing, not far from where he'd woken up. Inside the room was a large, cylindrical metal tube with small round windows. It reminded Rafael of a submarine.

"What the hell is that?"

"It's a hyperbaric chamber," Lucien answered. "It's full of pure, pressurized oxygen, to bathe the tissues of whoever's inside. Hospitals use it in burn wards, and to help speed up healing of other kinds of injuries. Also for people who've been exposed to carbon monoxide."

Julian quirked an eyebrow at him. Lucien shrugged. "I paid attention to Dr. Greene during that long lecture we got."

"You're a better man than I am," Julian said.

"So what's inside?" asked Rafael.

Lucien waved toward the chamber. "Take a look."

Hesitant, Rafael stepped up to the strange, steel cylinder. Still not sure he wasn't the butt of some practical joke, he peered back at the other two men before looking inside.

On a long, low, bench-like table within the chamber lay a human body. But not quite a body. There was no skin, no hair, and in many places only partial musculature. The long, flat, pink and red strands of muscle and connective tissue, with blue and red blood vessels threading in and out, both fascinated and repulsed him.

"I don't get it. What's going on here?"

"That was a bleached-white, four-thousand-year-old skeleton when we found it," said Lucien. "We took it out of the cave you were guarding as nothing but a bag of bones."

Rafael stared into the chamber, then looked at Lucien. "Samis."

"He went by Aanu when I knew him."

"When will he be . . . in one piece again?"

"We're not sure. I've never seen a regeneration with this kind of technology, or with the healing assistance Julian and I have been able to provide, though Aanu and I both went through a similar regeneration after the Great Flood."

"The Great Flood," Rafael repeated dully. This was nuts.

"The Black Sea flood. He disappeared not long after that. Now I know what happened to him." He smiled at Rafael's look of complete disbelief, then turned toward the door. "I'd better go check on Sasha. My guess is she's probably pretty damned pissed right about now."

Rafael watched Lucien go. And *felt* him go. The big man's aura faded gradually as he walked away. Like Ialdaboth's, Rafael thought again, but not quite the same.

"What is he?" he said suddenly, without thinking.

Julian laughed a little. "Not an unfair question. They call themselves the First Demons."

"'They?'"

"Lucien and Ialdaboth." He gestured toward the bones on the table. "Aanu and Ruha. They're brothers. Half-brothers, really. All sired by a demon on different mothers."

Rafael nodded. "I've heard the stories. I thought it was all a load of crap."

Julian shrugged. "We all have to come from somewhere. Vampires came from them."

Rafael mulled that over. He'd spent most of his four years as a vampire wishing he could be mortal, not absorbing the vampiric backstory. He'd heard some of the tales, the folklore, but it hadn't made much of an impression on him. It hadn't mattered. Now, to discover it was true—

"We've heard some odd stories, as well," Julian went on. "I was hoping you could confirm or deny them."

"If it's about Ialdaboth's enclave, I won't have much. Like I said, I just stayed low and tried to keep out of trouble."

"Lilith said you belonged to Brigitte."

Rafael tensed. Where the hell was this going? Had he escaped Brigitte just to end up a slave again, this time to Lilith? It didn't bear thinking of. He'd heard horrible stories about Lilith. He'd even met her once. She had been cold and pale and frightening.

"Lilith is here?" He couldn't keep a tremor of fear out of his voice.

Julian nodded soberly. "She's left Ialdaboth's enclave."

"She was—" He stopped.

"Tremendously evil," Julian finished for him. "She changed her mind."

Rafael decided not to ask how someone could just change her mind about being tremendously evil.

"Now. About Brigitte," Julian continued.

"What about her?" Rafael couldn't fathom what any of these people could possibly want to know about Brigitte.

"There was a litany. Something Ialdaboth knew and passed on to certain members of his inner circle. Lilith had not yet finished the initiation process, but Brigitte had. Am I right?"

Rafael eyed him narrowly. Things still weren't quite making sense. "She was one of his inner circle, yes."

"Do you know the litany? Did you ever hear it?"

Rafael was silent for a long moment, thinking. Could he remember the litany? And if he could, should he tell it to Julian? Hell, never mind the litany. Should he tell Julian anything at all?

"Why do you want it?"

"I want to kill Ialdaboth. The litany is, I believe, part of what will tell me how."

He schooled his features carefully. He'd gotten good at hiding his emotions, at keeping Brigitte, in particular, from knowing what he was thinking. "Why do you want to kill him?"

"Can you think of any reason why I shouldn't?"

Okay, that was annoying, that answering a question with a question thing. Then again, it was a good question. Meaty. Worth a bit of consideration.

"If you want to take his place," Rafael answered slowly, "to take over his enclave, use your power for—" He broke off.

Julian grinned. "Use my powers for evil?"

"Something like that. I mean, doesn't everybody?"

Julian sobered. "Not everybody."

"I'm starting to get that."

"Will you help us, then?"

"I'll do what I can."

Sasha sat up and rubbed the bump on her head, unsure what had happened. A second later, she remembered—she just wasn't prepared to believe it. Surely Rafael wouldn't be stupid enough to whack her over the head with a lamp.

Or maybe he would be. He was too damned pretty to have any actual brains. She rubbed the bump a little harder, feeling it disappear, along with the pain, under her fingers. Regardless of the speedy healing time, Rafael was in deep shit.

She was halfway to her feet when the door opened. She spun, ready to fly on the intruder if it happened to be Rafael. But it was Lucien.

"You okay?" he asked.

She straightened, adjusting her mussed blouse at the same time. "Yeah."

"You deserved it, you know."

His smile should have infuriated her, but she found it hard to be angry with Lucien. Maybe it was those blue eyes. Her annoyance at Rafael evaporated, as well. "Yeah, I suppose I did. Where is he?"

"He's next door with Julian and Aanu."

"Aanu's awake?"

"No. Not even close."

A shadow passed through Lucien's eyes, and she wondered, not for the first time, what Aanu must be going through right now. Enough to warrant Lucien's concern, certainly. She hated to think what it must be like to come back from a pile of bones. She wasn't even sure she, as an ordinary, run-of-the-mill vampire, could do it. That kind of destruction would probably kill her permanently.

"Do you think he'll be okay?" she ventured.

"Eventually." He stepped into the hallway, holding the door open so she could follow. "Let's go. You can apologize to Rafael."

"I will not."

Lucien only smiled.

Rafael looked up as they entered the other hospital room, but the expression on his face held more fear than contrition. Good. He *should* be afraid of her.

"Hey," he said. "You okay?"

"For the most part."

"Sorry about the lamp."

She shrugged. "Sorry about the rock. And the kidnapping—you know, all that jazz."

His lopsided smile appealed to her. "Would you like to talk?"

"Sure." With a glance at Lucien, who was smiling, she backed toward the door. "Follow me. I know a place where we won't be interrupted by these ancient, all-powerful geeks."

She'd found the little cavern a few years ago, in a bend of a tunnel off a side-corridor that branched into a little-used area of the Underground. She had no doubt Julian knew about it—he seemed to know a great deal—but he'd never interrupted her when she was there. Maybe he understood that she only went there when she needed to be alone. There were several such niches and crevices throughout the Underground, with various vampires laying claim to them as their private "thinking places."

She led Rafael toward her own secret alcove. He looked around at the corridors as they wound their way deeper into the complex. Occasionally they passed other vampires. One, who had the appearance of a ten-year-old boy with odd, mud-colored skin and dark brown, curly hair, gave Sasha a smile as they went by. Rafael eyed him reflectively.

"That's Daniel," said Sasha. "He's about five hundred years old."

"That's just not right."

"I know. Here, this way." They started along the first branch off the main corridor. It had a steepish downward slant. "Dr. Greene's working on some kind of procedure to make the Children mortal again."

She looked over her shoulder, judging Rafael's reaction. He was frowning.

"We don't have kids," he said.

"No one ever Turns kids in Ialdaboth's enclave?"

"No, we—they—Turn them all the time. But as far as I know, none of them has ever lived through the initiation phases." He spoke in a near-monotone, as if dissociating himself from his own words.

"So they Turn the kids just so they can kill them?"

He shook his head. "It's bad over there. I hated it. You did me a favor, braining me with that rock."

She wasn't sure what to say to that, so she said nothing. Neither did Rafael. They continued in silence until, finally, they took the last bend of the last narrow corridor and Sasha led the way into her small cavern. It was big enough for them to sit comfortably, with a few feet between them, but they both had to duck under the low entryway.

"This is nice," Rafael said, looking around. The cavern had rough, unfinished walls, and some of the bumps sparkled with embedded quartz. A small stalactite had begun in a concavity in the ceiling.

"It's quiet," she said, settling herself in her usual sitting-spot. The darkness, impenetrable to human eyes, presented no challenge to vampiric senses.

Rafael settled cross-legged against the opposite wall. "So what about this bunch of brats they're trying to make mortal again?"

"They're not brats," she said. "And we don't think of them as being kids anymore, either. They're the Children—a special group."

He shrugged. "Okay, if you say so. But what about this procedure for un-Turning them? What do you know about it?"

The question surprised her. "As far as I know, the doctor's still working on it. We don't even know for sure if it's possible. Why?"

"Just curious. It seems like a good thing to do."

"Yeah. I feel bad for all the kids. We've got about twenty-five of them, and most of them have been through hell."

He studied her curiously. "You spend a lot of time with them?"

"Technically, I'm one of them." She smiled at his surprise. "I was sixteen when I was Turned. I didn't choose it."

"Neither did I. I was seventeen." He folded his hands, settling them against his crossed ankles—good hands, well-shaped and with a certain grace to the way the fingers moved. "Why *did* you drag me out of Romania?"

She tilted her head, at a loss for an answer. "Would you believe it was because I thought you were cute?"

He laughed. "Yeah. From you, I'd believe it."

"What's that supposed to mean?" Her offended tone was mostly feigned.

"It means I find you a little hard to follow."

"I like the sound of that."

"So what do you say? Friends?"

He held out a hand, but she didn't take it. Instead she looked at it, considering. "I like to make up with a little more than a handshake."

"Kiss and make up?"

"That's a start."

He leaned toward her, and she was shocked to realize she was genuinely nervous. Why? In three hundred years she'd slept with more men than she could possibly count. Why should this one be any different?

Because he just was. And she couldn't come up with any better answer as her lips met his and she found herself involved in a careful, chaste kiss instead of the passionate tongue-tangle she'd intended to initiate. And that careful, chaste kiss sent heat through her body more intense than anything she'd ever experienced from a kiss from any other man.

She backed up, just a little, and looked into his dark eyes. "Can you answer one thing for me?"

"Yes." The breath of his answer fluttered against her lips.

"Do you have any desire whatsoever to go back to Romania? Back to Ialdaboth?"

"No."

She smiled. "Good," she said, and kissed him again.

Two

They talked for a while longer, about nothing in particular. Sasha had a strange urge to unload her heart to Rafael, tell him everything she'd experienced in her long, not necessarily happy un-life. But the urge frightened her as much as it drove her, so she held back. They talked about music, movies, books, and for the first time ever Sasha had some sense of what it might be like to be a modern teenager. They faked it pretty well, she thought, considering he was technically twenty-one and she was three hundred and sixteen.

After a while she grew tired of the darkness in the cavern and offered to take him to her room. The look he gave her made her dizzy. In spite of everything, he wanted her.

"How close is it to daylight?" he asked as they headed back up the long corridors.

"A few hours yet. Can't you tell?"

He shook his head. "I'm jet-lagged or something. I think I'm still on Romanian time."

She laughed, amused by the idea. "The nights are still pretty long here. Not as long as in Romania, but we have some time."

"Good."

Leading him into her room, she seemed to see it for the first time, and wished she'd cleaned up before inviting him in. There were bits of things everywhere—paper and wire, hemp cord, glass beads, stubby pencils—all remnants of projects she'd started and never quite finished. Inspired by conversations with Dina, she'd gotten the idea she could design jewelry for one of Vivian's profit-making ventures, but too often in the middle of a project she got distracted by something else. The TV was a huge culprit. It continued to fascinate her, because some part of her three century-old brain simply couldn't comprehend it.

Rafael didn't seem interested in the condition of her room, though. He closed the door behind him, watching her. She recognized the heat in his eyes and her body responded, tingling.

But for the first time in recent memory, she was having doubts about falling into bed with a man. As he reached for her she shrugged away, almost without realizing she'd done it.

He frowned, looking hurt. "What?"

"I don't know. I think— I think maybe I like you too much to just jump into bed with you."

He quirked an eyebrow. "Even though I clocked you with the lamp?"

"Maybe because you clocked me with the lamp."

"I'm flattered." He reached for her again. She held still this time and he ran a finger gently down her face. His expression told her he was struggling with something. Finally he spoke again, his voice soft and halting.

"I was a virgin when Brigitte Turned me. She taught me every-thing I needed to know to make a woman crazy in bed, but I can't say I ever really enjoyed it. I was her personal whore, basically."

His fingers trailed from her face down her throat, feather light. She wondered again why she'd decided to knock him on the head and drag him across the ocean. Had she sensed what they both were feel-ing now? Had she somehow known he wanted out?

"I've often wondered," he went on, his voice rumbling barely above a whisper, "what it's like to make love to a woman I actually want to be with."

"I would be . . . the first?"

"Yes."

"Now *I'm* flattered."

He smiled. His fingers had paused at the point of the V in the neckline of her sweater. "I like you," he said. "Plus I get the feeling you might just know what you're doing."

She grinned. "You calling me a slut?"

"Just acknowledging the fact you're about two hundred years older than I am."

"More than that."

"I was told to always underestimate a woman's age."

"Good policy."

He took his hand away, looking into her eyes. He had lowered something, some guard or wall he'd been maintaining, and she saw new depths in him. Pain, mostly, and threads of fear. Vulnerability above all. His openness made her feel vulnerable, as well.

"Would you do this for me?" he said, and for a moment she could almost swear he was afraid of her.

"Yes," she said, and then suddenly had no idea what to do next.

Nothing like an emotional preamble to make sex awkward, she thought. She'd never before felt this uncomfortable in this situation.

But to her surprise—and relief—he took over. Leaning forward, he touched his lips to hers, moved his mouth gently, as if experimenting with an action utterly new to him. She responded, moaning softly in the back of her throat. She felt as if she were about to cry. She felt almost like a virgin. Not that she remembered what that felt like.

She reached toward him, hoping to draw him closer, but he caught her hands. "I'd like to be in charge here, thank you very much."

She grinned. "Are you sure?"

"Absolutely. I mean, if that's okay with you."

"It's perfectly okay with me."

He kissed her again, harder this time, then bent and lifted her in his arms. Laughing, he tumbled her onto the bed, landing half on top of her. His fingers found the tail of her sweater and peeled it off her, pulled the cups of her bra out of the way so he could suckle her breasts.

He was going too fast, but she couldn't fault his enthusiasm. And once he'd gotten a taste of her, he slowed down a little, sampling her skin an inch at a time while she writhed under him. He maneuvered her out of the rest of her clothes, but when she reached for his shirt buttons he pushed her hands away. "I'm in charge, remember. For a while, at least."

"Sorry. You may have to remind me a few times."

"Brigitte always—"

She laid a finger against his lips. "Don't talk about her. This is for you and me."

"All right."

He kissed her again, thoroughly exploring her mouth. She let him take the lead, restraining herself when necessary, but it wasn't long before they were both so involved that it didn't matter who initiated what.

He hadn't exaggerated when he'd said he knew how to make a woman crazy in bed. He used his fingers and his mouth on her until she was nearly weeping in ecstasy. And when he pressed inside her, hard and deep, he drove her even higher, withholding his own climax until she had shuddered to pieces twice beneath him.

To her surprise, then, he started to pull out. She was certain he hadn't finished. She grasped his buttocks, stopping him.

"Don't stop," she said.

He stared down at her, his glazed-over eyes telling her that he hadn't been consciously aware of what he'd done. It took a few moments for her words to sink in, then the glaze changed to the intense, mindless look she was accustomed to seeing as he let his body take over, driving himself into her again and again, until he climaxed with a soul-deep moan.

"Oh, God," he breathed, sagging above her, propped on trembling arms.

She shifted under him, touched his shoulder to urge him down next to her. She curled her body into his arms, and he cradled her close, trembling. She couldn't tell if it was the aftershock of his orgasm, or if he was trying not to cry.

"Are you all right?" Her voice came soft, barely more than a murmur.

He nodded. "It's never felt like that before. It's never been that good. Thank you."

Smiling, she kissed him gently on the forehead. "You're welcome."

They lay curled together for a time, then Rafael sat up, rubbing his hands over his face. He *had* been crying, she was surprised to discover. His show of vulnerability touched her.

Apparently he'd had enough of it, though, because he pointed at the TV.

"You get a signal down here?"

She shrugged. "Sometimes. Nicholas spliced into a cable feed somewhere above ground for me. The picture's crap most of the time, when it's there at all. Mostly I watch DVDs."

"Wow. Where do you get them?"

"Different places. I buy them here and there, or rent them." She grinned, pointing to a stack of discs next to the chest of drawers. "Those are all from Blockbuster. Good luck to them, trying to collect late fees."

He laughed. "They must totally hate you."

"I keep forging new membership numbers so they don't know it's me. Plus I can put the whammy on them pretty good." She lowered her voice, imitating the vibrations of compulsion. "Give me three copies of *Gladiator*. I'm never bringing them back."

Chuckling and naked, he wandered to the pile of DVDs, glancing through the titles, then looked at a similar stack of music CDs that leaned precariously nearby. "I never had much of my own stuff. Wasn't allowed. We had to sneak stuff in or sneak out to find it."

"Ialdaboth runs a tight ship, huh?"

"Very. One of my friends got his hands chopped off for smuggling in old *Eagles* albums."

She winced. "Didn't they grow back overnight?"

He nodded. "He had a standing appointment. Hand removal every night at dusk for three months."

Sasha shuddered. "How did you put up with that place?"

"Not very well." He gave her an apologetic look. "I guess that shot the romantic mood all to hell."

"It wasn't exactly romantic. More like plain lust." She grinned wryly. "But, yeah, kind of."

"Sorry."

He joined her on the bed and put an arm around her. "Should we watch a movie and cuddle? We could act like mortals for a couple of hours."

"That sounds nice," she said, though she wasn't sure why. Not long ago she would have sworn that was about the last thing she would ever want to do with a man. "Pick a flick."

His choice surprised her, as had many other things about him, and they were a half-hour into *My Best Friend's Wedding* when someone knocked on the door.

"Shit," said Sasha.

"I'll get it." Rafael hit the pause button on the DVD player and went to the door.

It was Dr. Greene. Sasha peered around Rafael to see him standing in the hallway. He was wearing his white lab coat and a concerned expression.

"What's up?" Rafael asked.

"I've been doing some work in the lab," the doctor said. "I need to talk to both of you."

Sasha followed Rafael to Dr. Greene's office. Julian was waiting for them, sober, performing complex finger gymnastics with a stubby pencil. He said nothing, though, letting Dr. Greene run the show.

"I've been performing these experiments at Julian's request," Dr. Greene explained to Rafael, who nodded.

"Sasha told me something about it. It sounds like a good idea."

"Yes. Anyway, it looks like I've found the right combination of elements. I'm not sure how it works, exactly, but I've gotten a significant sample of juvenile vampiric blood to return to a normal, human state."

Sasha glanced at Julian. His expression told her nothing. He twiddled the pencil in and out, around and between his fingers. *That guy should have never stopped smoking*, she thought.

Dr. Greene passed around a sheet of paper with color pictures of blood cells in two different squares. The blood cells in the left-hand square were thinner and sparser than those in the right-hand square. Sasha skimmed the text below the pictures, but it was all in medicalese and made no sense to her.

"What does this have to do with us?" she asked.

"To put it bluntly," Julian said, "we need a guinea pig."

Sasha blinked. "But this is just for the kids. The little kids. Like Daniel."

"Yes, but I don't want the doctor to test the procedure on the younger Children."

"Daniel's, like, two hundred years older than I am," Sasha protested.

"Yes, but he's a ten-year-old, psychologically," Dr. Greene put in. "I've spoken with him, as well as several of the other younger Children, and I don't think any of them would be suitable candidates for this phase of the testing."

Sasha narrowed her eyes at him. "Because it might not work?"

"Partially, yes. But also because I don't think any of them are prepared to comprehend what a return to mortality would mean. They weren't mortal long enough to remember, so many years later, what it was like."

Julian switched the pencil to his left hand, which, Sasha noted, was nearly as nimble as the right. "You two were Turned as teenagers," he said. "You can remember mortality. Thus you're capable of making an informed decision."

Rafael looked flummoxed. "I thought . . . I mean, I was assuming that in order for this to work, the vampire would have to have been Turned before puberty."

Dr. Greene nodded. "I was working on that assumption, too. But it appears that's not the case. It has more to do with achievement of adult growth. I need to do some tests on both of you, but I have a feeling you'll both be eligible."

"What kind of tests?" Sasha asked.

"X-rays. Quick and painless."

She crossed her arms firmly over her chest. "What if I don't want to be mortal again?" The thought, quite frankly, repulsed her. She liked her power, her strength. She liked knowing she would never have to die.

"Then you don't have to participate," said Julian, balancing the pencil on the backs of his knuckles.

She stood. "Let's go, Rafael. I don't want anything to do with this."

But Rafael remained in his chair, looking not at Sasha, but at the doctor. "I'll take the tests," he said quietly. "If I'm eligible, count me in."

Mortal again. Rafael could barely bend his brain around the concept. But having been Turned only four years ago, he had no trouble remembering what being alive was like. It hadn't been that long ago. He remembered the sun especially, heat and light on his skin. And suddenly he remembered what pancakes tasted like—remembered so vividly it made his mouth water.

But Sasha was staring at him as if he'd completely lost his mind. "Are you nuts? Do you remember what mortality means? It means you *die*."

He frowned at her, the ghost-flavor of maple syrup still lingering on his tongue. "Yeah. Generally. What's your point?"

"My point is you're an idiot." She stormed out of the room, slamming the door behind her.

Dr. Greene blinked at the reverberation. "I'd say that was a 'no.'"

"How long before we know for sure? If we're eligible, I mean?" Rafael asked. He couldn't worry about Sasha's reaction, not with this huge, beautiful possibility looming in front of him.

"A couple of days," said the doctor. "I'll get back to you."

Rafael nodded. A couple of days. It seemed, suddenly, like a lifetime.

He lay in bed just before dawn, thinking about it. At least he didn't have to worry about it keeping him awake. As soon as the sun rose, he'd be asleep, regardless of what preyed on his mind. There was no such thing as vampire insomnia.

He didn't want to spend too much time obsessing about it, though. So he turned his mind to the other thing Julian had asked him about— the litany.

Brigitte had said it every morning just before daylight. Rafael knew it was a secret thing, something only the privileged few were supposed to know. This was precisely the reason he'd paid attention to it, since, otherwise, it had seemed like so much gibberish. But he wasn't supposed to know it, so of course he'd done his best to eavesdrop.

The one who feeds on life. What the hell did that mean? And what was the next line? *The one who feeds on life holds power beyond the one who eats death. Bring the First Ones. Feed.*

That couldn't be all of it. It was too short, and it made no sense. But that was all he remembered.

Ah, there was the sun. Weariness pulled him under in a deep, soft flood.

Three

He spoke to Julian the next evening.

The Underground's leader laboriously transcribed the brief, practically nonsensical words, then laid the piece of paper on his desk and frowned at it. Thinking, Rafael supposed.

After several minutes, Julian raised his head and looked at him. "You and Sasha have been staying fairly close to home, I hope?" he said.

Rafael gave a one-shouldered shrug. "Yeah, I guess." The farthest they'd strayed was Sasha's thinking place, and there he'd still been able to sense the thick layers of ancient magic that kept the Underground camouflaged. Even Ialdaboth's inner sanctums weren't as well-warded as this place.

Julian gave him a dubious look. "Well, if you have been wandering, I suggest you stop. A couple of our people went to Atlantic City night before last and haven't come back."

Rafael's stomach clenched. An overreaction, surely. "Atlantic City's a long way from here. Anything could have happened."

"It's not that far, but you're right," Julian said. "It could have been anything. Traffic, sunlight, the frigging Jersey Devil for all I know. Maybe they're still down there whoring. But it won't hurt you to be careful."

"How well protected are we here?"

"Very. But the protection I've been able to provide for the others may be less effective for you because of your blood ties to Ialdaboth. Lilith was tracked here—they might be able to find you, too."

"So it's best to stay under the city," Rafael concluded.

Julian nodded. "Yes. Most of Manhattan is fairly safe for most of us—the magic leaks upward, through the ground, and scrambles any interloper's sensing abilities pretty thoroughly. Still, if I were you, I'd be especially cautious. If you have no need to go to the surface, don't."

Rafael didn't even consider objecting. He had no desire to skulk around Manhattan looking for victims, anyway. Especially if there was any risk of being discovered by Ialdaboth's minions. "I'll keep that in mind," he said.

"Good." Julian gave him a vague smile. "Thanks for your help.

You can go now."

Relieved at the abrupt dismissal—he still felt unsettled around vampiric authority figures—Rafael made his way to the hospital wing. He let himself into Aanu's room and stood next to the strange, silver hyperbaric chamber where lay the bones he'd unwittingly guarded for six months, day in and day out, doing what he was told, to keep from being killed.

Except they weren't bones anymore. The body was almost completely healed. Muscles had formed, filling in the outlines of a large, strong body. Yesterday he'd sat for three hours watching lungs build, layer by layer. Today they were covered by a thin layer of muscle and connective tissue that bound the ribs together. If he stood at the front window of the chamber, he could see the heart beating. Aanu's heart. That was this body's—this man's—name.

What would it be like for him, coming back to life after four thousand years? Would he be able to remember how to walk? How to speak? How to breathe? What did it feel like, being remade layer by layer?

What would it feel like to be mortal again?

Rafael could understand Sasha's reaction. She'd been a vampire for three centuries, and in spite of Dr. Greene's assumptions that she remembered what it was like to be mortal, Rafael doubted she really did. Plus she seemed to enjoy being a vampire. That was fine, he supposed, if you could find a way to make peace with the darker aspects of the lifestyle. He'd never been able to do that, maybe because he'd had the misfortune of being Turned by one of Ialdaboth's followers. He had a feeling, though, that it wouldn't have mattered who Turned him. He'd never be totally at peace with vampire-ness no matter the circumstances.

Something changed inside the hyperbaric chamber. Rafael blinked, not sure at first what it was, then realized he couldn't see the beating heart anymore. Another layer of muscle had finished forming over Aanu's ribcage. It wouldn't be long, he figured, until skin started to grow. He wondered how long it would be before Aanu woke up. If he woke up.

"How is he?"

The voice startled him. A woman's voice. Brigitte. She was ready for him. Ready to hurt him. Old reflexes kicked in, and he spun around, hands crossed at the wrist protectively in front of him. Then, abruptly, he dropped them to his sides, embarrassed. It was only Sasha. He hadn't seen her since she'd stormed out of Dr. Greene's office the previous night. Strangely, he'd missed her. He shifted, looking everywhere but directly at her.

She frowned. "Are you all right?"

"Fine." He gestured weakly toward the silver chamber. "He's . . . I don't know. How do you tell? He doesn't have any skin yet."

Sasha walked up and looked in one of the small round windows. "Wow. He looks a hell of a lot further along than he did yesterday."

Rafael nodded. "I wonder what he'll say, first thing when he wakes up?"

"No telling. It won't be English, though."

He hadn't thought of that. But of course, the guy had been dead for four thousand years. What languages would he know? Some ancient Egyptian or Babylonian tongue? Would there be anybody here who could talk to him?

"Where were you born?" he asked her suddenly, not sure why he wanted to know.

"Belarus, I think they call it now," she said. She touched his elbow, hesitant. It was as if she barely knew him. Certainly she wasn't acting as if they'd been cavorting naked not that long ago. "I'm sorry."

"For what?"

"For shutting you out. I shouldn't have."

He shrugged. "Why not? We barely know each other."

"Maybe that's part of the problem." She backed toward the door. "Come with me. Please?"

"Are you going to hit me in the head with anything?"

She smiled. "Only if you don't come."

"What the hell, it's not like I have anything better to do."

She took him again to the quiet cave. He could tell she had something on her mind. He hadn't known her that long, but it had been long enough to know her silence wasn't typical. She liked to talk, to rib him and play verbal games. There was none of that now.

Instead, leaning against the cave wall, she said quietly, not quite looking at him, "If you go through with this, you won't see me again."

"I don't understand. Why?"

Her lip curled disdainfully, but there were tears in her eyes. "I don't consort with mortals."

"I'll still be the same person."

"No, you won't. You'll be human." She blinked and looked away from him. "You'll be out in the sun, eating whatever the hell it is they eat these days. And you'll die."

"Not right away. At least, that's not the plan."

"It's never the plan. But it doesn't really matter, does it? You will grow old and you will die." Her voice had gone thin-edged and bitter, with a trace of an accent Rafael didn't recognize and had never heard her use before. "I will not. Ever."

There were, of course, any number of ways a vampire could die, but this didn't seem like the time to point that out. On the other hand, he'd learned a few things in the short time he'd been in the Underground that did seem worth noting. "There are several human/vampire couples around here. Dr. Greene and Lilith, for instance. They seem to be doing okay."

"That is their decision." Her accent thickened, as did her voice. "It will never be mine."

It seemed, then, that there was little he could do. She'd obviously made up her mind. He turned away and started to leave the small chamber, then suddenly remembered.

This wasn't Brigitte. He could question her. Challenge her, even.

He turned around. "You would give up that easily?"

Her chin lifted. "Don't question me. I've been around a lot longer than you have."

"Don't pull that shit with me. You're scared."

She sniffed. "Of what?"

"Of hurting. If I'm mortal, eventually I'll die—I understand that—whether I get hit by a bus, or come down with the Ebola virus, or die in my sleep when I'm a hundred and twelve. And you'll still be exactly what you are now."

"I've been through it before. I don't want to go through it again. So, yes, maybe I am afraid. But for good reason."

She was right, in a way. She had been around a lot longer than he had. He couldn't conceive what it would be like to watch someone he loved age and die in front of him, while he remained unchanged. He hadn't been a vampire long enough to have experienced that. Maybe he hadn't been a vampire long enough to fully appreciate the consequences of his decision.

That didn't change one fact, though—the single fact that he could be sure of and that he didn't need a century of vampiric life to understand.

"That's too bad," he said, moving toward the door. "Because I think we could have had something. Something really good."

A tear had escaped and rolled down her face. "Yes. And we still could, if you just don't do this."

"I'm sorry, Sasha. I have to. Maybe there's no way you can understand, but I have to."

He couldn't look at her anymore, couldn't bear to see the pain on her face. He turned his back on her and left her there.

* * *

"Based on the X-rays, I'd say you're an excellent candidate." Dr. Greene pointed at the X-rays he'd hung on the viewing light set into the wall. "Based on the development of your femurs, you would have grown a few more inches if you'd been left to your own devices."

Rafael looked at the pictures of his leg bones. "Huh," was all he could think of to say. It was strange to have this, too, added to the list of injustices committed against him. Brigitte had abducted him, Turned him against his will, made him her sex slave, and on top of all that, she'd stunted his growth.

The doctor continued. "I'll want to monitor you throughout the process to be sure there are no problems and also to record exactly what happens during your transformation. Information we can gain from you will be vital in administering and regulating the treatment when we use it on the Children."

"So . . ." Rafael hesitated. "This procedure hasn't been tested at all?"

"Only under laboratory conditions. There's really no other way. It's not possible to, say, turn a lab rat into a vamp-rat and then change it back."

"So I'm the vamp-rat."

Dr. Greene unclipped the X-rays from the lighted screen. "I'm afraid so."

"What are the chances this procedure will kill me?"

"Based on my trials, extremely low."

"And if your trials are wrong?"

The doctor shrugged his shoulders. "I don't know. I'll be honest with you, though—this isn't risk-free. It's one of the reasons I wanted to try it with an older subject first."

Rafael nodded. "I get it." He looked at the X-rays, now dark and unreadable in the doctor's hands. "Do I have to decide right now?"

"No. Think about it a little longer if you have to."

Rafael stood. "Has Sasha talked to you at all?"

"No. She had no desire to participate. She wouldn't even come in for the X-rays." He paused, studying Rafael's face. "Does that have something to do with your own hesitation?"

"A little." He shrugged. "You know how it can be."

The doctor gave him a wry grin. "Yeah, I do."

"I just need to talk to her, is all." Rafael wasn't sure why he felt such a need to justify himself.

"Take your time."

Still, he felt odd about leaving, as if he owed the doctor more of an explanation.

But he didn't. He didn't owe anybody anything—except Sasha for dragging him out of Ialdaboth's hellhole. And even her . . . well, he owed her his life, but not eternity. No, he had to decide what *he* wanted, not what might be good for the Children or Dr. Greene or anybody else.

He left the doctor's office and went to Sasha's room, knocked on her closed door.

She opened it, looked at him, and let him in.

"Sasha," he began, but she cut him off with her mouth on his, kissing him hard and deep while her hands pulled open his jeans.

There was no fighting her. Well, he could have—she wasn't Brigitte—but he had no desire to. She dragged him toward the bed and pulled him down onto it, dragging his jeans half off him. Before he quite knew what was happening, she was on top of him and sliding him inside her, her sex clenching hard on his shaft. He could do little but respond.

She took him to the edge and then stopped. When one move would have meant his climax, she held utterly still. Somehow she knew the moment when he had moved back from the inevitable, for that was the moment when she slid off him. She took his hand in hers and pressed it into her own heat.

Her arousal stoked his, as he slid his fingers into her. She was slick with desire. He wanted inside her again, but she wouldn't let him. Instead she held herself over him while he worked her to the peak and over it, until she came tumbling down with tears in her eyes, her body shivering with aftershocks.

"Now?" he whispered. She nodded. He rolled her over, under him, and buried himself in her again.

He knew, suddenly, as he thrust his way to release, that this was the last time. He didn't know why she'd pulled him in here, but he did know, in a moment of sudden, unexpected clarity, what he would tell Dr. Greene.

Thoughts dissipated as he plunged inside one last time. His brain emptied as his body did, as he filled her.

Drained, satiated, he sagged over her. She looked into his eyes.

"Don't do it," she said. "Don't take this away from us."

He'd suspected as much. It had been a bribe of sorts, a practical demonstration of what she would so stubbornly insist on taking from him if he followed this path. The path he'd finally realized was the one single thing he most wanted right now in what passed for his existence.

More than love, more than sex, more even than her, he wanted life. If she couldn't accept that, then there had never been anything more between them than this—this sweat and heat and raw satiation of flesh.

His arousal faded, and he rolled away from her, groping for his jeans, which were somewhere on the floor.

"I'm sorry," he said. "But I have to do it."

He pulled his jeans on, found his shirt and shoes, and left. He didn't even look back to see if she was crying. Because if she was, he couldn't bear it.

Four

He left her, left the corridors where she slept, left the Underground altogether. He would stay in Manhattan, since Julian had said it was relatively safe. The danger didn't really matter to him now—he needed to make one last excursion as a vampire. Just to be sure.

Outside on the street he cloaked himself as Brigitte had taught him, disguising his presence from the mortals around him. He'd never been very good at it. Other vampires could slide noiselessly through crowds, unseen, unsensed. Where he passed, he left behind whispers of, "What was that?" "Did you see something?" "I thought I heard something."

He was a terrible, lousy, awful vampire. How could Sasha begrudge him the chance to reclaim the life that had been taken from him?

Maybe she was afraid of more than his death. Maybe she was afraid that she herself would kill him. But he didn't think so. She'd had human lovers before, she'd said. So she knew something about balancing that kind of relationship. She was just afraid to watch him grow old and die. No more than that.

He had to forgive her. If he truly loved her—and he was almost certain he did—he had to accept her fear as part of her and let her go.

He forced his thoughts away from Sasha and focused on other things. He wanted to use the time to make up his mind. He wanted to experience exactly what it meant to be a vampire during these hours, to be certain he could give it up. The power—or the potential for it—the heightened senses, the things about it that were beautiful.

There were colors in the darkness he'd never seen as a mortal. Deep, glowing indigoes. Reds so dark they approached black. Gorgeous, velvety blacks with blue, green, orange undertones. There was a particular shade of red that surrounded mortals in the dark, outlining them and pulsing with their heartbeats. He stood in the best vampiric silence he could muster and simply watched this for a time, imprinting the sight on his memory.

This, he decided after a time, was the only thing he would miss. The colors. But there were other colors, colors of sun and daylight, that were as beautiful and intense as these could ever be.

Just before dawn began to creep in, he realized he was hungry. He wondered why he hadn't noticed earlier when it was clawing so insistently in his stomach.

Blood. He needed blood. He'd had a couple of plasma drinks before he'd left the Underground, but that stuff didn't stick with him very well. He needed fresh, hot blood, to flow, copious and coppery, down his throat, to fill his dead veins.

He sat very still, watching the mortals. They would provide more than enough. A bit from the man, a bit from the woman, not enough to distress either of them. In spite of his training by the Dark Children, he had enough control for that. He didn't have to kill to feed.

He should try it, one last time, just to be sure. Maybe it really wasn't that bad. Maybe it was a reasonable trade for immortality. For power. For the colors.

But no. He didn't need to explore that possibility. He already knew where it led.

Time to go back. He could take a shortcut through Vivian's house and pick up more plasma on the way.

He woke that evening starving for blood. He'd taken a couple of extra plasma bottles yesterday, and they were ready for him, on the table next to his bed. He drank them quickly, then dressed and got out of bed.

He knocked once on Dr. Greene's door, waited, then knocked again. The doctor's bleariness when he opened the door confirmed Rafael's belated realization that he should have quit after the first attempt.

"When can we start?" he said.

The doctor smiled sleepily. "Give me a few minutes."

As he was closing the door, Rafael glimpsed, in the room beyond, the slim figure of a woman with long, near-white hair. She wore only a pink, filmy nightgown. Lilith. The human doctor's vampire lover. For a split second, a twinge of pain, a thought of Sasha, weakened his resolve. The remaining taste of the plasma in his mouth strengthened it.

Dr. Greene reappeared a few minutes later, dressed and with his glasses in place.

"Sorry about the timing," Rafael said.

"You ought to be," Dr. Greene replied.

The response surprised Rafael, but when he lifted his eyebrows,

Dr. Green said, "It's okay. I'm kidding. Vampire girlfriends aren't much for cuddling first thing when they wake up, anyway. They really, really need to eat first."

Rafael felt too awkward to laugh, but managed a vague chuckle. There was that twinge again.

Dr. Greene cocked an eyebrow at him. "You okay?"

"Yeah, I'm fine. Let's get this over with."

Stretched out on a hospital bed in a room a few doors down from Dr. Greene's bedroom, Rafael finally began to feel calm. Strange, because logically this was when he figured he should start getting nervous.

"I've been experimenting with some different delivery systems," the doctor was saying as he took an IV bag out of the small refrigerator. "In the past, I've trusted the 'natural' approach—fangs and suction—but my interviews with the Children made me pursue alternate methods."

"Why?"

"Too much 'drama and trauma.'" The doctor grinned. "They're kids. I wanted something a little less . . . scary."

"They're vampires," Rafael reminded him. "Some of them have been vampires for hundreds of years. I hardly think an exchange of blood is going to traumatize them."

"Yes, they are vampires. But they're also children. I did some extensive interviews with the oldest of the lot—Daniel and Treva—and I discovered some very interesting trends."

Rafael wasn't sure he really wanted to hear a report on the doctor's research. But Dr. Greene seemed determined to ramble on about it, so he asked, "What kinds of interesting trends?"

"Neither of them remember being Made. The process has been totally blanked from their memories. Also, although I know they must have killed at some point to stay alive, neither of them remember any such incidents. In fact, they were hard-pressed to remember their last meal."

Against his better judgment, Rafael found himself becoming curious. "Why's that?"

"The human mind is a fascinating thing, particularly with regard to memory. Now, I'm no psychiatrist, but I did a great deal of research pertaining to this project. I wanted to be sure I had some idea of what might be going on in these kids' heads before I subjected them to any other potential trauma. Anyway, it appears a child's memory functions differently from an adult's. It's more likely to close out traumas, to block them off. The mind of a typical underage vampire has basically been wiped of anything traumatic or distasteful, to protect the child's psyche."

"So they don't even know they're vampires?" The concept jolted him. No wonder Dr. Greene was being so careful. There was a great deal more to this than just changing the physiology of the Children's blood.

"In a sense, no, they don't know," the doctor replied. Intellectually, maybe. Superficially. But not viscerally. You see, it doesn't matter how long they've been alive, their physical brain development has been frozen in time. For five hundred years, Daniel has had the brain of a ten-year-old boy, his synapse growth arrested by the fact of his transformation."

"Much like I'm stuck in the brain of a seventeen-year-old," Rafael said, with a lopsided smile. "Perpetually horny." At the doctor's laugh, he added, "Not a lot of my blood goes to my brain, I can tell you that."

"Well, that's a common affliction for men of all ages." The doctor had hung the IV bag from a stand and was preparing other apparatus—needles and tubes and such that made Rafael uneasy.

"So exactly how does all this work?"

"That's a good question."

"Doc, this does not inspire confidence."

The doctor grinned. "I have a general idea. How much do you want explained?"

"As much as you like. I'm relatively intelligent for a horny seventeen-year-old."

"Okay." Dr. Greene was silent for a moment, frowning thoughtfully. "About two hundred and fifty years ago, Julian ran across a Native American shaman. Of a Sioux vintage, as I recall. Generations before, a vampire had given the tribe's holy man an herb, with instructions to pass it on to any vampire they might encounter in the future, as he himself lacked the willpower to use it to its full potential. The current shaman gave the herb to Julian and told him to smoke it. The stuff made it possible for Julian to abstain from human blood. And abstinence changed him—changed his blood, his feeding, everything. Now he can eat some human food and walk in the sunlight for long periods, and he has little need for sleep. He can feed on human energy, much as Lucien and Ialdaboth do, but without diminishing that energy in the process."

Most of it had sounded pretty weird, if not impossible, but that last bit rang a bell. "Hey," Rafael exclaimed. "That sounds a little like the litany. In a way."

"Yes. Which is why Julian wanted that information from you. To tell him about himself."

"So what does this have to do with me?"

The doctor took off his glasses, wiping them carefully on his shirt-tail as he resumed his narrative. "The next thing we ran into was Nicholas. He had been made by Vivian, who'd spent the last century or two feeding primarily on cancer victims. We were able to use Julian's blood in combination with Nick's to cure Dina, Nick's girlfriend, who was dying of cancer."

Rafael laced his fingers together, trying to twiddle his thumbs. "And this relates to me how?" He didn't want to seem impatient or ungrateful, but he was having a hard time figuring out how these pieces might fit together.

Dr. Greene smiled a little, as if amused at his impatience. "Well, inquiring minds want to know, so I started mixing little bits of this blood and that blood and ended up with a blood that, when mixed with blood out of a vampire's veins, brings it to life." He lifted the bag on the IV stand. "This is one of the components from Nick's blood. It'll cause your blood to remain alive instead of dying within twenty-four hours, as it normally does."

Rafael frowned. "That's why we feed every day? To replace the blood that dies?"

"Right."

"Do most vampires know this, or am I especially ignorant?"

"Most vampires don't take the time to think about it. When Julian happened upon those herbs, he didn't know they kept his blood alive, but that was why he no longer had to feed. And when he transformed, that ability became a part of his physiology—something he could pass on to others under certain conditions." The doctor picked up a needle and opened the sterile packaging. "The combination I'm going to use on you doesn't work on cancerous cells, but it does work on the blood samples I took from the Children, and on the sample I took from you."

"Works how?"

"It produces the appropriate transformation—turns a finite supply of harvested blood, like what you normally keep in your veins, into self-perpetuating red cells like a normal human's. Wakes up your bone marrow—all sorts of neat things."

Rafael watched as the doctor slid the needle into a vein at the bend of his elbow, then taped it down and connected it to an IV tube. "So we start with this," Dr. Greene said. "We put this bit of Nick's blood into you and see what happens."

"Excuse me—'see what happens?' I thought you knew what you were doing?"

"I do." Dr. Greene adjusted the IV bag, twisting the valve to start the bag's contents moving down the long, clear tube. It was red, but not quite blood-red. It had more of a bluish tinge than pure blood would have had. "I'm just not sure how intensive the exposure has to be. If introducing this element into your blood isn't enough to convert all of it, then I've got a dialysis machine in the other room we can use. We can run all your blood through the machine, wake it up with Nick's blood, and put it back into you."

"Why not just do that first?"

"Again, I'm trying to reduce the trauma as much as possible. If this works for you, it'll work for the Children and we won't have to subject them to that." He picked up his chart and wrote in it. "I don't worry as much about subjecting you to such things."

"Gee, thanks." Rafael settled his head on the pillow. "You got anything to read?"

An hour later, unhappy with the results from the straight IV, the doctor rolled Rafael's hospital bed down the hall to the dialysis machine. Within a few minutes, Rafael understood why they'd tried the other procedure first. The dialysis machine was painful, invasive, and almost enough to make him give up the idea altogether.

But it worked. Dr. Greene took samples of the processed blood from time to time, scribbled in his chart, and made pleased grunting sounds.

The first round of dialysis lasted five hours. Then Dr. Greene showed up with another IV bag. This time the contents were a milky white, the bag only half full.

"One more go," he said, and Rafael groaned.

"We can't go back now. If I don't do this stage, you'll be dead in a week."

"Go ahead," said Rafael. "I signed up for the whole thing."

Dr. Greene nodded. "Good man."

Rafael grimaced. "I guess it's a good thing we've got a long night to work with."

The second time was worse. He couldn't concentrate well enough to read anymore, so he just closed his eyes and tried to think happy thoughts. Mostly about Sasha.

Sasha lingered in the hallway outside Rafael's room. She'd been avoiding seeing him most of the evening, but as midnight approached, her curiosity got the better of her.

At least, she kept telling herself it was curiosity. She wanted to know if Rafael was all right. Just out of concern for a friend. Nothing more than that.

When Dr. Greene emerged from the room, a frown on his face, her heart jumped up to choke her. Involuntarily, she took a step forward.

"Is he all right?"

The doctor looked up at her, still frowning. It seemed to take him a moment to orient himself. "He's fine," he finally said. "It's just proving a bit more difficult than I'd hoped." He paused. "More painful for him."

"He'll be all right, though?"

"Yes. He's got another couple of hours on the dialysis machine, then I'll monitor him through the rest of the night, and all day tomorrow."

"Will he sleep tomorrow?" She knew the doctor understood the real question, the one she didn't want to ask. *Will he be a vampire tomorrow?*

The doctor smiled a little. "He may sleep. He may not. He may have to go through one more night of vampiric Sleep, just to heal. Or he may sleep naturally. I'm really not certain."

"Because you've never done this before." Her voice came out more bitter than she'd intended.

"No, I haven't done this before. But Rafael knows that, and so do you." He frowned again, the expression directed this time at her rather than at his own thoughts. "I understand why you chose not to do this, but why do you resent his decision so much?"

She tilted her chin haughtily. "I don't think that's any of your damned business."

"No, it probably isn't." He glanced at his watch. "Do you want me to let you know when he's finished? He'd probably like to see you."

"No." Taking a backward step, she added, "Thanks." Then she turned and hurried down the hallway.

When the doctor finally unhooked him from the dialysis machine, Rafael was so exhausted from the constant pain, and so relieved at its absence, that he immediately fell asleep.

Must be daytime, he thought as he drifted away, but it felt different. He had a feeling his body knew something his mind didn't. His body remembered this kind of sleep. His mind had mostly set those memories aside over the past four years.

He dreamed. He'd been told vampires dreamed from time to time, but he hadn't dreamed at all since he'd been Turned. The dreams made no sense, but he watched them with that strange, half-awareness that came with all ventures into the dream-world. It unnerved him at first, enough so that he felt the discomfort in his dream-state.

Then the colors started, and he could do nothing but sit back and enjoy the show.

He didn't recall ever having dreamt this vividly before. It was as if he were making up for the years lost. The dreams had little substance, but they shimmered with vibrancy, with streaks and flags of almost indescribable color. It was like being inside a kaleidoscope.

It seemed to go on forever, but eventually he did wake up. With a gasp of surprise, he sat bolt upright in the hospital bed. In a chair by the wall, Dr. Greene jerked awake.

Rafael smiled sheepishly. "Sorry."

"It's all right." The doctor straightened, rubbing the back of his neck. "How do you feel?"

"Okay." He stretched his arms out wide, folded them against his chest. "A little achy in the joints, maybe, but otherwise fine."

The doctor, as usual, went for a needle. "I want one more sample, just to see how things look."

Patiently, Rafael sat through the blood draw. With any luck, maybe this would be the last one. Dr. Greene took only a small amount of blood, then took it to the table at the back of the room, where he put some on a slide and slid it under the microscope.

"Looks good," he said after a moment. Turning to give Rafael a grin, he added, "If I didn't know any better, I'd think it was mine."

A sudden flood of emotion caught Rafael by surprise. He blinked a few times. He didn't know if he was about to laugh or cry, but he knew there would be tears involved.

"You okay?" the doctor asked.

"Yeah." He rubbed his face. "No. I mean—I just can't believe it's real."

"It'll take some time to get used to the idea, I'm sure." The doctor put a friendly hand on his shoulder. "Are you hungry?"

"Not really." Then it occurred to him—he didn't have to fight his hunger anymore. He could be hungry. He could go eat a cheeseburger and French fries instead of ripping someone's throat open.

The tears rimmed his lids, hot and heavy. There was no stopping them. They slid down his face, but he swallowed the thick sob that tried to follow them. Dr. Greene moved his hand along his back, turning his friendly touch into a half-embrace. "I've got some chicken soup in my room. Want some?"

The sob came up then. There was no stopping it. Around it, Rafael managed, "Yes. Oh, my God, yes."

In the hallway, Sasha saw the doctor escort Rafael down the hall. Rafael was crying—or rather, trying not to, dashing tears from his face. They walked away from her and never saw her.

Rafael looked different. His skin was pinker, and she could smell his blood even from here. Living blood. The kind she could feed on.

She wheeled and ran the other way, all the way up, through the corridors, into the last few hours of darkness.

Five

Dr. Greene had leftover pizza, too, and Rafael, not thinking of the possible consequences, chose that over the chicken soup.

"Maybe not the best idea," the doctor commented, but as Rafael had already stuffed half a slice down his throat, it was too late to do anything about it.

The flavors were incredible. He hadn't tasted anything in four years. Tomatoes, pepperoni, bread, cheese, garlic . . . he had just enough time to be swept up in the incredible richness before the pizza came back up.

He heaved it into Dr. Greene's toilet, then rinsed out his mouth and washed his face. When he returned to the small kitchenette, the doctor was holding up a can of chicken noodle soup.

"Are you ready to listen to your doctor now?" he said.

Rafael winced. "Yeah, I guess so."

So he had chicken soup. As he sipped the broth he found the same kind of intensity of flavor he'd found in the pizza, even though the soup was bland and unexciting. At least it would have been to a mortal. To his reawakened taste buds it had layers and depths he'd never imagined. Colors, even. He tried a noodle and the starchy thickness lingered on his tongue, too heavy for now. He left the rest of the noodles in the bowl.

The broth stayed down, though it was iffy for a time. He drank water with it, suddenly discovering he was unbelievably thirsty. One careful sip at a time, he drank nearly a quart of Evian out of Dr. Greene's fridge.

"Don't give any of the kids pizza," Rafael suggested.

"Yeah," said the doctor. "You should have thought of that."

"Yeah, I guess I should have." He finished off his last water bottle, looking longingly at the pizza. "Maybe tomorrow. It tasted damned good for about five seconds, there."

"Maybe rice tomorrow," said the doctor. "I don't think pizza would be a good idea for at least a week."

The quirk of his eyebrow told Rafael that a week was probably a generous estimate. "Well, hell, what's the point of being mortal if you can't eat pizza?"

Dr. Greene smiled. "It's two hours until daylight. Care to go for a walk?"

Again, Rafael found his throat full of unexpected tears. "Yes. Yes, I would."

The beautiful night colors were gone, but of course he'd known they would be. In their place was just darkness. The night seemed too quiet, as well. It took him some time to realize what was missing. There'd always been a sort of whispering undercurrent of thought, nothing discernible, but a sort of half-sensed, white noise that was as close as he'd ever come to telepathy. He'd barely realized it was there last night, but now he noticed its absence.

And the blood lust was gone. He could walk among the people on the streets without thinking of them as a potential meal. He couldn't hear their hearts beating or see their heat in a nimbus around them. They were only people. For the first time in a long time the odors of skin and perfumes, soap, cotton, wool, and leather, were not drowned out by the smell of blood.

"It's incredible," he breathed.

"You're okay?" the doctor asked.

"Yes. It's even better than I remembered it."

Dr. Greene nodded. "I thought it might be overwhelming at first."

"No. It's just . . ." He trailed off. "I don't know how to describe it." He sniffed, feeling tears gather yet again. Maybe the doctor could give him something for that.

Dr. Greene clapped him gently on the shoulder. "It's all right."

"So," Rafael ventured, "where's a good place to see the sunrise?"

Sasha careered blindly through the night, anger and despair searing her throat. She didn't know how to make them go away. She didn't know why they were there.

She thought about Brendan and Vince, who had never come back from Atlantic City, but it was only a fleeting thought. Manhattan reeked of Julian's wards. She was surprised the humans couldn't smell it, the air was so thick.

Besides, at that moment, she didn't give a shit about Ialdaboth's minions. Let them come. She would rip them to pieces with her bare hands.

Darkness was her realm. She knew how to move silently through it but didn't bother to try, half-running through the crowds with no awareness of where she was going. Mortals bounced off her, swearing. She made no effort to hide herself.

Finally she stopped, in a dark place not far from Central Park. She could see the park, the people in it even in the night, most of them not on honest business. Not at two a.m. She looked at her watch. Make that four a.m. She'd have to be careful. Dawn was far too close, and she wasn't sure where the nearest entrance to the Underground was.

Clumsy. Why had she let herself get so distracted that she'd lost her bearings? She wasn't even sure why the rage of emotion had overtaken her.

Or maybe she was sure. Maybe she was damned sure but refused to admit it, even to herself.

He had done it. The stupid bastard. He was mortal now, and there was no turning back for either of them. He certainly couldn't become a vampire again—or could he? Dr. Greene hadn't addressed that question. Did it matter? Would it matter to Rafael?

Probably it wouldn't. He simply had no desire to be anything other than a boring, ridiculous, fragile, death-doomed mortal.

And she still loved him.

There was no getting around that, no matter how hard she tried. She loved the pathetic bastard, and he'd made it impossible for either of them to do anything about it.

If she didn't love him, if she just enjoyed rolling around naked with him once in a while, it wouldn't be such a problem. She could have dealt with his mortality, somehow managed that scenario. They would have seen each other now and then, enjoyed the sex. And one day she would have come by and found he was too old. She would have sat next to him and chatted, perhaps, and that would have been the last time she saw him. Or perhaps she would have come by his house, looking for him, only to find it empty of all but his spirit, knocking around inside the four walls, waiting for her to come say goodbye.

But even that was overly romantic. Even when she tried to summon the image of an intermittent relationship based solely on lust, her true emotions leaked through. She loved him, and there was no way she could stay with him, now that he'd given up his immortality.

Except it was beginning to look as if there was no way she could go on without him.

How many times had she been in love in her life? She couldn't remember. Not because her memory had gone bad, like Lucien's, but because, in most cases, she'd simply chosen to forget. But each carefully constructed hole in her memory masked a hole in her heart that had never been allowed to heal. She was riddled with them.

A person could fall in love any number of times in three hundred years. A heart could be shattered to pieces equally as many times.

She couldn't let it happen again. She couldn't bear it. Not with Rafael.

Yet, she thought as she curled up next to a brick wall in the alley, there seemed to be no way around it. No matter what she did, she was doomed to hurt over this one.

She sat there for a long time, head pillowed on her knees, trying not to think but thinking anyway, about Rafael—and about Gaelin and Alexei and Walks-with-the-Wind-at-his-Back. The memories were too much to handle all at once—too much even one at a time—and she wept into her folded arms. No one noticed her, as she huddled in a shadow. People walked by her on the sidewalk, many of them two-by-two. She couldn't bear to look.

Much later, when she did finally lift her head, her heartache was swallowed by cold fear.

The sky was blue.

Not cerulean, but indigo. Not quite daylight but so close it made her breath come fast. Lost in the awful surge of her emotions, she'd also lost her awareness of the creeping nearness of the Sleep. She could feel it now, dragging at her eyelids, slowing her limbs. She forced herself onto the sidewalk, forced herself to run.

But she couldn't remember where to find the nearest entrance to the Underground. It had to be close—in that alley? Or that one?—but her frantic search seemed to take her in circles.

Finally, as the shadows around her began to fade, she felt it. The crazed hammering of her heart slowed and she honed her senses toward the soft hum. The doorway wasn't far.

And then she sensed something else. Mortals. They were following her. At least it wasn't vampires, Dark Children come to follow her to the Underground or torture the knowledge of its whereabouts out of her.

She had been so careless. Where had her three hundred years of experience gotten her tonight?

Into deep shit, apparently.

A group of five mortals passed and surrounded her. It was too late to slip by them in the near-invisibility she could have mustered had she been paying attention. There were too many to put compulsion on. She could have overpowered them one by one, but she simply didn't have time.

She ran. Preternatural speed gave her an advantage, and she reached the door to the Underground before they did. But the light was coming too fast. She could feel it on her skin. A hot itch had begun on the back of her hands.

She found the door and pulled at it. It wouldn't open.

"No," she breathed, too shocked to produce much more than a whisper. She grabbed the handle, jerked it, hauled against it with her full weight, but it wouldn't budge. Had she come too late? Had they locked this access door already? Or was it an abandoned entrance, no longer accessible?

Breathing fast and hard with panic, she turned, putting her back to the door. Her five would-be assailants made a line in front of her. Kids. Stinking asshole kids. Why couldn't the damned humans raise their offspring better? These little shits should have been home eating oatmeal or something, not lurking in the alleys trying to mug vampires.

One of them drew a knife and held it up, letting the pale dawn glint off the silver blade. A beam of light had entered the alley and lay on the ground at her feet. She stared at it, barely interested in the punk and his knife. Her skin was burning.

The kid with the knife took a step toward her. "You got a purse, bitch?"

"Do I look like I got a fucking purse?" Sasha spat back.

"That's too bad for you." He took another step forward, reaching for her. His friends, laughing, egged him on.

Her face hurt. She was going to die. Railing against the inevitable, she lashed out, hissing, spittle flying. In a snarl worthy of the most vicious of carnivores, she let them watch her fangs spring free.

"Beat it, you little punk," she said, her voice thin and laced with compulsion. "I'll rip your throat out."

The boy's expression changed from haughty to frightened in the space of a breath. He took a step back, the knife lowering.

"Shit," said one of the other kids. "She's got fangs!"

"Forget that," one of the others put in, also stepping away from Sasha. "Look at her face."

The kid with the knife squinted at her. Sasha could feel the heat on her face, the sun touching her even though she stood in a shadow.

"Shit!" said the kid, stumbling backward, his eyes now round with terror. "Is that smallpox?"

The kid scrubbed his hand on his jacket, then turned and ran, his cohorts pounding after him. Sasha let her head loll against the wall. A sign of the times, she thought, that her fangs only startled them a little, while the threat of biological havoc sent them running to their mommies.

She closed her eyes. The sun was almost up. Just a few more minutes and she would go up like a torch. She tried the door handle again, thinking perhaps she'd been unable to open it out of sheer panic. It still refused to budge.

Her fear had fled, leaving behind a stoic, resolute calm. She looked around for possible shelter. Had she not been facing the daylight, she could have kicked the door down, but without full dark around her she lacked the strength.

She saw another door. Not a door to the Underground but to a deserted warehouse. It was open. She staggered that way, keeping to the shrinking border of shadow along the sides of the buildings. She made her way through the doorway, into a dark corner, where she pulled slabs of abandoned plywood over her head. An instant later, Sleep swallowed her.

Six

The doctor took Rafael to Central Park. He'd never been there before—had, in fact, never been to New York City at all. The place intrigued him, once he got over his fascination with the changes in his vision, his hearing, his sense of smell. It was a great deal to assimilate.

They sat together on a park bench waiting for the sun to come up. Here, in the middle of the city, it was nearly impossible to see the stars, but he could see the slight changes in the color of the sky. The black became paler, then took on a blue tinge. He felt his heart speed up, felt a surge of panic. He took a deep, quick breath to quell it.

"It's okay," said Dr. Greene, his voice soothing.

"Are you sure?"

"I hope so."

Rafael shook his head, scowling. "You really need to work on that confident bedside manner, Doc."

Dr. Greene only chuckled.

But he stayed right there next to him. Under normal conditions Rafael would have felt the older man was too close, their thighs and shoulders brushing, but at that moment, the contact steadied him. He watched the sky turn from blue-black to indigo, from indigo to purple, from purple to deep blue.

"Getting close," Dr. Greene said quietly.

Rafael could only nod. He was too busy fighting the urge to run, to find a darkened house or at least a shadow of some kind. Every previously dead molecule in his body told him it was time to get up off his sorry ass and run like hell.

Then another aspect of the situation struck him. He wasn't sleepy. In his vampiric state, he would have been dragging with exhaustion right now, barely able to keep his eyes open as the Sleep overtook him. But he was awake and alert, full of adrenaline and ready to jump up and greet his first sunrise in four years. Actually, he couldn't remember how long it had been since he'd seen a sunrise. As a mortal teenager he'd rarely gotten up early enough to see it.

And it came. Slowly, then faster, until suddenly the sky was blue with pink clouds streaking through it. Beams of sunlight laid golden stripes across the grass in front of him. Birds sang in the trees. The park's sidewalks began to fill with people.

He could only stare, marveling at the beauty. The doctor had picked a bench that proved to be in the shadow of a large oak tree, so the sun didn't quite fall on his face, but the light filled his eyes with beauty the likes of which he had forgotten existed.

"You gonna cry again?" Dr. Greene asked.

Blinking quickly, Rafael gave the doctor a dark look. "Watch it," he growled.

Dr. Greene only smiled.

Rafael just sat for a time, absorbing the brilliant green of the grass, the pale, clear blue of the sky. Then he stood, giving the doctor a sideways glance. "I want to walk," he said, his voice still shaky. "I want to take a walk in the sun."

Even after he'd said it he was almost afraid to do it. If his skin had still been afflicted with the vampiric sensitivity to the sun, he knew he would have been dead already. The mere shade of a large tree wouldn't have saved him. But to step out, right into the direct sunlight . . . For a few breaths, he wasn't certain he had the courage.

The doctor poked him. "Just go. Get it over with."

Rafael went. Out from under the tree's shadow, out onto the sunlit grass, where the still-thin dawn light was brightest. He felt the warmth on his hands, his hair, his face. He stopped, turning his hands over, looking at his palms, at the backs of his hands. "It's beautiful," he breathed.

"It's sunlight. Get used to it. You'll be seeing plenty of it, I can guarantee you." He clapped Rafael's shoulder gently. "We should head back. I don't want you out here too long. There's no telling how your skin will respond after so many years out of the sun."

Rafael nodded. "All right."

They made their way to the sidewalk not far from where they'd been sitting, the doctor leading the way. A few joggers joined them, out for their early morning exercise. Rafael stared at them as they went past. Humans looked so much different in the daylight.

Humans. He was one now, too. He was going to have to get used to that.

"The Underground's sealed off through the day, isn't it?" he asked suddenly.

"Yes, but I can get in through one of the back ways. The Senior gave me access several years ago. There are times when I need to be out during the day, and I needed consistent and reliable access."

"Good. I was afraid for a minute we were stuck out here."

Dr. Greene grinned. "What? You don't want to go out for breakfast?"

Rafael's brain froze around the idea for a moment. Pancakes. Eggs. Bacon. Biscuits and muffins and syrup and jelly and toast. Oatmeal. Milk. "Could we?"

The doctor laughed. "Not just yet. Give your system some time to adjust before you start piling things into it."

He was right, of course. "What about toast? I could have toast."

"I can get you toast at home. And tea. And not much else, if you follow my advice."

Rafael really wanted pancakes. He thought about them as they headed up the sidewalk, conjuring the flavor from his memory. Sweetness, the fluffy texture, sticky syrup. "Pancakes tomorrow," he said stubbornly. "And pizza."

Dr. Greene shrugged. "Fine. Just go puke in your own toilet."

Rafael frowned. "I don't have a toilet."

"Ah. Yet another wrinkle."

"This is going to take some getting used to."

He was trying to remember what it felt like to have to go to the bathroom when frantic shouting suddenly broke the relative calm of the morning. He couldn't quite make out the words, but the man speaking them was obviously in a state of near-hysteria.

"What the hell is that?"

"Dunno," said Dr. Greene. "Shall we check it out?"

"Sure. Why not?"

A small crowd had gathered around a group of five young men— punks, Rafael thought, of the highly questionable type he'd hung out with in his previous life. One of the punks was talking while the other four nodded emphatically and occasionally chimed in to agree with his story.

"I'm tellin' ya, this bitch's got, like, smallpox or something. We gotta get outta here. That stuff's, like, contagious extreme."

A frown creased Dr. Greene's forehead. He approached the crowd at a half-trot. "Excuse me!" he called over their heads. "I'm a doctor. Please let me through. I need to find out what's going on."

The crowd obediently split, letting him into the inner circle. Rafael followed.

"You a doctor, man?" the kid asked.

"Yes, I am. Can you tell me exactly what you saw?"

"This woman, she, like, busted out all over all of a sudden with these blisters. Man, it was nasty, like pus 'n shit."

The other four kids, who looked genuinely terrified, nodded. "I think she was gonna die," one of them chimed in.

"You say this happened very suddenly?" the doctor said, and suddenly Rafael realized where he was going. His stomach went cold.

"What did she look like?" he demanded before the kid could answer.

The kid gave Rafael an angry look. "Yeah, it was, like, all at once."

"How long ago was this?"

"Not that long. Like, ten or fifteen minutes, I guess. The sun was just coming up."

Rafael grabbed the kid by the shoulders and shook him hard. "What did she *look* like, you damned little punk? You were shaking her down, weren't you? Gonna mug her?"

"Jesus, get your hands off me, ya psycho."

Dr. Greene said, very quietly, "Answer his question."

"Damn, she didn't have no money, and we didn't do nothin' to her. Whatever happened to her, we didn't do it."

"I meant the other question. What did she look like?"

"I dunno, like, some skinny bitch with black hair, I guess."

Rafael's fingers tightened on the kid's arm, until he felt the bones. "Did this happen right at sunrise?"

"Yeah, I guess."

He wanted to know if it been just these punks after her or if vampires had been involved. His heart contracted at the thought that she might have fallen prey to Ialdaboth's assassination squad.

"Take me there. Now."

"Man, I ain't goin' back there. I ain't catchin' no smallpox."

"It's not smallpox," said Dr. Greene. "Take us to the woman, please. I might be able to help her."

"Forget it, man—"

"Take us there, or we call the police and you get into deep shit for that knife you got stuffed in your pants," said Dr. Greene, still quietly.

The kid stared at him.

"Yeah, punk," the doctor went on. "I ain't stupid. Now get moving."

The kid jerked himself free from Rafael's too-tight grip, gave them both hard looks, then led the way back down the sidewalk.

A "skinny bitch with black hair" could have been just about anybody, Rafael thought, but the cold, sinking feeling in his gut made him more certain with every step that the woman was Sasha. If she'd been out in the sun, Dr. Greene probably wouldn't be able to do anything for her. They might not even find anything left of her body. But if she'd somehow been able to find shelter . . . It was a long shot, but it was all he had to hold onto at the moment.

The kid led them to an alleyway not far from the park that dead-ended against the back wall of a warehouse. There was no one there.

"She was here," the punk said. "I'm tellin' you, she was right here on the ground, all screamin' and shit."

Rafael looked frantically around the alley and saw another door along the left wall. He ran for it, shoved it open.

At first, he saw no sign of Sasha. Then, as his eyes adjusted, he made out a foot, protruding from underneath haphazardly arranged pieces of plywood. She had pulled them over her, for protection.

He ran to her, dragged the wood off her, making sure she was still protected by shadow. She lay on her side, her knees drawn up to her chest, her fists clenched in front of her face. And her face was streaked with wide, blackened burns.

"Dr. Greene!" he shouted. "In here!"

The doctor appeared at the door and hurried over. "Holy shit," he muttered, crouching next to Sasha's motionless body. She was barely recognizable under the brutal burns.

"She got caught outside," Rafael said, his voice sounding strange, unreal. All the fear, all the anger, had sunk to a cold lump at the bottom of his stomach. He reached toward her face, then drew back, afraid to touch her.

The doctor, of course, had no such compunctions. He laid fingers to her throat, checking her pulse, then took one of her hands, trying to uncurl the clenched fingers.

"Is she dead?" Rafael ventured.

"I don't know. It's hard to tell in this state. She could just be in the Sleep."

Rafael swallowed. "How do we find out?"

"We have to get her out of here." He let go of Sasha's uncooperative hand. "The other door in the alley is an old entryway into the Underground. That must be where she was headed. But it's been closed off for a long time, so she wasn't able to get through."

"How do we get her home?"

"We can't. There's no way to take her out of here without carrying her through direct sunlight. If I could get through that door . . ."

"So what do we do?"

Dr. Greene put his face in his hands for a moment. "Lucien."

"What about him?"

"We have to get him out here. He can teleport or something—I'm not sure how it works."

"But how long will it take to get Underground and bring him back?" Rafael had a scream inside him, growing huge just beneath his diaphragm.

"That might not be necessary." Dr. Greene closed his eyes. "Think. Think hard. Think, 'Lucien, get your ass here right now. We need you.'"

"And that'll work?"

"I don't know. It's an awfully long way from here to there, and he's still not back to full strength. But maybe that doesn't matter." He looked at Sasha again, peering more closely at the streaky burns on her face. Rafael could barely stand even to watch him looking.

"Go out," the doctor said suddenly. "See if there's any way to get through that door."

"But—"

"Just go. If Lucien doesn't make it, or can't, it might be her only hope."

Rafael went, trying to force from his mind the picture of Sasha lying there still as death, her face marked with angry red burns. If she was dead . . .

But when vampires died from exposure to sunlight, weren't they supposed to turn to dust or something? It occurred to him he'd never seen a vampire die that way. He'd never seen a vampire die, period.

He went to the Underground entrance and pulled at the door. It refused to give. And he'd lost his preternatural vampire strength. But Sasha still had hers yet apparently hadn't been able to open it, either.

Lucien, if you can hear me, we need you. He thought it as loudly as he could, making the words feel big and bold and black inside his head. Not that it seemed to do any good, at least not as far as he could tell.

They couldn't count on Lucien. Sasha needed to get out of that warehouse as quickly as possible, and that meant her best chance lay with Dr. Greene and himself. He stood still for a minute, thinking.

If brute strength wasn't the answer, maybe something else was. He slid his fingers along the doorframe, questing. If there was a trigger, perhaps it was only detectable by vampires. . . .

He heard a click—or thought he did. He pushed against the door, but it still wouldn't open. It did, however, move.

A sequence, then. He'd have to find one more click, or two, or ten. Whatever it took to get the door open. He tried again, fingers sliding all along the doorframe. Nothing. Okay, so it didn't really make sense for all the levers to be in the same place. He moved away from the door, questing between the seams of the wall's panels.

Another click. He turned immediately and shoved his shoulder against the door. It gave, but not all the way. Screw the third click. He shoved it again, hard, putting all his weight behind it. The door came open, slamming backwards into the room beyond.

Just a warehouse. His heart sank for a moment, then he saw the mark on the back wall. He wasn't certain what the mark's origin was—it was sort of a cross, sort of a whirligig—but he knew he'd seen it in the Underground, near exit doors. Finding the latches, he activated them, yanked the door open. Then he backed out, fast, half-running to the other building.

The doctor had found a tarp—a very dirty tarp—and had wrapped Sasha in it, covering her completely. He looked up as Rafael barreled in.

"Come on," Rafael said.

Dr. Greene scooped Sasha up in his arms and followed, no questions asked. Wrapped in the tarp, her skin was protected from the few feet of sunlight they had to pass through. The doctor carried her into the second warehouse, then set her gently down on the floor next to the entrance to the Underground. Turning toward the alley door, he closed it, cocking his head to listen as a series of clicks indicated the locks had reengaged.

"Let's go," he said.

The actual entrance to the Underground was small, barely large enough for Rafael to slide through sideways, on his knees. Dr. Greene eased Sasha through feet first, and Rafael carefully positioned her on the floor just inside.

Dr. Greene was halfway through when Lucien appeared, out of nowhere. The doctor wormed the rest of the way through and bent to pick up Sasha.

"Sorry," Lucien said. "I heard you calling, but I couldn't quite zero in on your location. It's hard to navigate from the Underground to outside." Rafael suspected the navigation problems might have more to do with Lucien's recent injuries. The right side of his face still looked like somebody had branded it with irons.

Lucien caught hold of the doctor's arm, helping him to his feet. Then he grabbed Rafael with his other hand and said, "Hang on."

And suddenly they were in the hospital wing, and the doctor was running with Sasha, leaving Rafael with Lucien to trail behind him.

Seven

Rafael paced the corridors, waiting for news. He didn't dare go too far, afraid he might lose his way. Without his vampiric senses it was harder for him to keep his bearings in the labyrinthine corridors.

It was hard, too, for him to stay focused. His thoughts were too full of Sasha. He could think of little else, his interior vision filled with the sight of her beautiful face, ravaged by streaking burns.

She might be dead. He thought she wasn't, though. Surely he would know if she was. But maybe he was deluding himself with unsubstantiated hope. He had no reason to think they had any kind of telepathic connection. After all, they hadn't been lovers very long, and he was nothing more than a useless mortal at this point.

Which led to the next question. If she wasn't dead, would she see him? Or would she continue to refuse to consider a permanent relationship?

He could bear even that, he thought, as long as she was alive.

"There you are."

Lucien's voice startled him, coming as it did a split second before Lucien actually appeared.

Rafael composed himself quickly. "How is she?"

"We're not completely sure yet."

"But she's alive?"

"Yes."

"I want to see her."

Lucien laid a hand on his shoulder. "Then I'll take you."

A breath later, they stood in front of the door to Sasha's room. Trepidation rooted Rafael to the spot for a heartbeat. Then he pushed the door open and went in.

Dr. Greene looked up from his work. He was replacing an empty IV bag with a new one full of clear fluid. Sasha lay with her face turned away from the door. She was utterly still.

"She's alive," said the doctor. "Her body is processing fluids, but very slowly."

"She'll be all right?"

"There'll be scars for a while. But maybe Julian or Lucien can help with that." He finished with the IV bag and took a step back. "In fact, I'd be surprised if they couldn't."

Rafael didn't care about scars. She was alive. That was the important part.

The doctor wasn't finished, though. "It remains to be seen, however, what will happen at nightfall."

"Why? I mean, she'll wake up, right? Just like always?"

"I don't know. Sometimes when a vampire experiences this kind of trauma, she remains comatose for a period of time—stays in the Sleep to facilitate healing."

"For how long?"

"Until her system revives. I've heard of it lasting a few days—or ten, even twenty years."

Twenty years? "But wouldn't it depend on the seriousness of the injuries?"

"It seems to depend more on the severity of the trauma." He poked the nosepiece of his glasses, pushing them into place. "Look, I'm sorry to be so blunt, but there are so many variables here. It's very difficult to predict what a vampire will do, what her response will be to a particular trauma or a particular course of treatment. Most of what I do is trial-and-error and guesswork."

Rafael nodded. "It's all right. I know you've done what you can."

"And will continue to do so." He hesitated, then nodded. "You'll stay with her awhile?"

"Yes."

"Okay. I'll be back."

Rafael heard the door click shut behind him, but his focus was on Sasha. He took a step closer, then moved toward the other side of the bed so he could see her face.

The wounds the sun had inflicted had not diminished. Whatever treatment the doctor had followed, it had done nothing to heal that aspect of her trauma. Her smooth, perfect skin bore streaks of red, brutal burns.

It would heal eventually, with or without help from Julian or Lucien. She would be beautiful again. But Rafael didn't care. Seeing her lying there, still as death in the vampiric Sleep, he didn't care about anything but that she was alive—and that he loved her. Anything else was inconsequential. The thought that he'd almost lost her—the immortal in their relationship—to something as common as the sun, made him angry and frightened at the same time.

He understood, then, why she'd left him. Because she'd imagined him like this. Still and silent, not breathing, brutalized by violence or illness or age. It was inevitable, now that he was mortal again.

She hadn't considered her own weaknesses, though. Yes, she was a vampire, technically immortal, but not invulnerable. In her own way, she was as fragile as he. They would both eventually die—she could just put it off longer than he could.

There was a chair by the door. He dragged it over, so he could sit where he could see Sasha's face. He was tired and hungry, but both could wait. Right now, he needed to be here, with her.

When Dr. Greene returned, he had a plate with plain white bread and a bowl of broth. Rafael's stomach was growling, but after one bite he stopped to look at the bread. To smell it. To analyze the taste it left behind in his mouth. As a vampire he had been able to do none of these things. This was Life.

And life was good. Immortality had its advantages, but eating good bread wasn't one of them.

The food went down smoothly. His stomach was starting to adjust to handling digestion again. He ate the bread and the broth and wondered if it was time yet to try that pepperoni pizza.

Probably not. He daydreamed about it, though, finally drifting off to sleep, thinking about some oddly erotic combination of pizza and Sasha.

Sasha woke with a stabbing pain in her face and sat bolt upright, heart pounding, ready to attack. But there was nothing to attack. Only a silent hospital room and Rafael sitting on a chair next to her bed.

They had gotten her to the Underground. Somehow they'd managed it. Had Rafael been there? Had he saved her?

She looked at his quiet face, and her heart twisted. This was why she'd driven him away—because, when she saw him, her resolve wavered and she was ready to let him into her life, to love him regardless of the consequences.

And now she was the one who'd walked on the edge of death. Irony sucked. It made her think too hard, threw all her carefully thought-out rationalizations out the nearest window.

Rafael twitched in his sleep. Sleep, she thought. Real, mortal sleep, including dreams. Where you tossed and turned and twitched and made funny noises, snored and drooled. She lay back down in her hospital bed, careful not to make any sound that might wake him, and watched him.

It wasn't until fifteen minutes later, when Dr. Greene entered the room, that she realized what was wrong. She frowned at the doctor.

"He doesn't smell good," she said.

"You're awake," said the doctor.

"Yes."

"How do you feel?"

"Not great. Why does he smell funny?"

Dr. Greene picked up a chart from the table near her bed. "Maybe he forgot that humans sweat and need to take showers."

"No, it's not that." She peered at him. "You don't smell good, either. But I know what that's about."

"Now, I *know* I took a shower." He examined her half-empty IV bag. "Are you hungry?"

"Yes. That's just it. I'm hungry, and he doesn't smell like a decent meal. Red-blooded, healthy male, and I have no desire to eat him."

He quirked an eyebrow at her. "Well, that kind of thing's a bit dangerous with fangs, anyway."

"You should know. Besides, that's not what I meant."

The doctor still looked smug. "I know what you meant."

Her eyes narrowed. "What did you do?"

"I doctored Rafael's blood a little. I put some of my markers in it. The ones that keep every vampire here from draining my veins."

"Why did you do that?"

"I thought it might smooth things out between you two a little. He's still mortal, but at least you won't have the urge to nibble on him for breakfast."

Sasha blinked, not sure what to think about the doctor's interference—or his assumptions about her feelings for Rafael. Her lashes felt moist. "So you're sort of a freakish, high-tech, geneticist-matchmaker type?"

"Something like that."

Rafael grunted. Sasha watched as he straightened in his chair, sniffling and snorting his way to consciousness.

The doctor stood. "I'll leave you two to it, then."

Sasha glanced at him as he closed the door behind him, then turned to Rafael, who opened his eyes and looked at her blearily.

"I dreamed about you," he said after a moment. He sounded surprised.

"Good dreams, I hope."

"No, not really." He grinned wryly, rubbing the back of his neck. "I haven't dreamed since—"

She understood both his wonderment and his reluctance to vocalize it. "So what the hell are you doing here?"

He studied her face. Suddenly she wondered what she must look like, what the pain in her face must mean. But there was no repulsion or even distaste in his expression.

"I wanted to be with you," he said. "You almost died."

"Yeah." She couldn't stifle the edge of bitterness to her voice. "I was stupid."

"You were. Stupid and careless."

"Rub my nose in it, why don't you?"

His expression had chilled, becoming unreadable. "I don't know if I can be with you if you're going to keep being stupid. It makes you careless, and sooner or later, you're gonna end up dead."

Tears rose too fast for her to stop them, but she refused to look away. "Touché."

"Damn straight. How does it feel?"

"If your blood didn't stink, I'd rip your throat out right now."

"You'd regret it later."

"Yeah, probably."

"Right about the time you wanted sex."

Her lips thinned. "There are plenty of men who'd be willing to help me out with that."

"Not many who love you."

She opened her mouth, closed it again. Rafael went on. "Don't close me out, Sasha. I love you. Human, vampire, whatever combination, I want to be with you."

"Rafael—"

"I'm talking, Sasha." His forced harshness made her smile. "Whatever time we have together, I want to spend it with you. Ten years, fifty years, six months. It doesn't matter. I love you."

"I love you, too, Rafael."

"Good. Then you're done with this nonsense about me being mortal and blah blah blah?"

"Considering I'm the one who almost died, I think I'll have to eat at least a few of those words."

"So I can kiss you, and we can call this whole argument over?"

"Yes."

He rose from the chair, leaned forward, and kissed her. She pressed into him, ignoring the pain of her burned face, savoring the flavor of his mouth. Hot, beating with the rhythm of his heartbeat. He tasted better than he smelled.

After a moment, he drew back and looked into her eyes. "Until death do us part," he murmured.

"Amen," she said, and kissed him again.

Julian's Journal

So it can be done. Rafael is mortal now, transformed by the catalysts of blood. This means the other Children—the ones Turned before puberty—can also be made mortal again.

I want it done as soon as possible. If Ialdaboth comes, and there are still little ones among us, he'll slaughter them.

We need a backup plan, though. A way to hide them if he comes before we're ready. Because I feel he will come soon, and their transformation will take time.

The pieces have begun to fall together. Rafael's contribution added weight to some elements, took my attention away from others I had previously thought were important. There's an answer here somewhere.

I can feel him. His power. Did I take something from him when I defeated him the last time, or did he mark me in some way? Or both? Maybe I am capable of killing him outright—I don't know. I don't know what power I have, what it means, what it can truly do.

Sometimes I think if I unleash it, it will kill me. Not exactly what we're after.

Lorelei worries, I can tell, but she won't talk to me about it. She can feel the babies inside her, she says. Moving, stirring. Dancing, perhaps. I have to save all of us in order to save them.

So the Children come first. Tara has agreed to help. I found her in the Senior's memory—didn't even know she existed until my concern over the Children made her face float up out of the morass I inherited—that I was forced to take—from my predecessor.

Tara has been important to the Children, helping to keep them safe, ever since her relationship with Dominic and his subsequent death—a shame; he was a decent vamp—led her to the Underground. She can handle what needs to be done. I'll send her to DeAngelo—after what Nick told me about him, and from what I've seen myself, he seems the most logical choice.

It's all about choices. The Children can have the choice now—the doctor and I can give them that. And from there we go . . . I don't know where.

Nowhere, if I don't find the secret to Ialdaboth's destruction. We're closer to it, with Lucien's litany and now Ialdaboth's, supplied by Rafael. Aanu's healing progresses well—it shouldn't be long, now, before we can find out what he knows, assuming he brings that knowledge back with him from the dark place he has been these past four thousand years.

But the enemy has come closer, as well. Jasmine died in Perth Amboy last night, and the two who hunted with her don't know what killed her. I had never even heard of her until she died. We've given up on Brendan and Vince ever returning from Atlantic City—so much for their little "vacation." Other reports have come in, as well, of vampires missing or being killed by "strangers."

I can offer no further protection for those who have chosen to live outside the Underground. I can't take the risk they might be agents of Ialdaboth. If they die, perhaps that is on my head. So be it.

Ialdaboth himself is dormant. I'm not sure how I know that.

No, I do know. I dreamed it. I dreamed he was sleeping, and there was a sort of dark curtain over his body. I think Lucien hurt him more than he knew, when they tangled in Romania. It will take time for the bastard to recover.

Time I must be certain to use wisely.

Tara

I sleep, but my heart waketh: it is the voice of my beloved that knocketh . . .

Song of Songs, 5:2

It's like I'm watching right through his eyes—though Liam's eyes—and he's looking at Felicity. "He's a vampire," I'm saying to her. "There's no question but that he must die."

Gray DeAngelo, past-life
regression journal

The past must always be considered, but often ignored. It can mutate and distort, until no one is certain at all of what may or may not have happened. Beware of this, O my too-certain children.

The Book of Changing Blood

One

The sign on the office door read GRAY DEANGELO, CERTIFIED HYPNOTHERAPIST. Tara looked at the ad she'd torn from the Yellow Pages. There, in addition to hypnotherapy, Dr. DeAngelo had listed, "Stop smoking, lose weight, recover lost memories, past life regression."

This appeared to be the place. She opened the door and went in.

Not long ago, she would have considered Dr. DeAngelo to be a quack and all his patients at least gullible, but more likely stupid. Since then, she'd dated a vampire, watched him die, and taken a lucrative job as part-time teacher, babysitter, and mentor to a group of pre-pubescent vampire children. As a result, past life regression seemed less weird than most of what she saw every day, and Dr. Gray DeAngelo was the most likely solution to a complicated problem.

The receptionist seemed friendly enough, but Tara felt unaccountably on edge. The whole situation was so precarious. She felt as though she could breathe wrong, look at someone the wrong way, and blow everything.

"I trust your judgment," Julian had told her. *"You've spent more time with the Children than any of the rest of us. If anyone is qualified to monitor Daniel's progress, it's you."*

It hadn't seemed prudent to argue with him. Not because he frightened her—though he did, still, just a little—but because, technically, he was right.

Sitting in Dr. DeAngelo's waiting room, she crossed her legs, folded her arms over her chest, and generally tried to make herself as small as possible. As if it would keep them from noticing her even though she'd already talked to the receptionist and signed in.

This was crazy. She had no reason to be so nervous. It wasn't as if Dr. DeAngelo could take one look at her and instantly know her innermost secrets. She picked a spot on the opposite wall and stared at it, easing herself into a semblance of calm.

"Tara Summers?"

It was a testimony to the success of her calming techniques that

Tara merely blinked at the sound of her name, instead of jumping out of her skin. She smiled gently, came to her feet, and looked at the man who had spoken.

Gray DeAngelo was tall, broad, and very pretty. An irrelevant thought drifted across her mind—that she was glad she wasn't here to discuss some kind of sexual dysfunction.

"Ms. Summers," he said, holding out a hand. "I'm Dr. DeAngelo."

She took his hand, liking the way it enveloped hers snugly. "Nice to meet you."

His smile seemed a little cautious, genuine but not entirely open. "My office is this way."

She followed him down the short hallway. He opened a door and gestured for her to precede him into the room.

The office was different than she'd expected. Though she wasn't certain what she *had* expected—big, intimidating furniture and musty books, perhaps, but not this light, airy room. The furniture was uphol-stered in pale blues and greens, and the sleek, modern desk was of a pale wood with white lacquered trim. A window let in a great deal of light, as well as a view of Manhattan. Tara felt instantly comfortable. Which, she assumed, was the point.

"Have a seat." The doctor gestured toward a chair. He looked at the date book on his desk. "You're here for a consultation?"

"That's correct. I need someone to treat my son."

Dr. DeAngelo settled on a corner of the desk. "How old is he?"

"He's ten. He's adopted." She added the last perhaps a bit too hastily, aware that she was, and looked, a bit too young to be the mother of a ten-year-old. That Daniel was, in fact, nearly five hundred was, at the moment, irrelevant. "He's been having some problems lately, and we believe it may have to do with something he experienced as a very young child."

"Something he's repressed."

"Yes. Some kind of abuse, most likely."

"That sounds like something I could handle. Have you spoken to any other therapists?"

"No. You were recommended."

"By whom?"

"A friend of mine. Nicholas Carrington. He saw you in connec-tion with an illness. He had cancer." Plus, Julian had agreed with the recommendation—Tara wasn't sure why.

"Ah, yes. I remember. I taught him self-hypnosis to handle the pain. How is he?"

"Unfortunately he passed away a few months ago."

"I'm sorry to hear that."

Tara lowered her gaze to her lap, hoping she looked appropriately distraught. Nick had asked her to tell the doctor that he'd died. "He spoke very highly of you, so when this situation came up with Daniel, I thought of you."

"I appreciate that. Have you seen any other doctors? Besides therapists?"

Tara grimaced. "They all wanted to medicate him. I didn't realize until recently that Ritalin and Prozac were such cure-alls."

Distaste rose in his eyes as he spoke. "They have their place, of course. I believe in being very cautious with drugs, though. Particularly with children."

Tara nodded. "It might have been a quick fix, but I wanted to get to the root of the problem."

"Good for you." He leaned backward from his perch on the edge of the desk to pick up a notebook from the opposite side. "I'd like to get some information, for starters."

"Of course."

"You said your son's name is Daniel?"

"Yes."

"And your husband's?"

"I'm not married."

His gaze flicked from his notes to her.

"Divorced," she clarified. "My ex-husband is very involved and will be helping me with the financial aspects of Daniel's treatment."

Dr. DeAngelo made no comment. "I'd suggest we get started as soon as possible. Make an appointment with my receptionist on the way out. Of course, you're more than welcome to attend all Daniel's therapy sessions. In fact, I encourage it."

"There was one more thing I wanted to mention. I'll have to make my appointments for the evening. Daniel has a very rare skin condition. He's extremely sensitive to sunlight."

Dr. DeAngelo's eyebrow twitched oddly. Tara had no idea what that meant.

"Of course," he said. "Just explain the situation to my receptionist. She'll make an appropriate appointment for you. But before that, I'd like to talk to you a bit about the exact nature of Daniel's behavior problems."

She told him the story she'd concocted with the aid of Dr. Greene. They'd spent hours on the Internet researching behavior problems to put together a logical scenario.

It had seemed to Tara at the time that Julian's input in the process had been based on some knowledge of Dr. DeAngelo, but then he'd told her to quote Nick as a reference. She wasn't quite comfortable enough with Julian to question him about it, though. And the plan they'd put together seemed rock-solid. If the doctor figured out what was really going on, he had a better imagination than any doctor Tara had ever met.

Still, if he did, they would deal with the situation. She just hoped Dr. DeAngelo made it through alive.

She'd intended to get home before dark, but she didn't quite make it. As she'd expected, but also feared, Daniel wasn't in his small, sun-tight bedroom. Looking at the empty bed, she sighed. It didn't matter that he'd gotten along fine without her for nearly five centuries. He was in her care now, and she felt responsible.

Julian and Dr. Greene had both warned her to expect Daniel to disappear during the night, but she couldn't help worrying. He was a vampire; but he was also a little boy, and she had developed a relation-ship with the little boy. So it was hard for her to think of him out, on his own. Harder still to think of him procuring a dinner of fresh blood. Hardest of all to imagine him being overpowered by one of Ialdaboth's evil followers. Never mind Julian's reassurances that Manhattan was safe; she didn't want Daniel's death to be the first indication that it wasn't.

She forced herself to make her own dinner, sit down, and eat, instead of pacing and worrying and wringing her hands, which was what she really felt compelled to do.

When she'd scraped the last bit of pasta from her plate, she looked fruitlessly out the window for a minute or two, then turned on the TV.

The evening news was half over when a deceptively small voice said, "Hey, Tara."

She turned around. Daniel stood behind her, a skinny little boy with disheveled curly black hair, his front teeth too big for him. He wore faded jeans and a bright orange Pokémon T-shirt. A smear of red next to his mouth might have been Spaghetti-O's, but it wasn't.

"Wash your face," Tara said mildly. "You missed a spot."

Daniel grinned sheepishly. "Oh, gee. Sorry."

Tara turned back to the TV, listening to the splashing sounds as Daniel washed his face in the kitchen sink. He returned to the living room and flopped onto the sofa next to her.

"Mind if I watch something else?" he said.

"Just let me watch the weather first."

"It's going to snow. I could smell it."

"Okay. Fair enough." She handed him the remote. Grinning, he explored the listings, then changed to a cartoon, one of the many specimens of Japanese animé he was fond of. Tara didn't care for it. It was too bright and choppy, the voices high-pitched and obnoxious. But he was engrossed in a matter of moments.

Kids, Tara thought. They were all the same. Even when they were five hundred years old.

He watched until the next commercial break, then hit the mute button on the TV. Tara, who had been drifting off to sleep, blinked at him in surprise.

"How did it go with the doctor?" he asked.

"I'll be taking you for your first session tomorrow night."

"I don't want to go," he said bluntly.

"It'll be all right." She put her hand on his shoulder, and he stilled for a moment, almost as if he were afraid of her. "We just need a few minutes, some flashes from those years."

"But there's so much more." His voice was small but not a little boy's voice at all. "I don't want to—" He broke off.

"I know." In truth, she had no idea what memories lurked within him. And she didn't blame him for his fear. "We can only do the best we can."

"Maybe I don't even want to be mortal."

"But maybe you do."

He bit his lip, fighting tears. Then he swallowed hard, and his face became stony and still. "Go on to bed," he said. "I know you're tired. I might go out again, so if you wake up and don't see me, don't get all freaked out."

Tara nodded, disappointed. She'd hoped he'd open up to her a little more. "I'll see you tomorrow night, then."

"Yeah." He hit the remote button again—the commercial break was over. "Unless I change my mind."

In his office, Gray DeAngelo re-read the file on Daniel Summers. Something wasn't quite right. Nothing he could pin down. He just felt vaguely uneasy in that way he'd learned, over the years, meant something was amiss.

Maybe it was the light sensitivity. Porphyria was an extraordinarily rare disease, and it was the kind of thing that would give a child a great deal of emotional difficulty. Surely Daniel would have been in therapy before, to help him deal with his inability to play in the sunshine.

Yet, according to the files Ms. Summers had given him, today was the first time Daniel's parents had consulted a therapist. Paperwork signed by a Dr. Jarod Greene confirmed the boy's porphyria, and an online search had found Greene listed as a hematologist. That seemed odd, too—why was Daniel seeing a hematologist when other specialists, like endocrinologists, usually cared for patients with his condition?

Rubbing his forehead, he wondered why he was making such an issue of it. Maybe some of Daniel's records had been lost somewhere, in the shuffle of a move or in the course of a custody battle. If Daniel had changed his name when Tara had taken full custody, the boy's records might not all be in one place. He'd have to look into that, as well. Searching the file, he found Daniel's father's name. Julian Cavanaugh. He typed it into the search engine to see what came up.

And was met with a big, fat zero. Oh, sure, there were Julian Cavanaughs on the Internet, but none who seemed to have anything to do with Tara Summers or her son Daniel.

"Leave it alone," he finally muttered to himself. He shut the file and prepared to leave the office for the evening. *Just help the kid, take the money, and forget about the rest of it.*

But he couldn't. And if he were really honest—which, as a therapist, he didn't want to be—he had to admit that his interest had nothing to do with Daniel. It was all about Tara.

He was certain he hadn't met Tara Summers before, but something about her had seemed eerily familiar. When she'd walked into his office he'd had one of those strange déjà vu moments. He'd known what her voice would sound like before she had spoken, but he was sure he'd never heard it before today.

He also, somehow, knew exactly what it would feel like to kiss her. And that made no sense at all.

He shrugged on his coat, then looked again at the file lying on the desk. He picked it up and took it home with him.

His face was shadowed in the darkness, but she could barely make out the line of his jaw, the glint of his eyes.

"It was a good day," he said. The timbre of his voice sounded as familiar as her own. "You were so brave."

"I wasn't." This voice seemed to come from her own lips, but it somehow was not her voice. "I was so afraid."

"But you did what had to be done."

A soft wash of pride swept over her, pride born of love. She was proud of him, proud of herself in spite of her modesty. But modesty had been ingrained in her from an early age, and it was hard to acknowledge her own accomplishments.

He loved her, though, and his praise made her feel warm. As did his arms, closing around her, protecting her in the darkness. His lips touched hers, then pressed more deeply. She could feel every soft contour of his mouth, the gentle caress of his lips and tongue.

He kissed her thoroughly, then shifted away from her to peer at her through the darkness. This close, even in the shadows, she could make out his face. . . .

Gray DeAngelo.

Tara started awake. Her heart hammered in her chest, the sound echoing in her ears.

"What the hell was that?" she muttered. She had absolutely no reason to think about kissing Gray DeAngelo, except that he was an attractive man.

Oh, well. It was only a dream. With any kind of luck, she'd forget it by morning.

Two

The next morning, Tara left Daniel asleep in his sun-proofed room and walked to the Underground. There was a doorway not far from her apartment—the Senior had created the portal specifically for her use three years ago, when her relationship with Dominic had led to her discovery of the vampire community and her eventual employment as a sort of nanny to the vampire Children. Back then, they'd been feral, most of them, making their way along the fringes of the Underground, avoiding the main areas because they knew too well what an adult vampire could do to them. She still wasn't sure she'd found them all. Some of them had been so hideously abused for so long that they trusted no one, and refused to come out of the dark, safe shadows they'd found for themselves.

The guards knew her on sight, and nodded as she walked down the narrow alley. The door at the back of the alley was locked with three padlocks. Tara fished out her keys and opened them, opened the door, then keyed the security code into the keypad just beyond it. There were three more checkpoints along the hallway behind the door, then another door with another keypad and another security code. After that, a long, narrow staircase, one more door, and then she was truly in the world of the vampires.

She could always tell, even on those rare occasions when she came in through a different portal. There was a certain smell or aura or thickness to the air—she didn't really know how to describe the sensation even to herself, but it was always there and always obvious to her. It grew thicker the deeper she passed into the Underground. At first, when she'd initially taken on the job of helping with the Children, the sensation had given her panic attacks. It still made her edgy, but she'd gotten used to it.

Julian's office was deep within the Underground, through what she liked to call the Geode Room. That was her favorite bit of scenery in the vampires' territory. The walls were covered with crystals that refracted the artificial light in gorgeous streams of blue-green. She always stopped there, just for a minute, even if she came at night and ended up with a flock of vampires staring at her while she absorbed the beauty.

Julian answered her knock immediately. She entered cautiously. She still wasn't used to him. She and the previous Senior had developed a sort of uneasy rapport. Julian didn't scare her as much as the old Senior had—she was more used to vampires now, and Julian seemed much more human in many ways than his predecessor. Still, he was a new face, a new personality to deal with, and she still hadn't quite accustomed herself to the idea that he was in charge.

"Tara," he said with a smile.

She was sure that smile was meant to reassure, but he seemed too edgy behind it. Things were brewing down here, she was certain. Things she, as a human being, would most likely never hear about. She wasn't even sure she wanted to know.

"How are you?" he asked.

"I'm fine, thanks. How's Lorelei?"

"Better. She's been sleeping enough for her, the baby, and me. Thanks for asking." He leaned back in his chair, giving her his full attention. "You've made some progress?"

"I consulted the therapist you and Nicholas recommended. I think he'll work out."

"Good. So you'll start seeing him when?"

"Tonight. I'll be observing the sessions with Daniel."

"He had no problem with that?"

"He suggested it."

"Good." He gave a quick nod, as if settling things with himself. "Keep me informed of Daniel's progress. If everything goes well, I might send Treva out, too."

Tara knew that Treva had been twelve when she was Changed, nearly two hundred years ago. On the initial evaluation, though, Dr. Greene had judged her less emotionally mature than Daniel. "We'll cross that bridge when we come to it."

Julian smiled at her hesitation. "Yes, we will. Do you need any cash? How are you holding out?"

One thing she liked about working for vampires—she was never short of money. "I'm good for the moment. There's enough money in the account to cover the first five sessions or so."

"Grocery money? Rent?"

"I'm good."

"All right." He glanced at his watch. "How about lunch? I'm dying for sashimi."

Surprised, Tara nodded. "All right."

It still surprised her that Julian could go out in sunlight. Apparently he wasn't quite used to it, either, because he blinked and shaded his eyes when they stepped out onto the sidewalk.

"Bright," he said.

"Doesn't it hurt?"

"Not so much anymore."

He led the way to a Japanese restaurant. They chatted over sushi and sashimi, about Daniel, about her own role in the vampire community. Tara felt more at ease with Julian after the conversation, which she assumed had been the point. In spite of the circumstances of his arrival, she liked him, and she sensed that the other vampires trusted him for the most part. She couldn't help wondering about Lorelei, though, or more accurately, about her pregnancy. What kind of baby was she likely to have, if it had been fathered by a not-quite vampire? She hoped all went well for them.

That night, sitting with Daniel in Dr. DeAngelo's waiting room, other worries occupied her mind. If possible, she felt even more uncomfortable than she had the day before, when she'd come alone. Never mind that Daniel was the patient. She wanted nothing more than to turn around and run. Surely this could do nothing but endanger Daniel, regardless of Julian's opinion on the matter.

Daniel seemed much more at ease. He sat in the waiting room next to her, reading a kids' magazine. She'd assumed, before she'd met him, that he'd be interested in adult fare, given his chronological age. But he spent most of his time devoted to pursuits appropriate to his apparent age. She had no idea why that was. Maybe his brain had been stuck for five hundred years at the level of a ten-year-old. Other things about him made her think that was the case.

He was so involved in the magazine, she had to nudge him when the receptionist called his name. He looked up at her with a very adult look of irritation. His voice, though, was a pre-adolescent whine. "I don't want to go."

"Then you'll have to talk to Julian." She grasped his elbow, urging him to his feet.

"I talked to Julian already. He's annoying." Shoulders slumped, he followed her toward the office.

Hanging back a little, Tara slipped an arm around his shoulders as they walked, and he leaned into her. He was more scared than angry, she was certain.

Dr. DeAngelo met them with a warm smile. "Good evening," he said to her, then turned his attention to Daniel. "You must be Daniel."

"Yeah, that's me." Daniel fell into a chair.

Tara sat next to him, patting his shoulder. "It's okay, sweetie," she said. He rolled his eyes at her. She smiled her apology.

"Girls," said Dr. DeAngelo in a commiserating tone. "They're always so mushy, aren't they?"

"Yeah." Daniel gave a wry grin. "Enough to make you barf sometimes."

"My mom was like that, too. Always wanted to kiss me in front of my friends."

Daniel made a face. Tara leaned away from him, partly to put him more at ease, partly to remove herself from the conversation. Time to let the doctor take over.

"So how are you tonight?" Dr. DeAngelo began. "Are you feeling okay?"

Daniel shrugged. "Yeah, I guess."

"I'd like to just talk a bit, get to know you a little, before we start anything too involved. Okay?"

Daniel shrugged again. Probably a typical reaction for a kid, Tara thought. In any case, the doctor seemed to be taking it in stride. He continued with his questions, asking things anyone might ask a ten-year-old boy. Tara kept half her attention on the conversation, in case Daniel might need her to intercede, but he handled things well. He'd been pretending to be ten for a long time—he was good at it.

Instead of watching Daniel, she focused on the doctor, looking for any indication that he might be suspicious, or ill at ease in any way. Certainly no sign of that, she thought, noting the movement of his finely cut mouth. He was a very handsome man, with dark, nearly black hair and eyes somewhere between green and hazel. He wore a dress shirt but no jacket, and he'd unbuttoned the top button of the shirt beneath the loosened knot of his tie. A long day, Tara supposed. As he continued to chat with Daniel, he unbuttoned his cuffs and rolled up his sleeves.

"So," he said after a time. "Let's talk a little about these problems you're having."

Daniel cut Tara a look. He'd been briefed ahead of time on what he'd supposedly done to warrant the intervention of a professional. She bit her lip, hoping he wouldn't suddenly decide to rebel.

"Yeah, okay," he said.

"This says you've been having trouble with your friends. Lashing out at them, calling them names."

"Yeah, and I hit a couple."

Tara suppressed a smile. He was going to cooperate, and with flying colors, too, apparently.

"I'm sure you don't need me to tell you this is inappropriate behavior." Gray's tone was neutral.

"No, sir."

"So can you tell me why you do it?"

Daniel shrugged. "They just piss me off, I guess."

"Does it have anything to do with your not being able to go outside? Are you feeling frustrated about that?"

Daniel's mouth curled at one corner. "I've been living inside a long time, Dr. DeAngelo. I guess I'm pretty much used to it by now."

"Then have there been any changes recently?"

"Yeah, my dad left. That was tough."

"You still see him, though, correct?"

"Yeah. He's a good guy, I guess."

Tara saw the curl in his mouth deepen. He was enjoying this. She'd discovered most vampires got a thrill out of extemporaneously inventing their personal histories. It amused them. Even Julian seemed to get revved when he had a good line going.

Confident that Daniel he could carry the conversation at least for a while, she relaxed in her chair.

And suddenly remembered the dream.

Had it really been Gray DeAngelo kissing her? With his soft mouth and fondling tongue? Thinking back, the voice hadn't seemed quite like the voice she was hearing question Daniel about his relationship with his father. But somehow it had been the same.

Uncomfortable, she shifted in her chair, trying not to stare at the doctor. What had they been talking about in that ridiculous dream? Something about being brave. What had they been doing that they needed to be brave? She wasn't sure she wanted to know.

"Ms. Summers."

Tara started. He'd called her name more than once, she suddenly realized. "I'm sorry," she said. "I drifted off there, for a minute."

The doctor smiled, but she didn't miss the small spark of disapproval in his eyes. She should be ashamed of herself, she thought, not listening to her own son in this kind of a serious situation.

"I'd like to speak to you alone for a few minutes," the doctor told her, "just to finish things off for the day."

"Of course." She looked at Daniel. "Can you wait for me in the lobby? You can finish your magazine."

"Sure." Daniel trudged off, equal parts obedience and reluctance. Watching him go, Tara wondered how much of that was an act put on for the doctor and how much was simply Daniel being himself. It was hard to tell with him.

"I think we've gotten a good start," Dr. DeAngelo said when Daniel had pulled the door shut behind him. "For our next session I'd like to try a little light hypnosis, get him used to the procedure before we try to isolate any trauma."

"That sounds reasonable."

"Whatever's bothering Daniel, I'd bet it's on a deeper level than current events between you and your husband. He seems at ease with his relationship with his father, and equally at ease with you. What do you know about his history before you adopted him?"

"He was abused. He doesn't like to talk about it. I think that's probably what we need to look at. I'm not sure he remembers everything that was done to him—or that he acknowledges what he does remember."

The doctor nodded. "I think that's probably a good guess." He hesitated, eyeing her just a bit too closely. "This isn't exactly kosher in my profession, but would you like to have a cup of coffee with me tomorrow? Maybe while Daniel's in school?"

Tara blinked, surprised. The dream rushed in for a moment, even more intense than it had been while it was happening. She could almost feel his breath against her lips. "I'm not sure, Dr. DeAngelo."

He gave a sheepish smile. "Forgive me for being forward. You're not really my patient, so I thought it might not be too untoward." He hesitated, then looked right into her eyes. The contact startled her. "To be honest, since you walked into this office I've been having the strangest feeling of déjà vu."

That startled her even more. "Well . . . as long as we're being honest, I've sort of been sensing the same thing. We haven't met before, have we?"

"Not that I'm aware of. But I've always made it a policy to figure these things out when they happen to me." He shrugged. "Sort of a therapist thing, I guess."

"So you're not really asking me on a date."

"No. Just for coffee. Some chat. Would that be okay?"

She couldn't deny the attraction. Had it been only that, nothing more than the primal pull of hormones, she would have refused. But it was more. She had the undeniable sense she *knew* him. "Yes. That'd be fine. There's a coffee shop around the corner from my building. Would that be good?"

"That'd be fine."

She wrote directions on a piece of paper, said goodnight to Dr. DeAngelo, then went to retrieve Daniel.

"I'm hungry," he said when they reached the sidewalk.

"Okay, go. I'll meet you at home."

She watched him disappear with her usual trepidation. Then, with a sigh, she turned and walked in the opposite direction, toward home.

Three

At seven the next morning, sitting at a table with a latte and a blueberry scone, Gray still wasn't sure being here was a good idea.

When Tara walked in, saw him, and smiled, he was almost positive it wasn't.

True, she wasn't his patient, but close enough. He didn't like to play fast and loose with the rules, particularly those he'd made for himself. And his own rules definitely disallowed involvement with a patient's mother.

Still, he found his attention drawn to her as she bought her coffee and approached his table. Her blonde hair, cut in a neat, chin-length style, bobbed prettily as she walked. Her blue eyes shone when she smiled.

But not the way they should have. They were bright with friendliness, but something inside him felt that was not enough. The light there should be colored by love.

And the eyes should be green.

He shook his head a little as she sat down, bewildered by the images in his head. Images that tried persistently to overlay the reality in front of him.

Tara settled across from him and frowned delicately. "Are you all right?"

"I'm fine." He schooled his features, wondering what kind of ridiculous expression they had held. "Just a little tired."

"Oh, me, too. Daniel had me up half the night." She broke off, as if she'd said something she hadn't meant to say. Then, in a different, less certain voice, she added, "You know. Bad dreams."

"That's not unusual. In fact, it's something I would expect to see more of as treatment progresses. I'm a bit surprised it's started so soon, though."

Tara's frown deepened. "So what causes them?"

"Sometimes the subconscious starts working on problems we can only brush on in therapy sessions. I'd like you to ask Daniel to start a dream journal. We can take a look at the imagery and see what his brain is trying to tell him."

"Okay. I'll tell him."

Gray settled into his chair, tapping his scone. Tara hadn't bought anything to eat, he noticed. "Ms. Summers, I'm sure you understand, but I want to stress anyway, that you and Daniel have to be in this for the long haul."

"Call me Tara." She sipped her coffee, watching him over the rim of the cardboard cup. The look in her eyes wasn't quite seductive, wasn't quite coy, but seemed to be trying to hide elements of both. "Did you really invite me here to talk about Daniel? Or is that your way of justifying it to yourself?"

Gray shifted uncomfortably. Honesty, he thought, was probably the best idea at this point. "Maybe a little of both."

Her smile was a little wistful, and she tilted her head, looking at him. "So. The déjà vu thing. What do you think it's about?"

"It's not that unusual," he said stonily. But the strength of it—*that* was unusual.

"What do you think it means? You do past-life regression hypnosis, don't you? Maybe we knew each other in another life."

He shrugged, reluctant to entertain the idea, even though it was, technically, his specialty. "I suppose it's possible."

"Is that something you'd be interested in exploring?"

Her teasing expression brought out the wicked in him. "I don't know. Is that the kind of therapy you'd be willing to pay for?"

"At your rates? I don't think so."

"Maybe that ex-husband of yours could finance it."

He immediately regretted the joke as her expression sobered. "I don't think he would see it as a wise investment." She paused, frowning thoughtfully. "Don't you think it's a bit strange, though, that I came to you for help with Daniel, and then we both feel this connection?"

"Yes, I do."

"Has anything like this ever happened to you before?"

"No, I can't say that it has."

"So what are you going to do about it?"

The question caught him off guard. "Maybe I should ask *you* to do a dream journal."

She flushed. Just as he'd suspected she would. He nodded smugly. "That's what I thought. The whole past-life thing is a big joke to you. But I've been doing this for a long time, and I've seen some pretty strange things. If we start looking into it, you'd better be prepared for what you might find."

Her gaze hardened. "Ditto, Dr. DeAngelo."

He quirked an eyebrow. The color of her eyes might be different from those eyes he remembered, but the sparks flying from them at that moment looked eerily familiar. "You think I might not like what I learn about you?"

"Yes. And about Daniel, too." She scooped up her coffee and, with one last flash of her eyes, left him.

Odd, he thought, and returned to his scone.

Tara spent the rest of the day wishing she'd kept her mouth shut. She had no idea what had possessed her, besides sheer anger at Gray DeAngelo's nerve. Something about the connection between them, and finding out he was aware of it, too, had rattled her badly. Badly enough that she'd opened her big mouth and said things she shouldn't have said. There was no point putting ideas in his head, after all, especially about Daniel.

There was also no point, she supposed, in dwelling on things she couldn't do anything about. She'd said what she'd said, and couldn't take the words back. Maybe she could just blame it on sexual tension. Or PMS. Or lack of breakfast. Regardless, there had to be some way to smooth things over.

When she went to his office that evening, though, there didn't seem to be a need for any smoothing. Dr. DeAngelo immediately started to work with Daniel, putting him into a light hypnotic state to be sure he was comfortable with the procedure. Tara watched with interest.

"Do you remember the first time you saw your mom?" The doctor's voice was soft, in keeping with the atmosphere he'd created in the room.

Tara was almost afraid to breathe. Easy questions, she thought. Start out easy, then get to the tough stuff.

"Yes," said Daniel.

"What did you think of her?"

"I thought she was pretty. But too young to be of much use to me."

The doctor's eyebrows compressed a bit. Tara bit her lip. Daniel didn't sound like a ten-year-old boy at all. "What do you mean by that?" the doctor went on.

"I mean that she didn't seem like she knew much of anything. She was twenty-something, just a kid I guess. She hadn't been around."

"And you had?"

"A hell of a lot more than she had."

"But you grew to like her."

"I don't know. Maybe. She's done some good stuff since then. She's smarter than she looks."

The doctor steepled his fingers, leaning his elbows on his knees. "What do you remember about the people you were with before?"

"A little. No one really watched out for me before."

"Do you remember the first person who loved you?"

There was a long pause. Tara held her breath, wondering how many centuries Daniel was sifting through to find the answer to that question. The plight of child vampires was often an unpleasant one, and she tried not to think about all the people who might have used, hurt or abused him through his long lifetime.

Finally he said, in a small voice, "My mother."

That startled Tara, but of course it seemed a perfectly normal answer to the doctor, who continued with his questions.

"You remember your real mother?"

"Yes. She was gentle. She had a soft voice. We used to go . . . outside. Into the sun."

The doctor nodded. "I see. This was before you were diagnosed with porphyria?"

"It was when I could still go into the sun." Daniel's voice held a reverent tone. "It was bright and warm, and it didn't hurt. And I could eat. Meat and fruit and—" He broke off, and when he spoke again, it was no longer in English.

The doctor exchanged glances with Tara, then returned his attention to Daniel. He let the boy talk for a while, in an odd language unlike anything Tara had ever heard before. Finally, when Daniel paused, a rapturous expression on his face, Dr. DeAngelo said gently, "Daniel, it's time to come back. I'll count backwards from ten. . . ."

When Daniel had returned to the present, the doctor discussed what had happened, asked him a few questions, then asked him to sit in the lobby while he talked to Tara. Daniel gave her a weighted look as he walked out. She nodded encouragement.

"That was weird," she said to the doctor when Daniel was gone. "Do you think he was having a past-life regression or something?"

"It's possible, but I wouldn't rush to that conclusion. Do you know anything about his biological mother? Maybe she spoke another language at home."

Tara shrugged. "I don't know. I'll see if I can find out."

"Great. That'll be your assignment for next time, then. That and the dream journal."

She gave him a narrow look. "Daniel's or mine?"

He grinned. "Both, if you like." He stood, effectively ending their heart-to-heart. "I'll see you tomorrow night, then."

The whole situation was eating at Gray. Something just didn't seem right to him. About Daniel spouting strange languages, about Tara and her blue eyes that should have been green. As he talked to Daniel, it had suddenly occurred to him that he knew where he might be able to find answers.

He wasn't sure why he hadn't thought of it before. It seemed obvious, once the idea popped into his head. Maybe he'd been repressing. He should talk to a professional about that.

At home, he went to his bookshelves and reached for a set of hardback journals on the top shelf. He wasn't sure which one he was after, and the dates weren't a great deal of help. There wasn't much for it but to skim through the books until he found what he was looking for.

The books were diaries recording his own experiences with regression hypnosis. He'd gone through several sessions with a trained hypnotist, exploring his own past, and eventually discovering a sequence of previous lives. Unfortunately, he didn't recall the details of the sessions. He'd been a difficult hypnosis subject, able to remember details immediately after the sessions but unable to retain them for very long. The journals had been written mostly by his therapist, but he himself had scribbled frantically, post-session, in many of them. Between the therapist's handwriting and his own hurried scrawls, reading the journals proved more of a chore than he'd anticipated.

The first two volumes yielded nothing. He moved on to the third.

Daniel was quieter than usual, barely speaking on the way home. He took the time to get a jacket, then headed out with little more than a farewell grunt.

Tara sighed, tossing her purse on the couch. Obviously today's session had disturbed him. She just wished he would open up to her.

It would be another long night spent with the television, falling asleep in front of late-night talk shows. Parenting was hard. Especially parenting a vampire.

Exhausted from dealing with Daniel's erratic schedule, she'd hoped to fall asleep quickly, but the buzzing in her brain kept her awake. She kept thinking about the evening's session, about Daniel's strange lapse into that strange language and the way he'd closed up after the session. He'd returned to where they'd wanted him to be, to the days before he'd been made into a vampire. He'd remembered the sun. Doubtless, Julian would be pleased, but Tara thought it was probably too much for Daniel to deal with all at once.

Or maybe his moodiness was due to hunger. On reflection, she'd scheduled his sessions a little too early in the evening. There wasn't time for him to get a significant meal before he went to the doctor. Maybe she should call in the morning and change the appointment.

She flipped channels for a time, finally settling on an infomercial. She finally drifted off to the over-excited tones of men raving about spray-on hair.

Gray found volume three of his journals more interesting. Skimming through the pages, he found the descriptions he'd been looking for—the green-eyed woman with pale hair, the man who'd been himself but wasn't. And, reading on, he remembered why he'd forgotten.

"Hell," he said to himself. "This can't be it."

She was certain the dark, narrow alley would mean their deaths. Their pursuers had deliberately driven them here. There was no escape.

Liam set himself in front of her, placing his body between her and the dark shadows approaching them. She clutched at his coat, fear bitter in her throat.

"Do we have anything left?" she asked. "Crosses, garlic, holy water?"

"I have garlic, but it doesn't seem to do any good."

"Nothing seems to work. I don't understand. We've followed the legends—"

"I think the legends are wrong." He drew his pistol. "This isn't supposed to work, but I'm going to try it. If nothing else, maybe it will slow them down."

"Trying is better than dying." She took a moment to appreciate her own unintentional cleverness, then grabbed the other pistol from under his coat. "This one's loaded, as well, I hope?"

"Yes."

So they stood their ground together. The shadows drew closer,

intent, growling, the faint moonlight glinting off long, feral fangs.
Vampires. She hadn't believed in them until Liam had shown
her. There were times when she'd regretted letting herself be pulled
into his dark world. This was not one of those times. If there was
anyone in the world she was willing to die with, or for, it was Liam.
And the vampires advanced. . . .

"'We're in the alleyway,'" Gray read aloud to himself. "'The vampires are coming closer. Our only defense is two pistols. Everything that's supposed to work on vampires doesn't work. Felicity is behind me, holding onto my coat. We fire.'" Shaking his head, he turned the page. "What a bunch of nonsense. 'I put a bullet between the eyes of the first one. Felicity fires with equal success. They stagger back, wounded more than I thought possible. Maybe, just maybe, there's enough space to slide by, to get out. . . .'"

He dropped the book and shoved back in his chair, letting his head bang against the wall behind him. No wonder he'd forgotten this. It hadn't been a genuine past-life experience—couldn't have been, with vampires crawling through it. As he recalled, he and his therapist had never quite figured out what this series of visions had represented.

The accounts he was looking for had to be somewhere else, he thought, eyeing the book he'd let fall on the desk. Volume four, maybe.

But this one, with its convoluted fantasy about vampires, was the one that felt in sync with the déjà vu memories he'd been having.

Besides, he wanted to see what happened next.

There was enough room, barely, to slide past the staggering
vampires and out of the alley. She took her chance, following Liam,
clinging to his coat. A rush went through her, of excitement more
than fear, making her heart beat hard and her breath come fast.

And they almost made it. Steps before freedom, a hand clamped
onto her skirts, yanking her back.

"Felicity!" Liam's voice roared in her ears as she was dragged
around to face the snarl of a vampire. A vampire with a bullet hole
right between his eyes.

It bent its head toward her throat. . . .

"'Suddenly there's another vampire. It's as if he's come out of nowhere. He grabs the vampire who has Felicity and flings him down the street. 'Go!' he shouts to us, and, God help me, I'm too frightened, too bloody scared, even to think about killing him. We run. We just run. But I look at him over my shoulder at him, trying to see what he looks like. He is a vampire and, therefore, a demon, and despite that he helped us escape, he still must die.'"

Gray vaguely recalled his therapist pausing there, asking him for a description. He'd done his best to provide one, but the figure in the dream had been shadowy, vague. A man of medium height and build, with dark hair. He could have been anyone.

"This is pointless," Gray muttered, slamming the journal shut.

The teeth were almost at her throat when hands jerked the vampire away, freeing her. She ran, following Liam, but took one last look over her shoulder, to see the face of the creature who had saved her.

Tara jerked awake, sitting straight up on the couch. "Julian."

Four

There was no getting back to sleep after that. Tara paced the floor for an hour, looking at her watch and muttering to herself about Daniel's continued absence. Sunrise wasn't that far away, after all. Yes, he'd done fine for himself for five centuries, but that hadn't involved her waiting up for him, worrying that he'd been abducted or killed by the Dark Children. Was he staying close to home, as she'd told him to do? Was he even staying in Manhattan, where it was supposed to be safe?

When he finally did come home, he looked so forlorn that she couldn't bring herself to chastise him. Instead she went straight to him and knelt in front of him, holding out her arms. "Oh, honey, are you all right?"

A moment after she'd made the move, a moment after the saccharine words had come out of her mouth, she cringed. Daniel hated that stuff, the Mommy stuff, the nurturing stuff. But he stepped right into her arms and let her hold him.

He said nothing for several long seconds, and she didn't break the silence. Finally he took a step back, looking sheepishly at the floor. "I'm sorry."

"No, it's okay, Daniel." Sensing the "Mom" moment had passed, Tara pushed herself to her feet. But she couldn't resist a last caress of his head, an almost-tousle of his hair. "Whatever's wrong, you can talk to me about it."

"Yeah." He went to the couch and sank into it. For once he didn't turn the TV on right away. "How come you're up?"

She shrugged. "I had a bad dream. It woke me up, and I couldn't get back to sleep."

He peered cautiously up at her. "About me?"

"No. Not about you." She frowned. "Why would you think I'd have a bad dream about you?"

"Because I'm a monster." He stopped, pressed his lips together, scrubbed angrily at his eyes. "You should be afraid of me. You should run and run and never stop running."

She'd heard a lot of strange things come out of Daniel's mouth, but never once had she felt threatened by him. And she didn't then. She sat next to him on the couch and slipped an arm around his thin shoulders. "You mean like this?"

He blinked rapidly, then buried his face in her chest and wept.

She let him cry, patting his back and stroking his hair. "There, there," she murmured. "It's okay."

"No, it's not okay." He sniffled, then suddenly gulped and pushed away from her. "Are you sure I can talk to you? Are you sure you can handle it?"

She wasn't sure at all. But she figured, after seeing her boyfriend staked through the heart, she could handle whatever Daniel had to say. "Just tell me. I'm a big girl."

"I'm a vampire," he said. "Vampires drink human blood."

Tara nodded. "Yes, for the most part."

"I go out every night, and I feed. I come home, and you talk to me like nothing weird is going on, like I went out for a hot dog."

"I don't really see how I can do much else. You have to eat, and Julian told me the plasma drinks make you sick."

For several minutes, Daniel remained silent, and she could see he was trying to work up the courage to say what he needed to say.

"Do you know—" He stopped, closed his eyes, swallowed so hard she could hear it. "Do you know if I kill people when I go out?"

"No. I don't know." She paused, wondering if she should ask the obvious question. "Don't you know?"

"No. That's the problem. I go out and feed, and I come home, and I have no memory of where I've been or where I've gone. It's always been that way. I don't know what I eat or who I hurt. Or kill."

"Oh. I see." She fought the urge to reach for him again.

"I've been alive for five hundred years." His voice had gone thin and choked again. "How many people have I murdered in all that time?"

Count on the little vampire kid to ask the tough questions. Absently, Tara stroked his hair again. He was just a little boy. Even his depiction of himself as a bloodthirsty killer couldn't change her perception of him as innocent, unblemished in many ways by his nature.

"If I had to guess," she ventured, "I'd have to say not very many."

He brightened a little. "Really? Why?"

"Because in all the time I've known you, you've gone out every night and come back apparently having had a satisfactory meal. But I haven't heard anything on the news, ever, about any mysterious deaths in the vicinity."

His eyes widened. "Oh, my gosh. You're right. I read the paper most mornings, and I haven't seen anything there, either."

"Right. You're a small person, Daniel. Even the big vampires can feed their hunger without killing if they want to, or learn how to." She knew that ability varied among vampires, depending on who had Made them, but she also knew without a doubt that it was possible. "My guess is you take what you need and go on, without ever actually killing anyone at all."

Relief swept over Daniel's face for a few seconds, then his expression hardened again. "I need to know. I need to be sure. Do you think that doctor can help me find out?"

Tara frowned. "I'm not sure that's such a good idea." At his sudden, crestfallen look, she added, "But I'll talk to Julian about it."

"Good. Because I need to know what I've been before I can decide what I want to be. I need to know exactly what's been going on with me for the past five hundred years."

"Okay. I'll talk to Julian. I need to see him, anyway, today. Now, you get to bed. The sun's going to be up soon."

He yawned. "Yeah, I can feel it." Standing, he headed for his small, sun-tight bedroom. "Wish I'd gotten home earlier. I missed that *Dragonball Z* marathon."

"Next time let me know, and I'll tape it for you."

He gave her a sweet, boyish smile. "Thanks."

As usual, Julian was awake and in his office. He wasn't working, though. Instead, the complex and colorful graphics of a fantasy wargame filled his computer screen. She wondered why he would be wasting time with such a thing, then realized the map on his screen echoed the layout of the Underground. He was using the game's map generator to work out battle strategies.

"Tara," he said as she entered. "How are you?"

"Things have taken an interesting turn." She sank onto the comfortable couch. "A couple of interesting turns, actually."

She told him about her conversation with Daniel, then, more hesitantly, about the dreams. "I don't really know what to think, much less what to do. I've never run into anything like this."

Julian smiled. "Not many have."

"That's not very reassuring." Her fingers were trembling; she folded them together to keep them still. "I almost called him 'Liam' last night. It's all so—" She broke off as Julian's eyebrows shot upward.

"What's wrong?"

He composed himself quickly. A little too quickly. "Nothing."

"Do you—or did you—know somebody named Liam?"

He shrugged, his expression once again inscrutable. "It's a pretty common name. Particularly in Ireland."

Tara wasn't about to settle for such a feeble answer. She started to ask for a definite yes or no, but at that moment, Lorelei wandered in, tousled and sleepy-eyed.

She kissed Julian warmly and settled onto his lap. "Anything like what?"

"It sounds as if Tara and I may have encountered each other in a former life," Julian said. "Well, a former life for her, anyway. Just my same old, really long one."

Lorelei made a face. "Oh. I thought I was the only one who could claim that distinction."

Tara perked up. "Really? You knew Julian sometime way back when?"

"He thinks so. I'm not so sure. I mean, I don't remember shit about it." She stood. "I'm going up for coffee. Anyone want anything?"

"Bring me down some milk, if you could," said Julian.

"I could use some coffee. Any pastries?"

"You betcha. So, coffee and donuts for the girls—and gross, disgusting, unpasteurized milk for the ex-bloodsucker. See you in a bit."

Julian followed her to the door and watched her go, a deep-seated warmth in his eyes. Tara cleared her throat, then smiled at his obvious reluctance in closing the door and turning back to look at her.

"So," he said, settling beside her, on the couch, "do you think Gray DeAngelo may have some memory of the same past life you remember?"

"Well, he *is* a past-life regression therapist," she replied. "I'd say it's a safe bet he's done it himself. And he's as likely to have remembered Liam and Felicity as any other past life he might have had."

Julian sighed. "Then you might need to level with him."

"You mean tell him the truth?"

He nodded, his lips quirking up at the corners in an almost-smile. "Sometimes it just has to be done."

"But the danger to Daniel . . ."

Julian sobered. "Yes, I know. The way I see it, this will go one of two ways. Either DeAngelo's knowing the truth about Daniel—and about the two of you, and about me—will ease the way for Daniel and actually be a great help in his therapy. Or the doctor will start to identify with the less fortunate aspects of his former personality and decide he has to slay vampires again."

"That doesn't sound like much fun."

"No, it wouldn't be. But if it comes down to it, I can deal with him."

"You mean kill him?"

"Only if it comes to that."

Tara took a long breath. "I really, really don't like this."

"I know." He paused, studying her face. "You and Gray—you were lovers in that previous life, weren't you?"

She felt her face redden. "It kind of looks that way, yes."

She wished he would look away. His scrutiny seemed to bore into her soul, and it only intensified as he spoke.

"You need to be prepared, Tara. If you knew me in a previous life, and you also knew DeAngelo, then it's possible—likely, even—that DeAngelo knew me, too. And if he's having these dreams, too . . ." He trailed off, reached to lay a hand on her shoulder. "If he figures out that vampires are real and reverts to Liam's policy of indiscriminate killing. . . . Tara, I won't let him hurt Daniel or anyone in the Underground. You need to be prepared for that."

She understood only too well. And she hated it. But she nodded, anyway, knowing he was waiting for it.

"Don't look so worried," Julian said. "From what you've told me, the doctor sounds like a reasonable person. If he starts channeling Liam, I'm sure we can talk him down." He squeezed her shoulder. "We're the good guys, after all. He'll understand that."

She knew he was trying to reassure her, but it wasn't working. Instead, she felt as if there were something—something important—that he wasn't telling her. Then again, between the weird past-life dreams and lack of sleep, maybe she was getting paranoid. Either way, she had to trust Julian.

And maybe it would all work out.

She laid her hand on top of his on her shoulder. "Okay. We'll just have to see what happens."

Frowning, Gray hung up the phone. Normally, he would have been excited about the news he'd just received, but for some reason, something didn't seem right.

He looked down at the notes he'd written on the pad next to the phone. *Possibly Australian aboriginal dialect previously unrecorded.* His linguist friend, Mark, whom he contacted whenever a mysterious language popped up in a past-life session, had been nearly bouncing off the walls with ecstasy. The language Daniel had spoken in his last session appeared to be a more primitive version of a language spoken by modern aborigines. Mark hadn't been sure how old it might be, but his colleagues were analyzing it.

Gray recalled a similar occurrence, a few years ago. He'd had a patient who, under hypnosis, had spoken for hours on end in a language Mark had finally identified as Etruscan. Another patient's tongue of choice had never been positively identified. Mark had theorized it to be an ancient precursor to Greek, but he could neither confirm that nor translate the language fragments.

So why did Daniel's speaking a foreign language seem so strange? Maybe because the other patients hadn't looked Etruscan or ancient Greek. Whereas Daniel actually looked as if he could be of Australian aboriginal heritage.

Gray dropped his face to his hands, rubbing his forehead with his fingertips. He needed to get a grip. The diaries he'd read, the strange reaction he was having to Tara . . . then being reminded that he'd seen vampires in his personal journey through past-life regression . . . he was starting to question everything he believed in.

No, he wasn't going to go there. He didn't think he could deal with it right now.

Instead, he called Tara. She sounded sleepy, but perked up when he explained what he'd discovered.

"So you think this really might be a past life experience?" she asked.

"I think there's a good chance." He paused. "Listen, I know you didn't bring Daniel to me looking to explore his past lives. And it sounds as if his current one has been traumatic enough. But sometimes past-life regression is helpful in solving current problems. Can we meet, maybe today for lunch, if you're free, and discuss this?"

"Another consultation?" She sounded wary.

"Informal." He smiled. "I won't charge you."

"All right." He could hear her answering smile in her voice. "It's a date. I'll meet you at your office."

She hung up before he could protest her use of the word "date." Bemused, he stared at the phone for a few seconds before he carefully replaced the receiver.

* * *

But maybe it was a date, Gray thought later. If the way his heart began to accelerate when he saw Tara walk into the reception area of his office was any indication, the term wasn't far off the mark. He really had to watch himself. Getting involved with her could cause him all manner of problems.

Still, as they walked to the diner on the corner, he couldn't resist carefully bumping shoulders with her. She didn't seem to mind. If she even noticed. She did seem rather absorbed in her own thoughts.

He found out why when they were seated in the diner, eating sandwiches.

"I've given a great deal of thought to your suggestion about Daniel. You know—the past-life regression thing," she said. She'd eaten only a few bites of her sandwich and was merely playing with her French fries. "He and I had a discussion yesterday after his session, and he has some specific goals he wants to address."

Gray frowned in sudden realization. "Where is Daniel, anyway? He doesn't go to regular school, does he?"

Tara's face froze, and she stopped chewing. Then, carefully, she said, "He's at home with a tutor. My ex-husband pays for private school-ing." Her words were even, as if she were reciting something. Then she laughed a little. "I can only stand so much second-hand algebra."

"He's learning algebra already? Bright kid." He paused, giving her a chance to respond, but she didn't. "So what are these specific goals?"

"He's aware of certain blank areas in his memory. He wants to fill those in. One of those was remembering his mother, and now he'd like to address other issues."

"So what are you proposing?"

"I propose that we do exactly what Daniel wants to do, and no more. If that leads us into past life stuff again, so be it. If not, then I think it's best to leave it alone." She dragged an abnormally long French fry through the puddle of ketchup on her plate. "I don't want to cause him too much stress. Not right now. The past life memories won't go away. He can dredge them up any time he chooses. Right now I think we need to focus on the immediate issues."

"All right, fair enough." He watched her for a few seconds, as she again attended to her food. Her eating pattern struck him as ner-vous—she was pulling pieces out of her sandwich instead of eating the whole thing, and she'd constructed some sort of complicated filing system with her fries. They seemed to be sorted by length, although some of the piles had fallen into each other.

Finally he said, "Speaking of immediate issues . . ."

"Yes?" she prompted.

"The déjà vu thing we were talking about. I went through some of my old therapy journals, just out of curiosity."

"And?"

"I found some strange things. I think that might have been what I was remembering. If so, it's all just a coincidence."

"You mean we didn't actually know each other in a past life? What makes you say that?"

"Because the journal I was remembering didn't refer to a past-life regression. It was something else." He waved vaguely. "Some kind of hallucination or dream recall, or something along those lines."

"Are you sure?"

"It has to be. There were vampires in it." He took a bite of his sandwich and shrugged.

She laughed, but the sound seemed false. "Really? You remembered being with me and hunting vampires?"

"There was a woman described in the visions, yes. As to whether it was you, well, I doubt it. But, yes, I was hunting vampires with her. How did you know?"

She dodged the question. "What kind of vampires?"

"Nasty ones with sharp, pointy teeth. What other kind is there?"

She looked at him levelly, her expression remarkably serious. "Well, I don't know. Because in the dream I had, there was a nice one who rescued us."

He gaped at her. "My God. You're kidding."

"Do I look like I'm kidding?"

"This is bizarre. Extremely bizarre. There was a similar scene in my journals." He shook his head slowly. "There has to be some logical explanation."

"And I'm sure you'll think of it sometime soon. When you do, let me know."

She stood and wheeled, but he caught her by the elbow.

"Why do you keep doing that?"

"Doing what?" she said.

"Storming off. You say cryptic things, and then you storm off. Is there something you're not telling me?"

She just looked at him. Something lurked behind her eyes, something that he thought might dissolve into tears. Finally she sat back down. "I'm afraid for Daniel."

Okay, unexpected change of subject, but he could handle it. "What does any of this have to do with Daniel?"

"I know things about Daniel that you don't. I'm counting on you to be able to help him. If you can't handle—" She broke off.

Gray was flummoxed. He didn't understand the intensity in her voice, or the way her eyes seemed about to overflow. "What does this have to do with ridiculous dreams about vampires?"

"That we're both having. The same dreams." She closed her eyes suddenly, squeezing the bridge of her nose with her fingers. "You know what? Never mind. I need to talk to Daniel. If he wants to continue with his therapy, you'll see us tonight."

This time she went, leaving half her sandwich behind. Watching her go, Gray realized he had no idea what they'd just been talking about.

"I want to go."

"Are you sure?" Tara felt she had to ask the question. But, truthfully, Daniel looked about as sober and certain as she'd ever seen him. "I mean, I'm not entirely sure he's going to be able to deal with you once the pieces start coming together."

"He already thinks I'm having past-life regressions. Why would he think any different?"

"Daniel, you said you wanted to remember feeding. You won't be able to pass that off as a past-life thing."

"I don't think there's going to be a problem. Obviously he's hunted vampires in a previous life, so he knows they're real."

"No, he doesn't know. He doesn't believe any of it's real."

Daniel frowned. "How could he not believe it if you're both having the same dreams?"

"Because he's a human being, and human beings can be unbelievably thick-headed and stupid."

Daniel smiled a little. "Except you, right?"

"Are you kidding? I went out with Dom for nearly two years without ever figuring out he was a vampire." She gave a wry grin, remembering what she'd come to think of as the Brain Dead Years. "I thought he was just afraid of commitment."

Daniel laughed, then suddenly sobered. "Dom. Dominic."

"Yes." She swallowed, surprised by the surge of emotion. It had been a long time since she'd cried for Dom. "It was because of him that I started believing in the existence of vampires. Some of his friends ended up introducing me to the Senior. You knew him?"

"Yeah. I'm sorry. I didn't know."

"It's okay. It was a long time ago."

"Not that long. Three years is . . . is a heartbeat to me."

Tara nodded. She hadn't thought of it that way before. So much had happened to her in the past three years, sometimes it felt like a lifetime.

The silence stretched, but she didn't notice until Daniel spoke again, his voice quiet and strained. "I need this, Tara. I need to know. I need to know what I am before I can decide what I want to be."

"Are you sure?" She wasn't sure she wanted him to know.

"I'm sure. And then . . . I think I'm going to do it. Change back." He paused. "Promise me you won't leave me. If I do turn mortal, I'm going to need you. I think I'm going to need a mom."

Blinking away sudden tears, Tara smiled and held her arms out to him. He came to her, let her hold him. "I can do that," she said.

He held her tight. "Thank you."

Five

It had been Daniel's decision, and that was the way it should be, so Tara sat quietly on her usual chair in the corner and waited for the inevitable drama to unfold.

Daniel looked Gray straight in the eye and said, "I need to know the truth about myself, Dr. DeAngelo."

"That's what we're here for," Gray said gently, exactly as if he were talking to a child. "I want to help you get to the root of your problems."

"Yes. And I think you can do that. Promise me you'll do that."

"I'll do what I can, of course." He looked toward Tara, a question in his eyes, but she looked away.

A few minutes later, the session was underway.

"I'm in the darkness again. The smell is thick. Alley smells. Garbage and, um, piss, I guess." Daniel spoke in a low monotone. Gray had been leading him deeper into the meditative state for the last half-hour. In spite of herself, Tara had become absorbed in the interplay. At times it seemed more like Daniel was leading Gray than the other way around. But Daniel knew what he wanted, knew where he had to go, and in spite of his memory lapses, she had the feeling he had a strength of mind unlike anything Gray had ever encountered before.

"What are you doing there?" Gray's voice, too, was soft.

"I'm hunting."

"For what?"

"For food."

"Your mother, your parents, where are they? Do they feed you?"

Daniel's blank eyes stared into space. He barely blinked as the mental image absorbed him. "They're dead. They died a long time ago. The one who Changed me, he taught me how to hunt, how to feed."

Tara held her breath. Gray said, "What do you hunt? What do you eat?"

There was a long pause. Finally, Daniel broke the silence. "Rats, mostly. Sometimes dogs and cats."

Carefully, slowly, Tara let her breath out. Gray's face had tightened in carefully controlled disgust, but when he spoke, his voice remained a gentle monotone. "Do you kill them yourself?"

"Yes. He taught me how. He killed people sometimes but he told me not to try. He said I was too small, and that animals were safer. But he said if I could get a human being, it would taste so much better. So maybe he would teach me later how to do it, even though I was small."

"Who was this man? What was his name?"

"His name was Reaper. That was what he called himself. I don't know what his real name was."

"Would you recognize him if you saw him?"

"He's dead. He fell asleep in the sun one time, and he caught on fire. I saw his bones the next morning. I think somebody tied him up so he couldn't get home."

Tara's gaze shot to Gray, and she held her breath. But his face remained impassive.

"All right, Daniel," he said, "I think that's enough."

He brought Daniel back slowly, as usual, but this time didn't ask him to leave the room right away. Instead he knelt in front of Daniel's chair. "Daniel, are you all right?"

Daniel nodded. "I'm fine."

"Do you remember what you saw?"

Daniel slanted a look toward Tara. "Just a little."

Gently, Gray took his hand. "Daniel, what happened to you wasn't your fault. Someone did something terrible to you, taught you terrible things. I think you might need someone besides me to help you with this. If I had known what we were going to find, I might have recommended another doctor."

"It's okay, Dr. DeAngelo. I'm glad I remembered. I'll be okay."

"I'm going to talk to some of my colleagues to see if one of them can take you on for intensive psychotherapy—traditional therapy, that is. I don't think I'm qualified to deal with this on my own."

Tara stood. "I don't think that would be wise right now."

Gray's gaze jerked toward her. "I think it's necessary."

For a moment, she drew a blank. What possible argument could she offer? Then the obvious solution came to her. "I need to talk to my ex-husband. He needs to know. He's paying, after all."

"This is extremely important, Tara. If there's going to be a problem with payment, then I need to talk to him. In fact, it might be a good idea for me to talk to him, anyway."

Daniel jumped a little, then looked at Tara. A faint smile rose on his mouth, a gleam of laughter twinkling in his eyes. "Yeah, Mom. I think it might be a good idea for him to talk to Dad."

Tara resisted the urge to roll her eyes. "I'll talk to him. I'll be sure this all gets taken care of."

Gray stopped her again on the way out. "This is very important. You need to be sure your ex-husband understands that. I've had some bad things come out of patients under hypnotherapy, but never anything like this. It's absolutely vital that Daniel get treatment—"

Tara grasped his arm. "I understand, Gray. I'll take care of it."

As they walked down the steps together, Tara rolled her eyes at Daniel. "Jeez. Did he overreact, or what?"

"Probably not many ten-year-old kids remember killing rats and dogs in an alley." His face lit up in a slow smile. "Rats. Not people." The smile faded. "I like dogs, though. That's bad. I don't want to eat dogs. And Reaper said he was going to teach me to eat people. Do you think he ever did?" His big eyes looked worried again.

Tara put her arm around him. "Remember what I told you. No reports of unexpected deaths. I think you're in the clear."

He nodded. "I hope so."

He remained thoughtful the rest of their walk home, and when they reached the door to the apartment building he said, "I'm not hunting tonight."

"Aren't you hungry?"

"I am. I'm going Underground. I want to see Dr. Greene."

"What about?"

"I want to get something to eat, and I want to talk to him about the mortality thing." He shrugged. "No decisions yet. Just information." He reached toward her, plucking shyly at her sleeve. "I'll stay down there all night. So you don't have to worry about me. That way you can get some sleep."

Tara smiled. "I'll do that. But first, I'll walk you to the entrance."

The entrance to the Underground wasn't far, making an escort seem unnecessary, but he tolerated her company. She watched him disappear through the entryway and wished somebody down there had a phone, so she could call and check on him later. At least she knew where he would be, which was better than most nights.

By the time she made her way to her apartment, she had decided to follow Daniel's advice and get a good night's sleep. It would be the first she'd had since she'd agreed to take him in, and God knows, she needed it.

By nine o'clock, relieved of the burden of worrying about Daniel, she could no longer hold her eyes open. She crawled into her pajamas, then into bed, and dropped off before she could wonder how long it would take her to fall asleep.

"Felicity, it is not my habit to take advantage of a lady."

She twisted her fingers in the neck of his white shirt. "You are not taking advantage, and I daresay I am not a lady."

He dipped his head toward her, kissing her, his mouth hard and hot. She tangled her tongue with his, glorying in the sensation. The evening's adventures had driven her to a place she knew well, where she craved the slide of skin against skin, the catharsis of relentless climax.

He drew back, looking into her face, the familiar heat smoldering in his eyes. "You most certainly are a lady, and I would put a stake through the heart of anyone who said otherwise." His hands slid up from her waist to pull at the hooks at the back of her dress, loosening them.

"Let's save the stakes for the vampires," she whispered, and grabbed him by the hair and kissed him again.

It was furious between them—it always was. Especially on nights like this, when their passion was fueled by the aftermath of shared danger. Tonight they had barely escaped death at the teeth of a gang of vampires, but they'd managed to kill two of them before they'd been forced to flee. Nearly losing Liam had made her want him desperately, so desperately she'd barely been able to wait until they returned to their small tenement house.

Now she pulled eagerly at his clothes, pulled him down onto the narrow bed. His mouth left her mouth and found her breasts as he peeled her bodice open. She arched into him, crying out at the tug of his mouth on her breast, the press of his tongue against her nipple. He pushed and pulled at her skirts until they fell to the floor. She tugged at the fastenings of his trousers until her fingers found his sex, thick and hot and ready. She cupped him, luxuriating in the velvety skin and the heat that filled her hand.

She had never been shy with him—she had never needed to be. She trusted him implicitly with her life, with her body. When his hand slid between her thighs, she shifted to allow him easier access. His fingers slid inside her, his thumb finding the center of her pleasure, and she gasped as he rolled and pressed her there, until she shuddered over him, her body melting into fire and ecstasy.

He pressed his fingers deeper into her as she pulsed against him; then he shifted her body, bringing her down onto the heat of his ready erection. He slid deep into her, and she moved on him, drawing him in as far as she could. She loved the way he felt inside her, loved possessing him and being possessed by him, the slide and the heat and the friction as he slaked his thirst for her body. When he finished she had ridden the wave again, and plummeted back down with him. . . .

Tara sat up in bed, shuddering. Not with fear, but with the aftershocks of powerful orgasm. Drawing her knees up to her chest, she hugged herself tight and closed her eyes as the pulsing faded.

That had been too damned real. Not a dream or even a memory, but something deeper, something stored in her cells. She was hot and wet and achy, exactly as if she'd actually experienced the events of the dream.

She should have been able to enjoy it. Under other circumstances, she probably would have. Knowing what she knew about Gray, though, she couldn't help but feel mortified at the thought that he might be having similar dreams about her.

She slept late the next morning, recovering from the sleep she'd lost in the middle of the night. The sun was up when she finally woke, and she jolted out of bed, rushing to Daniel's room.

He was there, curled up in bed exactly like a little boy, except he was deathly still and didn't appear to be breathing. Weak with relief, she took a moment to lean against the doorframe and collect herself.

Of course he'd made it home safely. He always did.

It was frustrating, though, knowing she couldn't talk to him about what he'd done last night. She was curious to know what he'd said to Dr. Greene and what the doctor had said to him. She wondered if he'd made his decision about whether to be mortal again. But at the moment, she couldn't ask him any of those questions.

Julian might know, though. And she needed to see him, anyway. So she went to get her morning coffee, intending to head for the Underground afterward.

Gray was at the coffee shop. Standing in line behind two other customers, staring at the menu board. Tara froze in the doorway, seeing him. The polite thing to do would be to go in, say hi, maybe share her coffee ritual with him, if he had the time. Yesterday morning she would have done exactly that. Today her brain burned with the memory of Liam and Felicity, Felicity crazed with wanting, Liam hot and hard inside her.

She turned around and walked the other way. There were plenty of coffee shops on her way to the Underground.

Julian didn't seem particularly surprised at her recounting of Daniel's last therapy session. Or, she noted, of Gray's dream. Again, she had the feeling he was holding something back.

"We knew it would come to this, or something like it, sooner or later," he said. "Daniel's subconscious is going to determine what he needs to know, in order to make the adjustment successfully, and if he needs to remember feeding, that's what this doctor's likely to find in his head."

"But he's freaking out and wants to call in a specialist."

"So make the arrangements. Then don't go."

"Gray will find out."

Julian looked at her, eyes narrowing. "Gray? He's not Dr. DeAngelo anymore?"

Tara looked at her hands, sheepish. "It doesn't mean anything. Not really."

"Are you dating him or something?"

"No." Defensive, she crossed her arms over her chest. "We had a cup of coffee and discussed Daniel's case."

"No more dreams?"

She didn't want to say anything. Didn't want to tell him at all. "Yes. More dreams. I don't know what to do about it, Julian."

"Sex dreams?"

"None of your damned business."

He laughed. "That's what I thought." The humor fled from his face as he lapsed back into thought. "Look, you just deal with the therapy thing the way you think you need to do it. If you need my help, let me know. We'll handle things as they come."

"And what am I supposed to do about Gray? He knows vampires are real—he fought them in a previous life. What if he figures out what's going on and decides to come after Daniel?"

"I think you're overreacting." He paused, studying her face. When he spoke again, his voice was gentler. "Dom was careless."

To Tara's surprise, she felt tears prickle her eyes. "Don't talk about Dom."

She'd spent a long time trying to forget about Dom. She'd cared a great deal about him, enough to accept him for what he was. When he had died at the hands of a gang of overzealous vampire hunters, she had been devastated. His friends—the vampire ones—had sensed her willingness to accept their world and had brought her to the Senior.

Julian's expression gentled. "Dom was killed by self-styled vampire hunters. Gray DeAngelo was a hunter in a previous life. You don't think the connection is what's upsetting you?"

She blinked until the tears had withdrawn. "I'm just afraid for Daniel. I don't want anything to happen to him."

"Daniel will be all right. I'll see to that."

Something in his voice made her look up. His gaze was hard and resolute, but it gentled as she met it with her own.

"It'll be okay," he said. "Just do what you have to do."

She nodded. "I'll let you know."

Six

When she got home, there was a message on her answering machine from Gray. Listening to it, she tipped her head back, stared at the ceiling with her lips in a thin line and reflected on the stubbornness of men in general and medical professionals in particular.

"Tara, I got the impression when you left last night that you didn't want to involve Daniel's father in this situation. But I think it's very important that he know what's going on, especially given the seriousness of Daniel's experience. He needs to know Daniel was abused, and I think a strong male presence, someone he can trust, will be important to Daniel's recovery, especially since his abuser was male. Please call me and tell me when the four of us can get together for a consultation." The slightly scratchy, recorded voice paused. "I really can't stress enough the importance of this, from a therapeutic standpoint. I'm going to have to turn Daniel's case over to someone with more experience in these matters, but I need to know everything's in order with your family before I do that. Call me. Please."

There was another pause before the recording ended, as if he'd thought about saying something else and had changed his mind. Tara pushed the button angrily, saving the message. "'I really can't stress enough the importance of this,'" she repeated in a mocking tone. Wonderful. Now she was going to have to traipse all the way back down to the Underground to talk to Julian. Again, she slung her purse over her shoulder and headed for the door.

Her hand was on the knob when the phone rang. Figuring it was Gray, she almost ignored it and continued out the door, but then decided to at least check the Caller ID. It was a pay phone. Curious, she picked it up. "Hello?"

"It's Julian. Did that doctor of yours call?"

"Thank God," Tara said. "Yes, he did, and I was about to drag myself down to your office again. You know, you really should get a cell phone or something."

"They don't work down there. And try telling the phone company you need a phone line miles under the city and partially in an alternate dimension."

"Yeah, I see the problem." She scrubbed her forehead. She was getting a headache. "Are you very far away? I think it'd be a good idea if you came over. We need to talk."

"I'll see you in a few minutes. I'm not far."

True to his word, Julian buzzed for her to let him into the building within fifteen minutes of hanging up.

"What's going on?" he said when she opened the door.

Tara peered at him. "Are you okay? You look flushed."

"It's the sun. I can't just traipse around in it willy-nilly like Lucien can. I've been out a little too much this week." He waved it off. "Don't worry about it. I'm not going to burst into flames."

"Yeah, but how will you get home?"

"I'll figure something out. Maybe I'll crash on your couch for a few hours, until I fade a little or the sun starts going down."

Tara wasn't sure she liked the sound of that, but decided to let it go for now. She went to the answering machine and played back the message. "This is what we're dealing with."

As he listened, Julian sucked his teeth. Fleetingly, Tara wondered if he could still produce fangs.

"Okay, I think we should do the consultation," he said when Gray's message ended. "I'll deal with it from there."

"But what if—"

He waved off her protest. "I'll play the money card—tell him I have a particular doctor I feel we should work with, and act like I was never very keen on using him in the first place. Hey, maybe we could argue about it."

Tara rolled her eyes. "You're enjoying this far too much."

"We do what we have to. If we manage to enjoy it, so much the better. Do you think we could see him tonight, after Daniel's up and around? I'd just as soon get it over with."

"Julian, what if he—"

Again, he cut her off. "Whatever happens, we'll deal with it."

She shook her head and sighed. "All right." She picked up the phone. "I'll call and find out if we can get an appointment."

As she'd suspected, Gray was not only willing but eager to meet with them that evening, in their usual time slot. Julian, deciding not to return to the Underground, stretched out on her couch and slept away several of the intervening hours.

"Won't Lorelei be worried?" she asked him when he woke, just before dinnertime. Daniel had awakened about a half-hour before, at sunset, and had left the apartment without a word. He'd looked grim. And hungry.

"I told her I might not be home until late. She's been sleeping a lot lately, so she'll barely miss me. And I asked Dina and Nick to look in on her."

"How's she doing?"

"Fine, as far as anyone can tell. Dr. Greene helped us find an OB, and that doctor hasn't found anything unusual about the pregnancy so far. Except that Lorelei's carrying twins."

Tara grinned. "Neat. I guess maybe that explains why she's been so sick." She paused. "Has it ever happened before? I mean, a human woman bearing a vampire child?"

"Not really. True vampires are sterile. Lucien and his brothers can father children, and have, but none of the rest of us can. Except me, because I'm special." He smiled smugly.

"You're also not exactly a vampire anymore," she reminded him.

"True. Which reminds me. Do you have anything around here I can eat?"

She had raw steak in the freezer, but she couldn't stand to watch him eat it. Obligingly, he went out on the balcony while she prepared her own dinner. She opted for a salad. Anything even remotely carnivorous made her stomach turn after watching Julian tear into his chunk of bloody sirloin.

Daniel came in the front door as they were finishing.

"Do we have an appointment tonight?" he asked, then blinked at Julian. "When did you get here? Are you going with us?"

"Yes, we have an appointment," said Tara. "It's at the usual time, and yes, Julian's going with us."

"Dr. DeAngelo's freaking out about that rat thing, isn't he?"

"Yes, he is, a little bit. So Julian's going to be your dad tonight for our consultation."

Daniel nodded. "Think you can get him off my back? I mean, shit, I shouldn't be sent off to the nuthouse just because I sucked down a couple of rats, right?" His mouth curled with amusement as he spoke.

Tara frowned. "This is serious, Daniel. And watch your language."

"It's not that serious." He headed into his bedroom. "Call me when it's time to go."

Julian grinned at Tara. "You're a good mom. You're right—he shouldn't swear."

"I don't think either one of you is taking this seriously enough."

"That's because both of us have been around for way, way too long to take much of anything seriously."

Tara crossed her arms over her chest, thoroughly annoyed now. "Well, then maybe there's something else you need to consider."

"What's that?"

"Gray saw you in his dream, too. It wasn't just me."

Julian's eyes narrowed. "And you're just now deciding to tell me? Even after I said to be prepared—that something like this could happen?"

Her belligerence faded. He was right. "He didn't *know* it was you. It was dark—in the dream, I mean. I only recognized you because I know you. He hasn't made the connection yet, and I'm hoping he won't." She shrugged. "But, yeah, I should have mentioned it."

"Yeah, you should have." He sounded more irked than angry, though. In fact, amazingly, he shrugged and said, "It'll all work out one way or another."

Still, Tara was undeniably on edge as they all walked into Gray's office. In spite of Julian's assurances that everything would work out, she had a feeling something was going to go terribly, horribly wrong.

The receptionist led them into the consultation room. "Dr. DeAngelo will be here in a few minutes. He's expecting you, but he went to get some coffee." Smiling, she left the room, leaving the door open.

Daniel gave a wicked, big-toothed, mischievous boy-grin. "So the doc needs a caffeine fix. Bet he's been dreaming about you, Tara. Bet it's waking him up at night."

Julian laughed.

"Oh, be quiet," said Tara, "both of you."

Daniel sat snickering while Tara's face flamed red and Julian watched both of them with one corner of his mouth quirked up. Daniel was still laughing when Gray came in, carrying a cardboard drink tray with three tall hot beverage cups and one smaller one. Tara gave Daniel a look—they were here to discuss his homicidal tendencies, and laughing hardly seemed appropriate. He pressed his lips together and composed himself quickly.

Gray set the drink tray on his desk and offered his hand to Julian. "I'm Dr. DeAngelo."

"Julian Cavanaugh," Julian said, standing to shake hands. "I'm glad you could see us on such short notice."

Retrieving the drinks, Gray replied, "No problem. It's good to see you all." He handed Tara one of the cups. "I didn't want to be rude, so lattes all around. Hot chocolate for you, Daniel."

"No, thank you," said Daniel. "Hot chocolate makes me barf."

"Daniel." Tara managed a chastising tone.

"No, no, that's okay," said Gray. "I'd rather know now than have to clean it up later." He held out a taller cup to Julian.

"No, thank you," said Julian. He winked at Daniel. "Coffee makes me barf."

Gray smiled. "The two of you seem to have a reasonably good relationship."

Daniel shrugged. "We get along."

"That's good." He sipped his coffee. "So let's get things underway, shall we?"

Tara relaxed a little as Gray briefed Julian on Daniel's last session. Thank God, Gray showed no sign of recognizing Julian. Based on what he'd told her about the encounter in his regression journal, she'd been certain he hadn't seen Julian clearly enough to recognize him. Still, it had worried her.

As Gray recounted Daniel's memories of the vampire who had Turned and trained him, Julian looked appropriately horrified. "My God, I knew he'd been abused, but . . . What could possess a person to do something like that to a child?"

"To be honest, Mr. Cavanaugh, I'm not certain if this is an actual memory or simply a construct Daniel has developed to deal with something more mundane but possibly more traumatic."

Daniel, whose attention had drifted while the others talked, perked up. "It was a real memory."

"That's not for me to determine. That's one of the reasons I've recommended that you see a specialist in this field." He picked up a sheet of paper from his desk. "I've made a list of therapists in the area who are qualified to take on this kind of case. I can start calling around tomorrow to see who might be available for extensive work with Daniel."

With a haughty frown, Julian took the paper from Gray's hand. He read over it and looked at Tara. "I'm not familiar with any of these names." He waved the paper at Gray. "I don't believe I'll be needing this list. I'll look into the matter myself and arrange for the doctor."

"Julian," Tara protested. "I think I'd be more comfortable following Dr. DeAngelo's recommendations."

"Perhaps so, but I want absolutely the best help for the boy."

Giving Gray a sidelong look, he leaned closer to Tara. "I let you pick this doctor—now it's my turn. Given the seriousness of the situation, I think I should handle it."

Tara pressed her lips together. Even though she knew it was just an act, Julian was irritating her. "I'm perfectly capable of taking care of it."

"Tara—" Julian broke off, straightened, and looked at Gray. "I believe it's for the best that we handle this amongst ourselves." He stood. "One of us will give you a call if we need further assistance."

"But—" Gray started, but Tara shook her head, giving him a cautioning look.

"Don't worry about it," she said quietly. "It'll be okay."

Julian folded the piece of paper and stuck it into his shirt pocket, then held his hand out to Gray. "Thank you very much for your assistance thus far. I'm sure you've been a great help to Daniel." Turning to his "family," he said, "Come along."

Tara trailed after him, Daniel right behind her. She took one look back at Gray as she left. He was frowning, his gaze intent on her. Not on Daniel, his erstwhile patient, but on her. It made her want to turn around and run to him and—what? Hug him? Beg his forgiveness for letting Julian appear to run roughshod over her? Throw him down on the floor and rip his shirt off?

Frankly, the last option sounded best, but it wasn't available to her at the moment. Still playing the part of the meek ex-wife, she reluctantly followed Julian out of the office.

Later that night, watching late-night TV and trying to recapture the weariness the evening coffee had driven from his system, Gray wasn't sure what to think about Cavanaugh—about the way Tara had let him run roughshod over her. He'd been certain, from her comments, that her ex-husband would be cooperative, but instead he seemed to have his head lodged thoroughly up his ass. And where the *hell* had Gray seen him before?

Gray could only hope Daniel got the help he needed. He would give it a week or so, then call around to see if he could find out who had taken the case. Just to be sure Daniel would be okay. As for Tara . . . He found it hard to imagine not seeing her again. But he knew what coffee shop she frequented, so it probably wouldn't be that hard to manage to bump into her by "accident." Now that Daniel was no longer his patient, maybe he could allow himself to step out of his stuffy doctor-tweeds and ask her out.

The whole evening, with all of its considerations, had left him muddled in the head. Finally, his eyes burning but his brain still not ready to settle down, he crawled into bed and forced himself to sleep.

It was time he asked Felicity to marry him. They'd been together nearly two years, constantly on the run, and she'd accepted everything about his insane life. But he'd offered her so little in return. He should give her some security about their relationship. At least that. The assurance that everything he owned would be hers if he died. When he died, as he almost certainly would if he continued in this line of work.

He watched her for a time as she lay in the small bed next to him. Everything he had wouldn't amount to much, but maybe it would be enough, at least, for her to remember him by.

Gently, he reached toward her, cupping her shoulder, caressing her until she opened her eyes and looked up at him. She smiled.

"Is it dark yet?"

"Just now, yes. Should we go, or should we stay here?"

In answer, she rolled him back into the bed and straddled him. "We could do both if you're quick about it."

It seemed like a reasonable plan. He let her wrap her legs around him, the heat of her sex caressing his shaft without allowing him entrance. He grasped at her shoulders, pulling her down to catch her breast in his mouth. His tongue rolled over her nipple, feeling the textures, tasting the warm muskiness of her flesh. "Marry me," he said suddenly.

She froze. "What?"

"I said, 'Marry me.'"

She laughed. "Make love to me first. I'll think about it." She looked down at him and, suddenly, her eyes weren't green anymore. They were blue, and she wasn't Felicity but Tara. . . .

Gray shifted in the bed, on the very edge of sleep. He was dreaming—he somehow knew that. But it was so real. . . . No, it couldn't be real. His name wasn't Liam, and he didn't hunt vampires. Yet when his conscious mind had finished interfering with his dream, he went straight back to the world that seemed so real but couldn't be. . . .

He was stuffing wooden stakes into a bag. "We hunt tonight. Where we saw the last one, the one that rescued us."

Felicity frowned. "You intend to kill him?"

"I intend to find out exactly what he is."

"He's a vampire."

"But then, why did he save us, rather than attack?"

"I don't know." *She hesitated before hefting her own bag onto her shoulder.* *"Are you certain all vampires are evil?"*

"How could they not be?"

They *were on the street then, and he was slipping around a corner. A shadow lurked near the back of the narrow alleyway. Smoke drifted from it and a small, orange ember glowed at the level of the man's face.*

"You!" *he hissed.* *"Come out where I can see you."*

The man stepped forward, out of the shadow, and he was, indeed, the man they'd seen on their last outing, with his dark hair curling a little against his shoulders.

"Can you see me now?" *he said.*

"Yes." *The man—the monster—was slim and handsome, his eyes bearing the slight slant of Oriental stock.* *"Who are you?"*

"I'm here to help you." *The man took another step forward, tapping ashes from his cigarette.* *"I know more about these creatures you seek than you could ever possibly hope to know. I know which deserve death and which should be allowed to slink away into the shadows."*

"They all deserve death."

The man smiled, shook his head. *"Not all."*

He lowered the stake he'd been holding. *"All right, I'll listen. Who are you?"*

"My name is Julian." *He took a long drag at the cigarette.* *"Julian Cavanaugh."*

Gray sat straight up in bed, sleep and dreams deserting him in a sudden rush. "Oh, my God."

Tara was dreaming and knew she was dreaming—of Liam, with his hands on her body, his mouth on her breasts, and she was no longer certain if she was herself or Felicity, if the dream was fantasy or memory.

The sound of the narrow bed protesting beneath them as they strained against each other intruded. Banging, banging. Louder and louder it grew, until it became a pounding in her head. Drawn ever more insistently by the reality of the sound, Tara drifted toward wakefulness. Finally, she opened her eyes.

Someone was knocking on her door.

"Good Lord, what time is it?" she muttered, rolling out of bed. The clock read 4:00 a.m. She got up and went to the door, glancing into Daniel's room on the way past. He wasn't home yet. A pang of worry struck, but she knew he had time. The year was winding into winter, and the sun rose late.

At the door, she peered out the peephole and was surprised—or really, not surprised at all—to see Gray in the hallway. She turned the deadbolt and opened the door.

"What the hell are you doing here at four in the morning?" Maybe she should have said, "Hello," or "My goodness, dear Gray, what seems to be the matter?" But she really wasn't in the mood.

Gray brushed past her, not seeming to notice the brusqueness of her greeting. "I just had a dream about Julian."

She blinked, shoving a hand through what felt like a truly spectacular case of bed-head. "I hope you weren't having sex with him."

"No, I was having sex with you—" He broke off, suddenly blinking at her in confusion. "I mean with Felicity. Liam and Felicity."

"Yeah." She slammed the door shut behind him, cranking the deadbolt into place. "You want some coffee?"

"No. Yes. Tara, do you have any idea what's going on?"

Tara opened the coffee pot, shoved in a filter and began to spoon ground coffee into it. "Yeah. I'm in the kitchen making coffee when I should be curled up in bed snoring and having stupid, annoying dreams about stupid, annoying Liam and Felicity. Who are, by the way, some former-life version of you and me, and if you haven't figured that out yet, then you're not half the past-life regression hypnotherapist you think you are."

He stared blankly at her while she ran water into the coffeepot. "I was dreaming about them, too."

"You just said you dreamed about Julian."

"I did. First it was Liam and Felicity." He waited until she turned around and looked at him to add, "He was going to ask her to marry him."

"Did she say yes?"

"I don't know. I didn't get to that part." He squeezed his eyes closed for an instant, took a deep breath, opened them again. His voice shook as he spoke. "She was . . . she was you."

Very carefully, Tara set the coffeepot down in the coffee maker. "Your point?"

He crossed the kitchen to stand right in front of her. Looking into his eyes, she saw, for the first time, unmistakable echoes of Liam. So she wasn't all that surprised when he ducked his head and kissed her.

She was more surprised when she kissed him back, and she was positively astonished when her hands shoved themselves inside his shirt. His skin was warm and smooth under her fingers, and she let herself explore higher, clutching the muscles of his back where they dipped into the groove of his spine. His tongue pressed against hers, hot and urgent, and she responded. The dreams, she realized, had left her wanting this. Aching for it. She wrapped a leg around his, and he lifted a hand, cupping her breast.

Suddenly he broke off, pushing away. "Tara, I'm sorry."

She pressed her fingers into his back, pulling him against her. "Why?"

"This is inappropriate."

"Am I your patient?"

"No."

"Am I related to any of your patients, as of this evening?"

He smiled ruefully. "No."

"Do you want me?"

The smile faded. "Yes."

"Then what's the problem?"

"The problem is, none of this is real."

"It feels real to me." She bumped herself against him, pressing her breasts into his chest. "I think you're overanalyzing."

Gently, he took her by the shoulders and pushed her away, at the same time taking a backward step. "I can't act on this. I feel like I'd be manipulating you because of dreams I don't even understand."

"What's to understand? You know the whole reincarnation drill thingie. I was her. You were him. We were lovers. We could be that again."

"But how can that be true when there are vampires in the dreams? You and I both know vampires aren't real."

"Maybe *you* know it."

He stared at her in silence.

She stared back. "I think," she said slowly, "that I might be falling in love with you. But I need answers to a few questions before I decide if I can let you into my life."

"What questions?"

"Some very, very weird and difficult ones. Do you think you're up for it?"

"I don't know."

"Well let's find out."

She finished brewing the coffee, and then they sat at her small kitchen table. Tara would have preferred to sit on the couch, but she was afraid that if she got too comfortable, she would just fall asleep and accomplish nothing. She let Gray take a few sips of coffee and get settled before she hit him with the first question.

"In your professional opinion, why was Julian in our dreams?"

Gray shrugged. "Maybe it was a projection of my resentment about his taking Daniel's case out of my hands."

Tara prodded. "But you mentioned him in your regression journal. The vampire who rescued Liam and Felicity."

Frowning, Gray seemed to look for enlightenment in the depths of the coffee cup. "The description in the journal was vague, and I don't remember the actual session very well." He cleared his throat. "Sometimes, in the dream I had tonight, Felicity looked like you, so, sure, maybe I was seeing Julian Cavanaugh's former identity."

"Closer."

Gray looked at her, eyebrows lifted in surprise. "I'm sorry. You have a particular answer in mind, here?"

"I have a particular answer in mind because this is one case where I know more about what's going on than you do."

"You're sure about that?"

"I'm positive." She pushed her coffee cup away, no longer interested in its bitter contents. It had to be the worst coffee she'd ever made. "If Julian was there, he was there. And he was Julian. The same Julian you met last night." She shrugged. "Well, not quite, but close."

"Your ex-husband."

"He's not my husband, ex or otherwise." Watching Gray slug down half of the horrible coffee without a blink, Tara figured he had to be completely befuddled.

Finally coming up for air, he said, "If Cavanaugh didn't appear in the dream as a representation of who he was in a past life—" He broke off. "You're saying he was the same person. That he's a hundred and fifty, two hundred years old."

"Actually, he's quite a bit older than that, but yes."

"That's impossible."

"You dreamed about vampires. Vampires are immortal."

"You're trying to tell me Julian is a vampire?"

Never mind trying to explain Julian's not-quite-vampire status. She offered Gray a definitive "Yes."

He came to his feet in a lurch, shoving a hand through his hair. "You're insane."

"Am I? You know what you saw in your dreams, and you know what those dreams are. You just don't want to admit it to yourself."

His face was set into hard lines. "There is absolutely no way I can possibly believe anything you're saying. It just can't be true. There's no way."

"Gray—"

Just then the front door opened and Daniel came in. "Hey, Tara," he called, his voice exuberant. "I just talked to Dr. Greene. I'm gonna do it. Tomorrow. He sent me home with one last celebratory bag o' blood when I told him how I was afraid I might kill puppies—" He stopped in the kitchen doorway, one hand raised high, holding a hospital bag full of garnet liquid.

Tara stared at him, fighting the urge to burst into hysterical laughter.

He stood for a few seconds looking at Gray. Then, slowly, he lowered his hand. "Ha ha," he said. "Just kidding."

Gray turned on Tara, fury filling his face. "You! You did this to him! How could you pervert a child this way? What kind of monster are you?"

The words hurt. Tara blinked back tears. "Gray, you don't understand—"

"Hey, Gray," said Daniel, and when Gray turned to face him, he added, "Don't you talk to my mother like that, you stupid prick." And with that, Daniel shot upward and slugged him in the jaw.

Gray dropped like a rock.

Tara put her hands over her face. "Oh, my God." She looked at Daniel, who was eyeing Gray's prone body smugly. "What do we do now?" she said.

"Can I eat him?"

"No! That's not funny," Tara chastised. Thinking quickly, she said, "We're taking him to Julian."

Gray drifted slowly back into consciousness. His jaw hurt. It took him a moment to remember what had happened, although the memory only confused him further. How the hell had a ten-year-old boy hit him hard enough to knock him unconscious?

Then, around him, he heard voices. He opened his eyes and tried to roll toward the sounds, but he couldn't. He was bound hand and foot, lying flat on his back, on the floor. He turned his head. Tara, Daniel, and Julian Cavanaugh stood a few feet away, talking. The room smelled odd, and the décor reminded him of displays he'd seen at the museum of ancient African art.

"Where am I?" he said.

The others turned. Cavanaugh looked at Tara, then stepped toward him.

"You're awake." He dropped to the floor, sitting with his legs crossed. "How do you feel?"

"Confused." Gray slanted a look at Daniel. "My face hurts."

"Good," said the boy.

"Daniel." Tara gave him a sharp look and shook her head, causing his grin to fade—but not completely.

"Dr. DeAngelo," Julian said. "We appear to have a slight problem here. I need to know if you want to try to solve it."

"Maybe if you'd untie me I could consider my options a little more clearly."

Cavanaugh studied him closely, then loosened the knots binding his hands. "There. Why don't you sit up so we can talk?"

"Feet, too, would be nice."

Cavanaugh looked over his shoulder at Tara, apparently seeking her opinion.

"No," she said. "He can't be running off."

"He wouldn't get far," Daniel put in. "He doesn't know his way out. Someone would eat him before he even got close to figuring out where he was going."

"Where the hell am I?" Gray demanded. "What are you people doing to me?"

"We don't want to hurt you," said Tara. "We just can't risk you hurting us."

"Could somebody please untie my damned feet?" When their three faces remained set, he let out a beleaguered sigh. "C'mon. I won't run. I really don't want some nutcase to kill me."

"We're not nutcases," Daniel said. "You just smell like food."

God, what a creepy little kid. Gray was beginning to think he was beyond any psychiatrist's ability to rehabilitate. "Are you in on this, too, Cavanaugh? Have you been part of whatever horrible thing has been done to this little boy?"

Julian looked grim. "What was done to Daniel was done a very long time ago. I had nothing to do with it. What we're doing now is attempting to correct that wrong. You were part of the solution. You still could be."

"I don't understand."

"If you promise not to run and not to try to hurt any of us, we'll explain. Then you can decide what you want to do."

The sincerity in the other man's face made Gray wonder, just for a moment, if there might be something going on here that he was simply incapable of understanding. Then he looked at Tara and realized, if that were the case and it meant she were innocent, then he wanted to hear their explanation. "All right. I won't run. No point in making myself a meal on the go."

Daniel's cold smile made him queasy. He'd seemed like a normal kid a couple of days ago.

Gray's attention shifted as Cavanaugh leaned over to untie his legs, saying, "Come with me. We'll go to the office. Daniel, you might want to get going. Sunrise is in about an hour."

Daniel nodded and headed for the door. "Shoulda let me eat him," he said, and grinned. Gray blinked at the long, feral fangs that had suddenly appeared next to the boy's oversized permanent teeth. "He woulda tasted good."

"Daniel," said Tara sharply. "Quit acting like a brat. If you're hungry go talk to Dr. Greene."

Daniel looked abashed. "Sorry." Hanging his head, he left the room.

Cavanaugh helped Gray to his feet. "My apologies for trussing you up like a turkey. It seemed necessary at the time."

Gray had no idea what to say to that. So he asked the question foremost in his mind. "You're a vampire, too?"

The other man shook his head. "Technically, no, not anymore. But I was. And I can still do the fang thing." He demonstrated. Up close, the long teeth looked wickedly sharp and brutal.

"God," said Gray. "This is freakish."

Cavanaugh grinned, the fangs retreating. "You're telling me? And call me Julian."

Dazed, Gray nodded and followed him and Tara through a doorway that led to what he assumed must be Julian's office.

Julian took a seat behind the computer desk and dropped his feet onto it, next to the monitor. Tara motioned Gray to the small couch, and he sat. She sat next to him.

"My ex-boyfriend was a vampire," she said. "That's how I found out about this."

"Not big on preamble, are you?" said Gray. "How the hell do you end up dating a damned vampire?"

"First off, he wasn't one of the damned ones, but I guess you wouldn't know the distinction since you refuse to open your eyes and see what's right the hell in front of you."

"Sorry. I didn't mean to cast aspersions on your ex. If he's so great, where is he now?"

"He's dead."

The very real anguish in Tara's eyes left him speechless. She stared at him a moment, letting him see her pain; then anger flashed through it, and she looked away. "His name was Dominic. He was a nighttime deejay at a club where I used to go. We dated nearly two years before he told me what he was."

"Two years? There were no clues? Like the blood-drinking, for instance?"

"He was nearly a hundred years old. He figured out long before I met him how to blend."

"We're really quite good at it, if we try," Julian put in.

"Anyway, I was floored. I couldn't believe it. But I really cared about Dom. He was a good man. So I decided to deal with it. He introduced me to this place, the Underground, and to the Senior, who ran things before Julian. It was a scarier place then, but when I saw the Children I knew I had to do something to help. So the Senior hired me to teach them."

"Teach them?"

She nodded. "A lot of them didn't even speak English. They had no idea how to blend in with people, and they'd been here for decades, some of them, never seeing the outside world. I helped."

"So you were like, uh, the vampire day care lady?" The story was getting crazier by the second, but at least it had its endearing elements.

"I still am. Except now, with Julian's help, these kids can become mortal again. That's what we were doing with Daniel."

Julian dropped his feet to the floor, leaning forward into the conversation. "I wanted him to be absolutely sure before he accepted the procedure. The Children, as a rule, have very little, if any, memory of what it was like to be mortal. I wanted him to remember, so he could decide if he if he wanted to be mortal again."

"Thus the therapy," said Tara.

Frowning, Gray said slowly, "Okay. I guess that makes sense. But why did you pick me?"

"I told you. Nicholas recommended you."

"And how the hell do you know Nicholas?"

"He's here. I lied to you. He's not dead. When his cancer progressed far enough to leave him with no hope, he chose to be Changed rather than die. One of the elements in his blood helps catalyze the process we're using to cure the Children."

Gray took a breath to speak, let it out, shook his head. "This is crazy."

"But you know it's true." Tara's looked implored him to believe. "You told me you wrote about it in your past-life regression journal. And you dreamed about it. You know the vampire part of is as true as . . . as the rest of it."

As true as Liam and Felicity, she was saying. As true as their love. He studied her face, looked into her eyes, her blue eyes that, in his memory, had once been green. In them he glimpsed possibilities he'd never seen in another woman. He could love her. She could love him. They'd done it once before.

"This is part of my life," Tara went on, her tone desperate. "If you can't accept this . . ."

"You mean, if I can't accept that you're the vampire day care lady?" His voice came out bitter. He'd been going for sarcasm.

Her lips thinned in determination. He was relieved to see anger in her eyes—it was easier to deal with than the big-eyed, near-weepiness she'd given him a moment ago. "And I will be until all of these children are taken care of. They need me."

Gray couldn't hold back a small smile. In an odd, surreal, freakish, deranged fantasy sort of way, it was endearing. "So you have a mission."

"I do."

"And what happened to this guy, this Dominic?"

"He was murdered. Some self-styled vampire hunters figured out what he was, and they chased him down and staked him in the heart." She blinked hard and no tears came.

Gray didn't know what to say, but he was saved from having to respond when Julian chose that moment to enter the conversation.

"The people who murdered Dom were like you were back then,

when you were Liam. Didn't have half a clue what the hell they were doing. They just thought, 'vampire—evil,' and acted."

Looking at Julian, Tara said in a small voice, "Dom died three years ago. You weren't around then."

"I heard the stories," Julian said. "I knew Dom, if only in passing. He was a decent guy."

"He was a vampire," said Gray, feeling something of Liam creeping into him—the driving hatred, the anger. "Vampires slaughtered my family."

"Liam's family," said Tara softly.

"He wanted justice. Vengeance." Gray's brows compressed. "He never quite got it, though, because . . ." Suddenly, shock flooded him, and his head jerked up, his gaze locking with Julian's. "I just remembered how he died."

Julian said softly, "That's right."

"What?" said Tara.

Eyes still focused on Julian, Gray said, "You killed him."

Seven

Tara couldn't believe what she was hearing. "Julian? You *killed* Liam?" But even as she said it, she remembered, because Felicity had been there. She had seen Liam die. "You didn't feed on him."

"No. I broke his neck."

"Why?"

"Because I figured it would be quick and relatively painless." Julian shrugged, still looking at Gray. "Anything I tell you won't mean squat unless you can remember for yourself."

"I don't see how it matters, in any case. I know what you are. You're a murderer."

"Am I going to have to kill you again?" Julian's question was matter-of-fact.

Tara couldn't believe the turn the conversation had taken. She had a horrible feeling Gray wasn't going to walk out of this room alive, and she knew she wouldn't be able to deal with that. "Julian, please."

"You knew the risk when you brought him down here. He has to decide what he's going to do. If he chooses to be a threat, I'll eliminate that threat."

"Julian—" She stopped, her voice choked by tears. But Julian wasn't even looking at her, wasn't listening. His attention was focused totally on Gray, waiting.

Gray smiled grimly. "Your point's taken."

"Julian, don't do this." Tara couldn't hold back the tears any longer.

Finally, Julian swung toward her, his eyes flashing. "I'll say it again—you knew what you were doing when you brought him down here. If he's a threat, then he's a threat not only to me and you and Daniel, but to Lorelei, and guess what I am perfectly willing and capable of doing if my woman and unborn children are threatened?"

Tara swallowed. She'd made a mistake. She never should have brought Gray here. Perhaps she never should have taken Daniel to him in the first place. "I'm sorry, Gray."

"Don't be. How could you have known?"

"Yeah," said Julian. "Past-life regression can be a tricky, tricky business. I thought it might help us in this case, but maybe I was wrong."

He leaned forward in his chair, looking right at Gray. His expression was placid, almost friendly, but Tara could feel the danger oozing from him. "What are you going to do?"

Tara watched Gray's face, holding her breath. Nothing in his expression told her what he was thinking.

Finally he said, "You knew." He said it bluntly, holding Julian's intense gaze.

"Not really. Not at first," said Julian. "When Nick told me about you, I had a feeling. I can't explain it, but it was there. So I spied on you for a while, and the feeling got stronger. Although I can't say it was anything as definite as my knowing I'd met you in one of your past lives. I wasn't sure of that until Tara told me about the dreams she's been having, and about the journal you kept of your past-life regression sessions, where you and Tara—Liam and Felicity in those days—were vampire hunters."

Gray was silent for a moment, studying Julian skeptically. Then— "You spied on me." His tone was accusatory.

Julian threw up his hands. "Hey, it got you the job. Think of it as an audition, rather than me stalking you. And you passed." Quirking an eyebrow, he added, "I wouldn't trust just anybody with Daniel, you know."

Gray fell silent again, eyes narrowed. Then he said, much to Tara's relief, "I think maybe I should try to remember. Tara seems to trust you—maybe you had a good reason for putting me down like a dog."

Julian's smile was relieved, though his gaze remained intent and cautious. "Fair enough. Let's get to it."

Gray hated the idea of being hypnotized in the middle of Vampire Central, but it seemed prudent to go along with Julian's suggestion. At least Julian hadn't objected when he'd asked to keep Tara with them. Right now, she was the only one he had any trust in at all, and even that was wearing thin.

Julian took them to a small room not far from his office. At least, Gray thought it wasn't far. Once he got there, he wasn't sure how long they'd walked, how far they'd gone, or in what direction. Certainly there was no way he'd ever find his way out of this labyrinth. They had him well and truly under their control.

"What do you want me to do?" Tara asked.

Gray looked around the room. It looked as if it, too, might have been someone's office, but no one had used it in a long time. He drew a line in the dust on the desk top with his finger. "Take notes." He looked at Julian. "You said there was someone here who could hypnotize me?"

"He's on his way."

"Is he a vampire?"

"No."

They fell into silence for a time, waiting. Tara stood near the desk, staring at the line he'd drawn in the dust. She looked tense and worried, rubbing the back of her neck and frowning down at the desk—or at the air molecules between it and her eyes, for all he knew. He had no clue what she was thinking.

Finally the door opened and a man entered. In his mid-thirties, with a slightly receding hairline, he was wearing glasses and carrying a briefcase. He looked human enough, but then, so did Julian when he wasn't flaunting his fangs.

"Hi," he said. "I'm Dr. Greene." He held out his hand.

Gray took it reluctantly, remembering the name "Greene" from Daniel's file. "How did he tell you he needed you?" he asked the doctor "Is he telepathic or something? Because I read somewhere that vampires are."

Dr. Greene looked at Julian, who shrugged. "Actually, I hate to disappoint, but he sent me an email before he led you over here."

Remembering the computer in Julian's office, Gray gave a soft "Hmph."

"Just like Liam," Julian said. "Don't know what the hell you're dealing with."

Dr. Greene smiled. "No offense, Julian, but this might go better without you."

"Okay. Whatever." With no further protest, Julian left.

Gray took a long breath of relief and turned to the doctor. "I saw your name in Daniel's file and did an Internet search for it. You're a hematologist, correct? Do you have any experience in hypnosis?"

"A little," the doctor replied. "When you work with vampires you have to learn to be flexible."

"If I write you a script, do you think you can take me through it?"

"I'll do my best. I'm guessing you've been hypnotized quite a few times, so it should be fairly simple to get you where you need to go."

Gray gestured toward the briefcase. "You got paper in there?"

Dr. Greene laid the briefcase on the table. "You bet."

Gray spent a few minutes writing out a script, then handed it to the doctor. "This should do it."

"All right." Dr. Greene looked over the sheet. "Tell me when you're ready."

The chair in the small office wasn't comfortable, but it would have to do. Gray had been under hypnosis so many times he could practically do it himself, so comfort wasn't as big a factor as it might have been. And Dr. Greene seemed to know what he was doing, more or less, as he read through the script in a gentle, even voice.

And Gray let himself go. . . .

"I have a lead," he told Felicity. "Patrick, down at the docks, told me there's been a great deal of activity at one of the old tenement houses, one that was abandoned a few years ago after most of it burned down."

Felicity, sitting behind him on the bed, put her arms around him, setting her chin against his shoulder. "Vampires?"

"A nest. He said there've been reports of as many as twenty."

"Liam, how can you handle twenty vampires?" Her tone was worried.

"In daylight."

"Oh, of course." She slid off the bed, coming around to face him. "They'll just lie there unconscious while you stake them. Do you really think you can bring yourself to do that? Kill defenseless creatures, in cold blood?"

He set his jaw. "They're vampires. Vicious, merciless killers. Demons. Yes, I can do it."

Then it was several hours later, and he was coming back into their room. He fell into a chair and dropped his face into his hands. "I couldn't do it."

Felicity's forehead crinkled in concern. "They're demons, you said. Merciless killers. What stopped you?"

"They were children."

She slipped into his lap, curling against him, her breath warm against the side of his neck. "If they were trying to kill you, do you think you could do it?"

"Yes. But there were so many."

"They're only children."

"But still demons." He nodded resolutely. "We go back at sunset."

And then it was later, and the sun was dropping below the city skyline, and they were setting out together. He had a horrible sense of doom but pushed it aside. He'd been hunting vampires for a long time—he knew what he was doing. As distasteful as the task seemed, these children had to die. All of them.

Still, he swallowed bile as they neared the burned-out tenement house. Children. Six, eight, ten years old some of them. How could these innocents have become demons? Who would do such a thing to a child?

Another demon, of course. One who held no compunctions about feeding on the living, beating blood of a human being. These children would have no more mercy than the ones who had Made them. They were just as capable of taking life as the vampires who had the appearance of adults.

He readied his weapons. "Felicity, wait for me here. I don't want you involved."

"I won't let you go alone." Her jaw was set with stubbornness. "I've killed vampires before."

"Not like this. You would kill one of these, and because it looked like a child you would hurt with the deed for the rest of your life. I won't let you. You wait for me."

The truth of his words must have reached her, because she only kissed him and said, "Be careful."

"Always."

He slipped down the narrow alleyway, the smell of soot heavy in his nostrils. He had a sickening feeling he was going to die here, overcome by a swarm of demon-children.

"Hello again."

The voice made him jump, coming as it had from what he had been certain was an unoccupied shadow. He spun to see the vampire who had saved them in the alleyway, the strange one who'd smoked cigarettes that smelled like cloves. The one called Julian. He was smoking now, the orange glow of the cigarette eerie in the near-darkness.

Clenching the wooden stake he held, he glared at the vampire and said, "What do you want?"

Julian drew hard on the cigarette before lifting it away from his lips. "I want to talk to you."

"About what?"

"About what you're planning to do."

"I'm about to rid the world of a nest of demon-children."

"You have no idea what's going on here."

His gaze never wavering from the vampire, he set his jaw and prepared himself. He would charge this creature if he had to, bring him down and stake him right here. "You're harboring demons."

"I am a demon." The vampire gave a menacing smile. "Or I was. Do you know I haven't tasted human blood in nearly a hundred years?"

"Am I supposed to be impressed?"

Julian shrugged. "I don't know. I am. I believe I have demonstrated a great deal of restraint and courage." He sucked hard on his cigarette, as if it were a lifeline to his very existence. "Especially with regard to you, right now, at this moment."

"Why is that?"

"These Children are under my protection. I'm teaching them to feed without taking human life. If you kill them . . . well, it would interrupt my lessons, now, wouldn't it?"

"I don't believe you."

"Then believe this. If you come into this place with the intent to kill, I will kill you. I might even decide to be mean about it and torture you a little first."

Liam could feel sweat breaking out on his face. He outweighed the vampire, and he had no doubt what the outcome of a fight between them would be, if the creature were human. But vampires were strong, quick, and without mercy. He should turn around and go, now. But he could think only of the vampires he'd seen earlier that day, piled around the inside of the building in small, comatose bundles. He should have killed them then. He should have steeled himself to the apparent horror of slaughtering children and just done it.

"How can I believe you?" he said.

Julian smiled. "I'm an honorable homicidal demon. I wouldn't lie to you."

"I—" He broke off. A figure had appeared behind Julian, a boy of about ten.

Without turning, Julian said, "Daniel, go."

The boy took a few steps forward. "What's going on?"

Julian lit another cigarette from the butt of the one he was smoking, stubbed out the old one and put the butt in his coat pocket. "This is Liam. He wants to kill us all."

"Bastard," said the young demon, and suddenly flung him-

self forward.

He saw the attack coming but stood unmoving while the boy grabbed at his coat, small white fangs gleaming. Then, regaining his composure, he wrapped his arms around Daniel, turned, and ran with him.

"Daniel!"

He heard Julian's shout behind him as he raced full-tilt down the alleyway, the boy pounding him with his fists, sinking teeth into his chest, ripping. Ignoring the pain, he ran, then suddenly stopped, tore the boy from his chest and slammed him to the ground. Daniel looked up at him with hatred on his face, his fangs and face bloody.

Just a demon. Not a child at all. A merciless, sadistic killer. He raised the stake over his head, ready to bring it down into Daniel's chest.

And hands closed on his head . . . and wrenched. . . .

Gray jolted back to the present, gagging, hands at his throat. Dr. Greene reached out to catch him as he collapsed out of the chair.

"Are you all right?" the doctor asked.

Gray couldn't gather enough breath to speak. He sat there on the floor for a minute, an echo of Liam's pain still flashing through his throat. Finally he managed to look up at Tara, who sat on the floor in the corner, a notebook balanced on her drawn-up knees, her eyes wide.

"Felicity saw you die," she said.

"I know."

"You would have killed him. Daniel."

"I know."

She just looked at him, her face stricken, as if he were someone she didn't know and didn't want to know. But she had never really known him, had she? The man she'd known was that self-righteous, would-be child killer. He couldn't bear it.

"I'd like to go," Tara said. "Would it be possible for me to just go?"

Dr. Greene gave her a sympathetic look. "Can you find your way out?"

She nodded. Her lips were pressed firmly together, her eyes brimming. "I'll be fine. Gray—"

He shook his head. He couldn't say anything to her. Not with her looking at him with such condemnation, as if she were holding him responsible for the actions of his former self. But then, how far was he, really, from Liam's self-righteous, comprehensive denunciation of vampires? The whole thing was too fresh in his mind, as if it had just happened. Everything seemed surreal. He should be dead—he'd felt the crunching of the bones in his neck. He'd come out of the hypnosis only a breath before the actual moment of death.

"Gray . . ." she began again.

"Later," he managed. "Just . . . later." He let the doctor lead him from the room, noting the sympathetic look Dr. Greene cast Tara as they passed.

They had walked a few yards when the doctor cleared his throat. "I'll have to take you to Julian," he said. "The final decision is his."

"About what?"

"About whether we can let you go."

Gray stopped, stood stock still in the middle of the corridor. Dr. Greene slowed to a halt and looked back at him questioningly.

"Damn," Gray muttered, then caught up with Dr. Greene. There didn't seem to be anything else he could do.

"You saw?" Julian asked when they arrived in his office.

"I saw."

"Are we good?"

Gray nodded. "We're good. You had good reason to kill Liam." And Liam might also have had good reason to do what he'd done. Gray wasn't sure about that yet. The larger part of him still said vampires were evil, but maybe that was just Liam inside him, doing the talking. And years of Dracula movies. Reality, in the form of Julian and Daniel, told him vampires were just like people—some good, some bad. And fate had led him to the former variety. That much, he was sure of. Vampire or not, Julian Cavanaugh was a good man. Gray couldn't fault him for protecting a nest of children—then or now.

Julian studied him for a long time, and when he smiled, Gray knew the vampire was satisfied with whatever he saw.

"Go home," Julian said, gesturing with a nod toward the door.

So Dr. Greene took him home. But even there, he didn't know what to do. Could he return to his life, burdened with the knowledge of the existence of the ancient caverns, filled with vampires, far below his feet? Could he walk away from all that had happened in the past week, knowing Tara existed in this city? Both questions seemed unanswerable.

He needed time. Time to get used to what he knew and what he should do with that knowledge. Not that he would tell anyone about the enclave of vampires. He just needed to figure out how to assimilate their existence into his view of the world. To make it make sense.

A big job, he thought. Especially for a psychiatrist.

* * *

Two weeks. Two weeks, and nothing from Gray. Tara didn't know whether she was frustrated or angry. But, in truth, she had to admit she wasn't surprised.

It was his own fault they'd arrived at this crossroads. His own damned fault for having been a vampire hunter in a previous life. His fault for refusing to believe the truth of his dreams, his visions, his memories. His fault for forcing the issue with Daniel.

Then again . . . maybe it wasn't anyone's fault. Maybe it was destined. She'd thought for a while that they'd been fated to meet and find each other again, and for love to blossom between them as it had between Liam and Felicity. But things didn't seem to be shaping up that way. It was looking more like, boy meets girl, boy meets girl's vampire friends, boy runs off screaming into the night.

She should just forget him. Which would be a lot easier if she could quit having those damned dreams. Nighttime had become a regular sex-with-Gray fest. He didn't even have the decency to appear as Liam anymore. He was just Gray. Big and sexy and solid, gorgeous, devoted, and very, very skilled.

Luckily, she'd gotten used to sleeping during the day, to make up for what she missed during the night.

Besides, at night she also had Daniel to occupy her now.

He was mortal, having undergone the same procedure that had transformed Rafael. She had stayed with him throughout, helping him deal with the pain of the dialysis. The transformation had left him weak for a few days, disoriented, barely able to eat. He'd stayed in the Underground until he felt better, and Rafael had offered assistance. Having recently undergone the procedure himself, Rafael provided more insight than she could have, Tara knew, although she'd stayed close by, if only to reassure Daniel and to keep him company.

"So you haven't heard from Gray at all?" Daniel asked on day fifteen, when he had graduated from clear broth to noodles and white bread. He was eating at the kitchen table, blinking at the noon sunlight.

"No. I've left a few messages, but nothing." She went to the window to close the blinds, afraid the sunlight might hurt Daniel's newly changed skin.

"He's a creep," said Daniel matter-of-factly. "Is it too soon for pizza? Rafael said pizza is the best stuff ever."

"No pizza yet, hon. Give it some time."

"I'm just sick of this broth. The same thing over and over, every day, every meal."

She gave him a dry look. "And what kind of variety did you have before?"

"I guess that's a point." He paused, poking at his soup. "Could you not call me 'hon?' I mean, I'm, like, five hundred years old."

"From here on out, you're a ten-year-old boy. That means you get schoolwork, you go to bed at a reasonable hour, and as long as you're living in this house, I get to call you sweetheart, honey, pumpkin, or whatever nickname I feel is appropriate."

He made a face. "Gross."

"And that's exactly how a normal ten-year-old boy should react."

He finished his soup, frowning reflectively. Finally he looked up at her and said, "If you're going to call me all those things, could I call you 'Mom?'"

She smiled, touched. "That would be fine."

He was there, in a misty darkness, strong and solid, and she was drawn to him. She went to him and his arms closed around her, until her face was pillowed against his broad chest. He was warm and beautiful, and he bent her backward over his arm and caught her breast in his mouth, drawing at her, making fire pool between her thighs. She wanted him inside. . . .

And he was there, deep inside her, and she was pulsing around him, the fire flying through her veins, through her heart, up to shimmer over her skin. . . .

Tara woke abruptly. It was nearly sunrise. From the living room, she heard the television. Daniel was watching his usual Japanese fare, and had likely been up much of the night. She was never going to get him on a regular schedule, so she could send him to school. Maybe she should home school him. Julian certainly wouldn't be likely to protest. She'd had a feeling one of his biggest concerns about Daniel's change was how to assimilate him into regular culture. Easing him into a version less mainstream than he'd be exposed to at a public school might be the way to go.

And thinking in long-winded, excruciating detail about the pros and cons of home schooling Daniel just might drive that dream out of her head.

Wishful thinking. It was hopeless.

She got up and dressed, then joined Daniel in the living room. "Good show?" she asked. To her, it looked the same as the other shows he watched—bright colors, fast movement, and characters with big eyes and irritating voices.

"It's a new one. It's the middle of the series, and I'm not sure what's going on." He shrugged. "Lots of action, though."

"That's good. What do you want for breakfast?"

"Eggs. Could I try eggs?"

Tara nodded. "Sure. Boiled eggs should be a good step up for you."

She went to the kitchen and put water on to boil. "When that show's over, could you turn to the news?"

"Sure."

It was so domestic, she thought. Just her and her little boy. She could devote her attention to him because Julian was footing the bill. And, based on her last discussion with Julian, he might be sending her a few more kids to take care of. At least three had decided to look into the change. It would be a while, though, before any of them were ready. With the loss of Gray's services, Julian had decided to let Dr. Greene take over the psychologist's duties. The doctor had agreed but had insisted on taking some classes first, afraid his amateur efforts might do more harm than good.

If only Gray were still in the picture. He'd done a good job with Daniel, after all. But apparently he'd decided to bow out.

Or maybe Julian had killed him—a thought she tried hard to deny but couldn't. Julian had said he hadn't, and Dr. Greene had concurred, but recent events had made her a little wary when it came to trusting Julian.

When Daniel's eggs were done, she peeled them, dropped them into a bowl and put them on the table in front of him. "Eat slowly," she said.

He did. "These are good."

"I'm glad you like them."

"Food is cool." She could tell he wanted to wolf down the eggs, but he restrained himself. "Food is very, very cool. I can't wait to try more of it."

"Do you feel okay? It's not disagreeing with you?"

"It doesn't seem to be."

"Good." She considered. "Will you be okay by yourself for a bit?

I was thinking about running out for some coffee."

"I could come with."

"Would you want to?"

"Sure. Why not? Any chance to see the sun."

"Put on some sunscreen."

He rolled his eyes. "Jeez, *Mom*."

Tara smiled. She had to admit, she really liked the sound of that.

They went to the coffee shop together, the one where she'd met Gray. Tara hadn't been in it since Gray's ill-fated trip to the Underground. She wasn't sure why. Maybe she was afraid of seeing him. And maybe she was afraid of *not* seeing him, then having to confront Julian about whether or not Gray was even alive.

"It smells really good in here," Daniel said when they got to the counter. "Can I try something?"

"How about some tea? Tea's easy on the stomach."

"I'm game."

They sat together at a table, and Tara looked out the window at the people passing by.

"Do you think he'll show?" Daniel asked after a few minutes.

Surprised, Tara looked at him. "Do I think who will show?" Her voice sounded guilty.

"Santa Claus," said Daniel. "Give me a break." He looked out the window. "Oh, there he is."

"Santa Claus?"

"No, Gray, you big grown-up goof."

She looked where Daniel was pointing. Gray was walking up the sidewalk, hands buried in his pockets, gaze focused glumly on the ground.

"He misses you," said Daniel.

Tara gave him a sharp look but detected no sarcasm in his voice or face.

"I said that because I know you miss him," Daniel went on. "What's a few vampires compared to the course of true love?"

"You're a nosy little brat."

"I've had five hundred years of practice."

Still, Tara couldn't bring herself to approach Gray directly. If this was meant to be, if the greater powers of the universe really wanted them to have a chance, he would see her, and he would stop, and maybe he would take her in his arms and kiss her, right in the middle of the coffee shop.

He bought his coffee, turned away from the counter, and walked right toward them, still completely oblivious of her presence. So much for the greater powers of the universe. She blinked back tears as he took a seat at another table.

"Just go talk to him," Daniel suggested. "I really don't want to watch you mooning the rest of the week because you didn't."

She considered. He was right. If she didn't go, she would regret it. "All right."

Gray was more than lost in his thoughts. He seemed to be wandering in a separate dimension. He didn't look up or respond to her presence in any way until she actually sat down across from him, touched his hand, and spoke.

"Gray?"

He looked up, blinking himself back to reality. "Tara?"

"Good. You remember. I thought you might have forgotten while you were off in la-la land, there."

He smiled a little. "Sorry. I was just . . . thinking."

"About what?"

"You."

That surprised her. "Why?"

"Because I'm still having dreams."

Desire hit her hard, out of left field, and she had to take a long breath before she could talk again. "You, too, huh?"

His rueful smile faded into smoldering sobriety. "Vampires or no vampires, I don't think I can walk away from this."

"From what, exactly?"

"From you." He looked down at the table, then leaned closer to her, his voice low and barely audible in the rumble of the coffee shop. "I think I'm in love with you. I think it's more than bleed-over from Liam and Felicity. I think it's just me."

There were those annoying tears again. "I think it's mutual."

"Could we talk? I think I need to talk."

"Sure. Let's go."

"Let me get Daniel."

"Daniel? I thought—"

Tara smiled. "The Blue Fairy granted his wish. He's a real boy now." She waved to Daniel, who picked up his cup and joined them.

"So," he said. "Is the mooning over?"

Tara cocked an eyebrow at him. "I'm going to start giving you an allowance."

Daniel shrugged. "Cool. Why?"

"So I can take it away when you say stuff like that." She rolled her eyes toward Gray. "Let's go."

Gray followed Tara to her apartment, Daniel trailing after them, seemingly absorbed in watching the sunlight. Gray felt intensely awkward, not sure what he was going to say to Tara when they actually sat down to talk.

"It's so bright," Daniel said.

"Which is why you need to stay out of it until you get a little more used to it." She gestured toward the shade of the building. "This way a little?"

"Aw, jeez," he muttered under his breath but spent the rest of the walk in the shade, only letting his hand drift out into the sunlight from time to time. Gray watched him, curious, as he turned his hand in the light as if trying to catch it.

"Something new and different, I guess," he ventured, not at all sure how Daniel would respond.

"It's been a long time. I didn't really remember what it was like. I mean, you helped a little, helped me remember some of it, but that was nothing compared to actually being out here in it." He made a face. "Except Tara wants to keep me in the house all the time."

"It's probably wise," said Gray. "I'm guessing you could sunburn pretty badly, if you don't take it a little at a time."

Daniel shook his head in disgust. "Grownups suck."

Tara led the way into her apartment. "Daniel," she said, giving him a meaningful look.

"Yeah, yeah, I'll be scarce." He went into his room and closed the door.

"How is he doing?" Gray asked. It seemed as good a way as any of avoiding the actual subject.

"He's doing well. He thinks I'm being overprotective, though."

"You probably are." At her arch look, he smiled. "Most good moms are, a little."

Tara settled into the couch, sipping her coffee. "Correct me if I'm wrong, but I don't think you came here to talk about Daniel."

"No, I didn't."

"I got the impression you really didn't want to see me or my weird vampire friends ever again."

"You, yes. Your weird vampire friends, no."

"We kind of come in a package."

"I worked that out. Among other things I worked out over the past two weeks."

"What things?"

He looked at her, into her eyes, then discovered he couldn't talk at all while he did that, much less say what he had to say. So he looked away, then closed his eyes completely. "I love you. I know it took me way too long to figure it out, but it's true."

"I said it before—I think it's mutual," she said, and when he looked to see her carefully sipping her coffee, he noticed that her hand was shaking. "So what are we going to do about it?"

"I was going to come here and tell you I couldn't be with you if you continued working for vampires." She started to protest, but he raised a hand. "I was going to give you a big ultimatum. Them or me. Prove you love me by never seeing them again."

"I think you know what I would have said."

He nodded. "You seem to have a certain . . . loyalty to Julian."

"And to Dominic's memory." She paused. "He was a good man. Vampire or not, he was a good man. I loved him, and I owe him this. If you can't understand that—"

"I said I *was* going to do that. I changed my mind."

"Why?"

"Because I knew it was the best, fastest way to lose you."

"So . . ." she ventured, "you're willing to accept what I do?"

"I've seen what you've done with Daniel. I assume there are other children who need the same kind of help?"

"Yes, there are."

"And they need the same kind of therapy I gave Daniel?"

"Yes."

"Have you had any luck finding anyone else qualified?"

"Dr. Greene's taking classes. Julian decided not to trust anybody else."

Gray drew a deep breath. "I want to help. And not just because it's the best way to be with you."

"Why, then?"

"I almost killed those children, when I was Liam. The least I can do is help them now."

A smile began to form on her lips. "It seems fair. And the part about you being with me—that works for me."

"I was hoping it would." He bent forward and kissed her gently. "Because it totally works for me."

Julian's Journal

Cryptic. I'll bet when these guys wrote this stuff down, they thought it was fun to make it as obscure and cryptic as possible. Or maybe, since it came from dreamtime, it was just hard to translate it into words. I'd like to give them the benefit of the doubt.

I'm starting to get the picture, though. Two litanies, now, plus additional study of the Book, over the past several days, and the theme is beginning to emerge. I don't like where it seems to be going, but it's too much to hope that I am wrong.

There is also still the question of my own memories. Or not so much my own but the Senior's. They become less painful to access as I dig deeper, but there's so much there—places I don't have time to go. Places I don't want to go. Especially places where memories of William lay buried. It's hard enough to look him in the face as it is, knowing how my possession of the Senior's memories violates him.

We're racing the clock here. I don't know how much time we have left, but it can't be a lot. The latest disappearance was in Jersey City—still far enough away to consider Manhattan safe, but there's no doubt that Ialdaboth's strength is growing. I can feel it. I dream it. I feel it lurking always in the background, stronger every day. He'll be coming for us. Soon.

Julian — Redux

All thine enemies have opened their mouth against thee: they hiss and gnash the teeth: they say, We have swallowed her up: certainly this is the day that we looked for; we have found, we have seen it.

Lamentations 2:16

Ialdaboth's insane. It gives him a bit of an edge.

Email—Julian to Lucien

If the darkest of the dark days come, and the Children of the Dark turn the earth to ashes, it will be because one of the Light has not come forth, and offered himself, and said, "Here. I am he who will change the tides of pain."

The Book of Changing Blood

One

Aanu had skin, and hair. Eyelashes, even, if you looked closely enough. Julian wasn't sure. The glass panel in the hyperbaric chamber distorted his vision so that he couldn't quite tell about the eyelashes. He could see eyebrows, though.

What lay inside that regenerated brain? Could they really expect the man to remember what he'd known four thousand years ago, before he'd been reduced to a bag of bones? Was there anything even remotely realistic about that expectation?

Aanu's eyes moved a little under his lids. The lids still seemed too thin, not quite opaque enough, as if they were missing a layer or two of cells.

Julian sensed rather than heard movement behind him. Without turning, he said, "What does it feel like?"

"The regeneration?" Lucien stepped up beside him. "Hurts like hell."

Julian nodded. "I drowned once. It wasn't like this."

"No. It wouldn't be. Closest I came was the volcano. I lost a good deal of flesh in that one." He tapped the chamber's glass panel absently with a big finger. "Didn't have the benefit of one of these things, though."

"You think it's made a difference?"

"Hell, yes. This would have taken months under open air conditions. And I'm sure your additional work has helped, too."

"Not just mine," said Julian, out of politeness, if not accuracy.

He and Lucien had spent hours with their hands on Aanu's gradually regenerating body, manipulating the warm flow of his life force. He himself had been experimenting to a great degree, testing and finding the nature and the limits of his power. But it hadn't taken long to discover that his abilities went far beyond Lucien's.

Julian studied Aanu's face, quiet in repose, raw, not quite whole. "Do you think he'll be able to tell us anything?"

"Maybe not right away. There'll be some disorientation."

"For how long? We don't have a lot of time, here."

Lucien grimaced. "I know. I can probably help with that, or, more likely, you can."

Julian took a long, slow breath. The air tasted different these days—cleaner, sweeter. Strange, he thought, when it seemed as if it should be full of fear. It should, he thought, taste like Ialdaboth.

"He's close," said Lucien. "Not here yet, not ready, but close."

It was hardly worth the effort it took to talk to Lucien, Julian thought, when the Demon could pick thoughts out of the air like that. Annoying. "I can feel him."

Lucien nodded. "Yes."

"Too bad you didn't kill him in Romania."

"I would have if I could have." Lucien shook his head slowly, his gaze, still seemingly focused on Aanu, going distant. "We're hard to kill. As you can see."

"What does it take?"

"I'm not sure. Two of us together against one, possibly. I remember . . ." He stopped, frowned.

"Remember what?"

"I forget."

"Nice." Julian stepped away from Aanu's silver, coffin-like resting place. More like a womb than a coffin, though, really. "You think on that. I need to see Lorelei."

Lorelei was asleep. She slept a lot these days—day, night, afternoon, it didn't matter. Softly, Julian settled onto the bed next to where she lay curled around herself, one hand cupping her stomach. She'd only barely started to show, even with two babies growing inside her. They seemed to sap her strength, drain her beyond her ability to recuperate. Having no experience with any sort of pregnancy, he couldn't help wondering if that was normal or a sign of something very abnormal.

Of course, one could argue that any child of a not-quite-vampire would be strange and abnormal. That didn't matter to him. These children were his, whatever they turned out to be.

He caressed her hair. She shifted a little under his touch but didn't open her eyes. A vague smile curved her lips, and he bent to kiss her forehead. Her skin felt too warm under his lips, but then, it always did. He could sense the swirling of her energies, moving light of vivid blue and magenta hues, the power that lay there. The babies had an energy, as well, that swirled in soft pastels throughout her body, mingling with her own life force. He had only begun to see the colors recently and assumed it had something to do with his growing powers; but he could tell the colors had changed since her pregnancy—there was more to her than there had been before.

He'd wondered often over the past few months exactly what had changed in her and what power she might have that they had yet to explore. Her power seemed not to have manifested in the same way his had. It was subtle, not there if you looked for it, only there when she needed it. He'd finally figured it out—her power was for this, for the children. Her body had known, even before she had quickened, that it would need to protect her babies.

That answered one question, at least. She would be of little use to him in the final confrontation he knew was coming. Hers was a specific power, defensive, a mother-power. Lorelei could stand against Ialdaboth—she'd proven that when he'd kidnapped her and threatened her life—but she couldn't attack him. He couldn't hurt her, but she couldn't hurt him, either.

Satisfied that she was contentedly asleep and safe, Julian went to his computer. He'd sat in front of it nearly every waking hour of every day since Lucien and the others had returned from Romania, trying to make sense of the pieces of the *Book*, trying to find the answers. The additional material Rafael had supplied fit with what they already had, but it still wasn't enough for the clues to make sense.

He booted up the computer, reflecting. It was as if there were something missing, as if the *Book* had a code, and he needed the key to break it. It would make more sense, he thought, than the idea that all these cryptic phrases and convoluted narratives actually meant something practical.

He pulled up a file in which he had concatenated some of the meatier passages. He would figure it out eventually. He would have to.

Otherwise, they were all dead.

He wasn't able to keep at it for long, though. He was tired, exhausted, drained down to his bones. When the words on the screen began to blur into incomprehensible blotches, he shut down the computer, slipped into the bed next to Lorelei, and let the weariness drag him under.

He dreamed. He dreamed a great deal these days, when he took the time to sleep. Floaty, disconnected images, usually, lacking both color and sense. But these dreams were memories.

Not his own memories. The Senior's. He had absorbed every

memory the Senior had owned when he'd taken the ancient vampire's blood. The blood had facilitated his transformation, but the memories had plagued him, adding several thousand years to his eight hundred.

In the dream, he saw a face, looking into his own. He'd seen the face before, in attempts to delve through the Senior's past, and he knew it to be Ruha, the fourth of the First Demons. He'd been the Senior's lover for a time before choosing the darker path favored by Ialdaboth.

The face was made of harsh lines, the pale eyes a strange contrast to the low, glowering forehead and dark brows. He looked more like Ialdaboth than Lucien.

"The Book *holds the key. . . . "* he said, and the last word drained out into a sort of broken, wordless mumble.

Julian blinked awake, immediately alert and focused on what he'd just heard. So there *was* something from the *Book*, something they hadn't yet found. Of course. No point in having everything be straightforward or easy. There were verses still missing, and he would have to find them.

At least, now, for the first time, he had some idea where to look.

Lorelei woke abruptly. Something was wrong, but she wasn't sure what. Inside her, one of the babies moved. It was a subtle sensation still—a sort of wave motion—not enough to have awakened her. Slowly, she sat up.

Vaguely, she remembered Julian having come to bed, remembered moving up against him in the night. But he was gone now, and she was once again alone. She'd gotten used to waking alone, since Julian wasn't much for sleeping these days. But for some reason, this time, his absence bothered her.

She sat up and turned, still under the covers, putting her feet on the floor. Her head spun a little. This morning sickness was never going to go away.

She heard Julian mumbling in the other room. He couldn't get his head out of the *Book* these days. The answers were there, he insisted, though she wasn't so sure. She had a feeling he was missing something. He must be. If he'd had all the pieces, as much time as he'd spent working on the puzzle, he would have solved it long ago.

Slowly, Lorelei stood. Her head went revolving again, and she waited for it to settle, then padded into the other room.

Julian sat hunched over the computer, fingers tapping softly on the table in a meaningless rhythm. His brow was creased in a deep frown of concentration and frustration.

"Shit," he whispered, then closed his eyes. After a moment he opened them again and started tapping the table again.

"Julian?" Lorelei ventured.

He turned to look at her and smiled wearily. "Hey."

"Making any progress?"

"Not so you'd notice." He leaned back in the chair and stared up at the ceiling, then looked at her again. "How are you doing?"

"Okay."

"You look a little pale."

"I kind of feel like I'm going to vomit," she admitted with a wry smile. Then the smile faded. "Is something wrong? I mean besides the usual. Is he closer?"

Julian frowned. "Why?"

"I just feel . . . I don't know. I woke up scared, sort of, I guess."

"He's closer." The soft matter-of-factness of his voice bothered her more than any overt indication of fear he might have displayed. "He's closer and I don't know what to do about it."

She slid a hand protectively over the soft swell of her abdomen, not aware she was doing it until her fingers brushed across the silk of her pajama shirt. "Aanu will be awake soon. He'll help."

"Maybe. But what if he doesn't remember anything?"

Another slow, rolling sensation in her womb made Lorelei clench her fingers against herself, holding the movement closer, protecting it. Warmth passed into her palm, bringing with it a feeling of certainty, of reassurance.

"He'll remember," she said, and she knew it was true.

Morning was climbing the sky. Julian could feel it. He'd left behind the involuntary vampiric Sleep, but his strong sense of the rhythm of the daylight hadn't faded. The knowledge that it was bright outside made him twitchy, restless. So when Lorelei elected to return to bed, he headed for the medical wing of the Underground.

Halfway there, he nearly collided with Dr. Greene, who was hurrying down the corridor, looking harried.

"He's awake," the doctor said, breathless. "At least, I think he is."

They half-ran the rest of the way together, Julian wishing his new powers included Lucien's neat teleportation trick. "Where's Lucien?"

he asked.

Dr. Greene shook his head. "I'm not sure. He was by earlier, but I don't know where he went when he left."

"We need to find him."

"He'll find us," Dr. Greene said, pushing open the door to Aanu's room. "He always does."

The doctor was right, for Lucien was already there, standing next to the hyperbaric chamber, peering in through the glass. "He's awake."

"Thanks for the news flash," Dr. Greene said dryly.

Lucien quirked an eyebrow. "I don't think he's entirely conscious yet, though."

Julian went to stand next to him, looking down at Aanu's face through the window in the hyperbaric chamber. His eyes were open, but he looked dazed, disconnected.

"I can help him," Julian said.

"Are you sure?" Dr. Greene eyed him narrowly. "It's been less than twelve hours since your last session with him."

Julian shrugged. Sometimes the healing sessions left him drained, but more often, he was manic in the aftermath, energized to a point that it was sometimes hard to control. "I know. It doesn't matter. I can help him."

Dr. Greene nodded. "All right, then. I'll get him ready."

It was different, in an odd way that Julian couldn't quite define. It just felt different. He laid his hands on Aanu's bare chest, and Aanu's eyes flicked toward him, looking into his face without recognition or visible comprehension. As if the acknowledgement were little more than a reflex.

"It's all right," Julian murmured. "It's going to be fine."

He let his palms shift, until both hands were in complete contact with Aanu's skin, and wondered what exactly was going to be all right. Aanu? Certainly he would be fine, probably within a matter of hours. A day at the most. But how long did they have until the shit that was Ialdaboth hit the fan?

He pushed that ever-present question out of his head. He couldn't afford the energy required to think about it, not if he wanted to help Aanu.

Aanu's skin was warm. That surprised Julian for some reason. It had been warm before, but not this warm. It was human-warm now. Lorelei-warm. He closed his eyes, feeling the energy moving beneath his hands. It, too, felt different today, less fragmented, its rhythms steadier. Aanu's heartbeat was stronger, as well, more regular. Julian let himself fall into that rhythm, the slow, steady drumbeat. The indigo pulsations seemed to wrap around his hands, where he drew them in, magnified them, fed from them, let them drain back out of him and into Aanu.

It was endless, a suspended, eternal moment, like an orgasm. Then Aanu took a deep, gasping breath, and Julian opened his eyes. Aanu was looking up at him, lucid, his pale eyes full of disbelief edging on fear.

"It's all right," Julian said again. "It's all right." But Aanu only stared, uncomprehending.

From behind him, Julian heard Lucien speak, his tone gentle and reassuring but his words incomprehensible. Julian withdrew his hands, and Lucien stepped a little closer, leaning over Aanu. Aanu's expression changed to one of relief and understanding.

"Belial," he said, and Lucien smiled.

"Lucien," he corrected, and suddenly Julian could understand him, though the language was still the same foreign tongue. "Welcome back, brother."

* * *

"He's not ready for extensive questioning," Dr. Greene insisted for about the tenth time.

He could be right, Julian thought, but under the circumstances, it struck him as unwise to take the conservative approach. "We don't have time to wait any longer," he said. "He been conscious and alert for twenty-four hours and hasn't shown any signs of relapse. I believe he's in better health than you think."

Dr. Greene took off his glasses and wiped the lenses on his sleeve, giving him a less-than-friendly look. "I suppose you would know," he conceded. "Your contact with him has been on an entirely different and much more intimate level than mine has been."

Julian shrugged a little. "The energy—the levels seem safe to me. I'm sure he could withstand a few questions, and he'd probably be okay out of the chamber, too."

"How does Lucien feel about it?"

"I think the question is, how does Aanu feel? I'm sure he can tell us if he's up to answering questions."

The doctor sighed and put his glasses back on. "All right. No more concentrated oxygen, no more overprotective doctor. He's breathing, his heart's beating, his blood's moving, and he seems fairly lucid. Give me a couple of hours to get him situated in a new room, and he's all yours."

Julian nodded decisively. "Good."

An hour later, Lucien met him at the door to Aanu's new room. "You didn't invite me?" Lucien said, sounding a little hurt.

"Since when do you have to be invited anywhere? You generally just show up."

Lucien grinned a little. "Well, I *am* a vampire. An invitation would be helpful."

"No, you're not. You're a First Demon proto-vampire biological half-blood freak or something. And that having-to-be-invited thing is bullshit, anyway."

"True." Lucien glanced at the sheaf of papers Julian was carrying, papers on which were painstakingly recorded all the most pertinent—and a few impertinent—questions Julian could think of. "Let him talk first," Lucien said. "Let him get out what he needs to get out. He's been dead a long time."

Fighting a quick stab of irritation, Julian nodded. He realized he was being impatient. He couldn't help it. He felt naked, vulnerable, unprepared, uninformed, and many other very uncomfortable conditions. If Ialdaboth popped in right now, he would take down the entire place.

"We have a little time," said Lucien. "Not much, but I think it'll be enough."

"Get out of my head," Julian groused, then added, "How do you know that?"

Lucien shrugged. "Like it or not, Ialdaboth is my brother. There's a connection. A small one, but still a connection. And my beating the living shit out of him in Romania strengthened the bond. He still hasn't quite recovered. I can tell."

Julian struggled to compose himself. "Okay. That helps—a little, anyway."

With an odd smile, Lucien tapped his knuckles against the door to Aanu's room.

"Enter," said Aanu.

Julian was again surprised that he understood the language. He had no idea what tongue it was, but it translated itself in his head when he heard it. There was a bit of a delay, though, as if it had to go through a relay process to hit the correct part of his brain. He'd figured out that was because he himself had never heard the language before yesterday. All knowledge of it came from the Senior's memories.

"Are you ready?" Lucien asked.

Julian nodded. "Ready as I'll ever be."

Lucien pushed open the door. Aanu sat in the bed, wearing clothes that had to have come from Lucien's wardrobe, given the fit. Julian knew his own or Dr. Greene's clothes would have been too narrow through the shoulders. Aanu looked up as they entered, his attention immediately focusing on Lucien, and he smiled a little.

"Belial," he said, then corrected himself. "My pardon. Lucien."

"You have caused no pain," said Lucien, tilting his head forward a little. "This is our leader, Julian."

"Not really the leader," Julian corrected, a little stunned that the words came out in the same language Lucien and Aanu had used.

Lucien turned to him with an eyebrow cocked in surprise. "I didn't know you spoke this tongue."

"I don't." Julian lapsed back into English, his concentration disrupted. "The Senior did. It's a bit hard to dig up. I don't even know what language it is."

"It's an ancient Sumerian dialect, I think," Lucien answered, also in English. "Probably been dead for centuries."

"What do you speak of?" Aanu said.

"Nothing of great concern," Lucien assured him. "I was simply surprised at Julian's facility with our language."

"Not a great facility. His accent is hideous."

Julian laughed. "No doubt."

Lucien smiled at him and pulled a chair from a corner of the room, pushing it closer to Aanu's bed. Julian sat and arranged his pages of questions while Lucien retrieved another chair for himself.

"How long has it been?" Aanu asked. His gaze slid from one to the other of his visitors as he tried with little success to hide his uneasiness, his fear.

Lucien spoke gently. "Do you really want to know?"

"I *need* to know. How long has it been?"

Silence dragged through the room as Lucien eyed his half-brother. Finally, slowly, he said, "Four thousand years."

Aanu gaped. "Four . . ." He stopped, closed his eyes.

Again the silence came. Schooling himself to patience, Julian followed Lucien's lead and waited it out.

"Ialdaboth," Aanu finally said. "And Ruha. They did this to me."

"I thought as much." Lucien shifted forward in his chair, leaning his elbows against his knees. "Two pitted against one. Is there any other way to defeat one of us?"

"I was not defeated." Aanu's tone was mildly offended, but more amused. "If I had been defeated, I would not be speaking with you now."

"Fair enough." He started to say something else, but Julian broke in. A memory had floated to the surface of his mind.

"When did Ruha turn?"

Aanu frowned. "Turn? What do you mean?"

"I remember Ruha." The memory was fleeting and faded, one of the Senior's that Julian had no desire to pursue. "Ruha was not with the Dark Children."

"You cannot possibly remember Ruha," Aanu protested. "He has been gone for . . . since before you were Made, certainly."

But Lucien understood. "The Senior?"

Julian nodded. "Yes. Ruha Made him, I believe."

"Interesting. Did I know that? Maybe I didn't."

Aanu was staring at them in frustration now, as both Julian and Lucien had switched to English. Julian rummaged for the words in Sumerian. "Ruha was not always of the Dark Children."

"No," Aanu conceded, "but he chose that path a long time ago."

"When he was with the Senior . . ." Julian trailed off. "But no. That was why the Senior left him."

"Ruha came to believe that we followed the wrong path." Aanu looked at Lucien as he spoke, as if seeking comfort in a more familiar face. "He partnered with Ialdaboth for a time, and then he disappeared. I believe that he and Ialdaboth also had an ideological disagreement, though one different from the one he had with us."

"He's not dead?"

"There are stories. Someone told me once he'd been overcome somehow, and cut to pieces. But that might just be legend again, like the Osiris story."

Julian frowned. "If he were dead and we knew how he died, we might use that knowledge against Ialdaboth."

Lucien shook his head. "My guess is, he's been incapacitated in some way, much as Aanu was. Where, how, why, even when—nobody knows for certain." He turned again to Aanu. "Do you remember the *Book*? The one we dreamed when we were under the mud?"

Aanu nodded slowly. "Parts. I remember parts."

"Good. We need those parts. Maybe if we get enough of them, we can figure out what they mean."

"Let's hope it's soon," said Julian.

Lorelei was waiting for him. She sat at his computer, playing a card game. On the desk lay an opened package of corn chips and a bowl of guacamole. Julian made a face.

"What?" said Lorelei, moving a card into position with the mouse.

"That stuff's just way too green."

"It's delicious."

Julian eyed it skeptically. He could smell it, and even though he had become accustomed to eating a wider variety of foods of late, guacamole didn't smell like something he wanted to try.

With no such compunctions, Lorelei scooped another large helping onto a corn chip. "Did you guys make any progress?"

"A little. I think I know where to start."

"With Aanu, of course. Hell, I knew that much. Because you were supposed to question him, and he was supposed to pass on some information that would put you on the right track."

"And he did. I'm fairly certain at this point that each of the four original brothers held a piece of the puzzle. Some of what they knew came out in the Books, when Lucien and Aanu dreamed them under the mud. But there's another piece of knowledge that was either left or taken out of the *Book* at some point. That's where our answers are, I'm sure."

Lorelei had turned away from the computer and was listening with some interest. "Really? What makes you think that?"

"We got one piece from Lucien. Then there was the bit that Rafael remembered from Brigitte's nightly ritual—that's Ialdaboth's piece. Aanu has a piece, I'm certain, and once he gets a little more lucid, he'll remember."

"So where's the fourth piece?"

"I have it." At her startled look, he went on. "It's there, somewhere, buried in the memories the Senior passed on to me. His memories of Ruha."

Two

The power continued to flow into him, filling him again, making him strong. He had been weak long enough, and now the healing process was almost finished. Only a matter of time until he had the power, the focus, the strength, the magic, to confront the enemies of the Dark Children. They were deluded, broken people, searching for hope where there was none, dispatching love where love could touch nothing, grasping at the falling straws of repentance where repentance was impossible.

They would bleed, and they would die, and he would devour the shredded fragments that remained. . . .

Julian opened his eyes. Had he been asleep? Perhaps, though it seemed rather unlikely, given his state of mind. Perhaps he had only been dreaming, without the benefit of sleep.

Or perhaps, as he'd suspected for quite some time, he was actually tuned into Ialdaboth, his brain picking up signals on the Evil First Demon frequency.

He was sitting in front of the computer, as he had been for the last several hours. Lorelei, satiated on chips and guacamole, had gone to bed a long time ago.

He had typed the fragments from Lucien and Rafael into a file, where he could play with them. He'd looked at them frontward, backward, upside down, sidewise, next to each other, one above the other, superimposed on top of each other, and nothing had clicked. Not yet. He had a feeling that wasn't the right approach, anyway. There seemed to be a narrative element in the fragments, which meant they needed the rest of the story. So he would have to wait until the last two bits came in. And hope they made sense.

Frankly, he was less worried about the piece they needed from Aanu than he was about the one he would have to extract from himself. Aanu would remember, and he would pass on the information, and they could add it to the collection. Maybe that would be enough, but Julian doubted it. He was going to have to dive into his own brain, and dive deep.

No great surprise. He'd known since the day he'd realized the

Senior's blood had brought memories with it that he would have to use those memories. So far, he'd dipped into them to arrange the trip to Romania, to protect Lorelei, and to perform a few other mundane tasks in maintaining the stability of the Underground. Surface stuff only, like wading ankle-deep in ocean surf. Getting to the memories he needed now would take a headlong plunge into the mental and emotional equivalent of the Marianas Trench.

He wasn't entirely certain he could do it. There were the headaches, for starters. Every time he tried to access the Senior's memories, his brain rebelled violently and painfully, and it seemed to get worse each time. After Lucien's party had left for Romania, he'd spent several days recuperating, and the painkillers the doctor had provided had done very little good. The truth was, he was afraid of what would happen next time.

But that wasn't the whole truth. In fact, it was probably just an excuse. Because it wasn't the memory retrieval itself that caused the pain. It was his own stubborn, full-fledged fight to limit the memories that caused it. When he accessed the Senior's legacy, he carefully looked for only the information he needed—the bits and pieces relevant to the specific situation, and no more. Because even in those limited incursions, he could feel the Senior as if he were still alive, lurking there in his head. And Julian knew that what really terrified him was the thought that, if he went too deep into that ocean of ancient memories, he would lose himself entirely, and no longer be Julian Cavanaugh.

The babies were afraid. Lorelei sensed it the moment she opened her eyes, realized it was, in fact, what had awakened her. The babies, too small even to be called babies yet, without fully developed brains, according to the developmental charts she'd been studying so diligently, were afraid. Terrified.

She sat up in bed, laying both hands on her slightly rounded abdomen. She could feel the taut walls of her growing uterus, a little larger than a grapefruit but clenched hard on itself. Gently, soothingly, she rubbed the tight muscles, trying to communicate comfort through her touch. The babies moved as she eased her fingers over her belly. She could feel the movement inside her, but not against her palms. The babies were still too small to disturb the surface of her skin with their kicking and swimming.

"Shh," she said, her voice little more than a whisper. "Shh. It'll be all right. It'll be all right."

Next to her, Julian sat up. She jumped a little—she'd been so absorbed in the babies that she hadn't even noticed he was there.

"Is everything okay?" he asked.

"They're afraid," she whispered.

He frowned and reached toward her, laying his big hand over her belly, next to hers. "Afraid of what?"

"I don't know. Him, I think." She looked earnestly at Julian, suddenly afraid, herself. His frown hadn't budged. "Is he closer? Can you tell? Are we running out of time?" Suddenly she could think of nothing but her tiny children, helpless there, inside her, and of the threat Ialdaboth posed to them. To everyone.

His fingers tightened a little on her, strong, comforting. His words, though, were anything but. "Of course we're running out of time. We've been running out of time since the day you let me drink you."

"If I hadn't, we'd all be dead by now."

His lips twitched a little. "Don't confuse me with the facts." Leaning forward, he kissed her softly. She let his lips play against hers, let the taste and feel of him comfort her. Then he drew back, lay his face against her belly, and began to sing.

She smiled at the soft sound of his slightly off-key crooning. The music vibrated through her nightgown, against her skin, and the babies began to ease under its effects. Their movements slowed, becoming lazy and, finally, stopping. They were asleep. She knew it in the same way she had known they were afraid. Just a sense, clear but strange, disconnected in a way from her own emotions and senses. Their fear had dissolved, eased away by the sound of their father's voice.

"The babies can feel him," Julian told Lucien in the morning, when Lucien showed up at his door, as usual, just after sunrise. "So can I. We're running out of time."

Lucien snorted. "Tell me something I didn't already know."

"You didn't know the babies could feel him."

"True," Lucien conceded with a shrug. "Anyway, I know we're running out of time. We need a solution before Ialdaboth comes blasting up through the floor or falls through the ceiling onto our heads or whatever crazy stunt he's likely to pull next."

"Do you know if Aanu has remembered anything?"

"Not sure." He stood and stretched, his spine popping rather alarmingly. "I talked to him again last night, and he's still having some retrieval problems. Anyway, I sent William to spend some time with him, just for a change of pace."

"William?"

"Turns out William knows that Sumerian dialect. Not sure how he learned it, but he knows it about as well as I do. Certainly better than you."

Chagrined, Julian said, "It's not exactly easy sifting for vocabulary through what effectively amounts to someone else's brain."

Lucien sobered. "You need to make it your brain. We're not going to solve this thing if you don't."

"I know."

"And I know why you don't want to. Get over it."

Julian looked up sharply. "I don't think you have any idea."

"I know a hell of a lot more than you want to give me credit for. And unless you want everybody here to die, you're going to have to get over your little personal problem and start using the Senior's memories—all of them."

"What if—" Julian started, then broke off, afraid to say the words.

"What if what?" Lucien's voice had gentled, almost as if he knew the words without them being spoken. Maybe he did. Lucien was that way.

Julian swallowed hard, and said it. "What if I get lost in there? What if I can't get back?"

Lucien laid a hand on his shoulder. "You will," he said. "You have to."

"Do you really think it's that dangerous?" Lorelei asked him later.

They sat in bed together, Lorelei in soft, satin pajamas the color of a ripe peach. Unable to resist the urge, Julian reached out to cup his palm over the soft curve of her belly. She'd told him she could feel the babies moving, but he felt only her warmth, the tautness of her skin.

She laid a hand over his and went on. "Or are you just afraid?"

Startled, he looked up to meet her gaze. Her eyes were wide open and ready for him to tell her the absolute truth. And they had a look in them that made him think she already knew it.

"Both," he finally said, "but maybe more of the latter."

She nodded, her fingers tightening over his hand. "I thought that might be the case. What are you afraid of?"

"If I go deeply enough into those memories to find what we need, what's to guarantee I'll be able to come back?"

"Me."

She sounded so certain, so resolute, that he could almost believe she knew more about it, somehow, than he did. She shifted a little closer to him, her mouth curving just a little at the corners. Her clear blue eyes, as always, entranced him, but lately they'd held more than simply her love for him. There was something else there—mystery, more than even the usual mysteries of a woman.

"You could never leave me." Her voice was little more than a whisper, but it thrummed with power. "And if something did happen, if you were lost there, even for a moment, I could bring you home."

"How do you know?"

"I know. Whatever you did to me when you drank me, it bonded us. There's power, but it's only protective power. I can protect myself, the babies. And you."

Hadn't he had the same thought just the other day? All the more reason to believe her.

She leaned toward him, until he could taste her breath on his lips. "You can't get away from me that easily."

Her kiss held a smile, and he returned it as his mouth moved against hers. He savored her mouth for a long moment, a hand sliding up her back, the other unable to resist the temptation to cup her breast. Her nipple sprang taut into his palm. The contours of her breasts had changed already, filling out a bit, and she'd told him to be careful touching them, because sometimes they hurt. But she was leaning into him now, pressing harder into his palm.

He wanted her. But he only kissed her, caressed her. They'd agreed reluctantly that it might be best to abstain during her pregnancy, because it was so odd and impossible and neither of them wanted to risk losing the babies. It was hard to resist her, but he had gone decades at a time without sex. He was certain he could go a few more months.

At least, he'd been certain when they'd made the decision. Now he wasn't so sure.

After a time, she withdrew, with a small sound of regret. "It would probably be okay," she whispered.

"But what if it wasn't?" That scared him, too. And it was one thing he could control in the midst of the out-of-control spiral that had become his life. He could keep his hands off Lorelei, keep himself from endangering their children.

She smiled a little, and he knew she understood. Her hands moved gently down his arms, until her fingers tangled with his. "Go where you need to go. I'll be sure you come back. I promise."

He kissed her softly. "Thank you." Then he settled onto the bed. She stretched out next to him, curled her small, peach-colored self against him, and he put an arm around her shoulders, drawing her in a little closer, until he could feel her heartbeat.

"Go," she whispered, and he closed his eyes.

Worried, Lorelei watched as Julian drifted off. He seemed to be asleep, but she could tell he wasn't. His alertness made a kind of echo in her own head, so she always knew when he was awake and when he had entered the slower, meditative state that, for him, passed for sleep.

It concerned her that he was afraid to look into his own mind. He so rarely seemed truly discomfited, and that he would be afraid of something as simple as another man's memories was, to her, disturbing.

She understood, though, or began to, as he let himself sink into himself and she followed him into the subconscious that had been blended with his own by his taking of the Senior's blood. She could feel the rhythms of his mind actually change, until he felt like a different person.

No wonder it frightened him. It scared her, too. Scared her that her lover, her mate, seemed to be disappearing. Suddenly she wondered if she'd been too confident in herself. How could she bring him back if she couldn't feel or see or even recognize him?

The memories were there, clear and accessible but hidden behind the long stretch of memory Julian called his own. He'd dipped only into the more recent of those other memories. To get what he needed, he had to go back hundreds, maybe thousands, of years. And to do that, he had to let go of his own memories, his own sense of self.

To do it without the intense pain, he had to do it willingly.

But . . . how?

Even with the reassurance of Lorelei's presence lurking on the edges of his awareness, he didn't know how to let go that completely. And if he did—if he even could—how was he supposed to know how to come back? He had no road map. It would be so easy to get lost.

He could sense Lorelei, though, on the other side, a beacon to guide him home, when it came time to return. The lifeline gave him courage.

So he let himself sink deeper than he'd ever sunk before, past the edges of memory beyond which he previously hadn't tried to venture. Twenty-five . . . fifty . . . a hundred years of another man's life. . . .

It was like wading through an underwater jungle, with tendrils hanging down from above, touching him from time to time. A quick current of memory occasionally trembling over his skin. Darkness amongst the threads of light. Odd muffled sounds in the distance, the voices of other, more distant memories.

It was so hard not to be afraid.

Lorelei.

I'm here.

He clung to her, a mental sensation that felt as if he were holding her hand, and headed for that dark place where he had no desire to go.

He found William there, as he knew he would. He'd been avoiding it since he'd first sensed the Senior's relationship with William in the sea of inherited memories. It was too intimate, too painful, and too alien to anything he had ever experienced. But it stood like an insurmountable reef between him and his destination. And somehow, he had to get past it, past William, back to Ruha.

Go on. I'm with you. Lorelei's voice was distant, a faint, wispy sound.

I can't.

He lurched toward the surface, abandoning the quest in what he knew full well was an attack of cowardice. He just couldn't do it. Not now.

He opened his eyes and looked at Lorelei, who regarded him with some sympathy but more disappointment.

"You have to," she said.

Julian sighed. "I know."

Sitting on the bed next to Julian, Lorelei drew her knees up under her chin and watched him sleep. That he had fallen asleep worried her—he almost never really slept—but it didn't worry her as much as his reluctance to find his way through the Senior's memories. He kept delaying it, when he knew there simply was no time for delay.

Somebody needed to talk some sense into him, somebody who understood better than she what he was facing.

She reached over and touched him lightly, the tips of her fingers in his hair, barely touching his scalp. Then she rolled carefully out of the bed and went into the front room of their living quarters.

She needed to talk to Lucien. Of course, she had no idea where he was—he was one of the most elusive people she'd ever met—but if she thought about him hard enough he usually showed up. So she took a seat on the soft couch, closed her eyes, and thought about him.

She had almost drifted to sleep when a knock fell on the door. Jerking awake, she got up and went to let Lucien in.

"You rang?" he said, smiling a little.

"You could say that," she answered. Glancing over her shoulder toward the bedroom, she stepped into the hallway, closing the door behind her. "Let's talk somewhere else."

He nodded and headed down the hallway. "How are you feeling?" he asked.

"I'm okay. For the most part. But Julian's a mess, and you need to do something about it."

"Cutting to the chase, are we?" He stopped walking. "Should we just talk here, or do you want to sit somewhere?"

Lorelei's teeth clenched involuntarily, responding to what felt, at first, like mocking from Lucien. But it wasn't, she realized, looking at his face more closely. He was concerned. He wanted to be sure she was comfortable.

"Let's sit." She tried to keep the fear out of her voice, but it was hard. Damned hormones, anyway.

He held out his hand. She took it, he squeezed her fingers lightly, and they were in his office. "Have a seat," he said, and she did.

He leaned against the desk. "So what's up?"

"We need what's in Julian's head, and he won't go get it. You need to talk to him."

Lucien grimaced. "It's a lot of memories. A lot of time to wade through."

"It's not just that."

"I know." He pushed away from the desk. "I'll talk to him." Then, to Lorelei's surprise, he took a step toward her and laid his hand over the curve of her belly. "How are you really?"

She held still, fighting the urge to flinch away from his touch. His long fingers were warm against her. "Scared."

His hand shifted, his fingers tightening a little. "I can feel them."

Her gaze jerked to his face to see a soft smile curving his lips. "Can you?"

"Hmm. They're . . . so small. Sweet. Lovely."

Lorelei swallowed tears, not certain where they had come from. "They're not. . . ?"

"They're not human, if that's what you're about to ask. Not quite, and frankly that's not unexpected. But they're not dangerous. Not evil." His hand slid away. "It'll be all right."

"No, it won't. Not if you can't get Julian to do what he has to do." Lucien sighed. "I'll take care of it."

"Good. Then that's one less thing I have to worry about."

"Just worry about the babies. They need you."

Again with the damned tears. Lorelei forced a watery smile. "Thank you."

Three

Across the ocean, under the ground, the power grew. Black and strange, crawling, filling all the space it had, then breaking through a dark carapace to grow again.

Had you taken your rightful path, you would have this power, too.

The path of darkness, of death. Julian could feel the thick blackness that was Ialdaboth's mind. He fed from death. Created it so he could devour it. Hatred and anger like honey in his mouth, bringing him the strength he needed to exist, to grow, to dominate and become.

Become what?

You wish you could know. But you have no ability to know, because you have sought life.

But Julian knew there was strength in life. He had felt the power growing within him, though, as yet, he only knew it existed, not what he could do with it or what it made of him.

Death feeds us. We kill to live. We are demons, and we should never try to be anything else. It is not what we are meant to be.

But we feed from life, he thought. Life's blood, flowing dark and red, full of the pulses of living. Ialdaboth had chosen the wrong metaphor.

You are a fool. You will die, all of you. You with your self-righteousness, all your misguided followers. The girl. And your children. I will tear them from the womb where they grow. . . .

Julian jolted awake to find Lorelei's warm body spooned against his back. She was sleeping soundly, her breathing slow and steady. He rolled toward her and watched her for a few minutes, absorbing the familiar lines of her face, her soft smells, the sounds of her breathing. Finally he leaned forward to kiss her gently, tasting her mouth without waking her.

Reluctantly, he rose to get dressed.

Lucien wasn't in his office, so Julian went on to Aanu's room in the hospital wing. Lucien was, of course, there.

So was William.

Julian hesitated at the door. William sat in a chair next to Aanu's bed, where Aanu sat listening intently as William spoke. Lucien leaned against the wall, watching.

Apparently, William was teaching Aanu English. Or trying to. From the sound of things, it wasn't going very well.

Silence fell as Julian stepped into the room. Lucien pushed away from the wall and met him at the doorway, waving him back into the hall.

"What's up?" Julian asked.

"We're trying to get Aanu up to speed." Lucien laughed a little. "Not that there's much chance that'll actually happen. But Aanu can use the company."

"Where did William learn ancient Sumerian?"

"Ask him yourself." Lucien's gaze slid sideways, toward him.

Julian tried not to be irritated by Lucien's too-obvious subtext. "Yeah. I should talk to him."

"Lorelei says you're having difficulty accessing the Senior's memories of Ruha."

Well, at least he'd left the subtext behind. Text was always easier to deal with. "You think talking to William will help?"

"You've let this thing with William go on way too long, Julian. Get it past you. Particularly if it's keeping you from Ruha."

Julian wanted to argue, would have done anything to avoid the excruciatingly awkward confrontation he knew any heart-to-heart with William would be. But he couldn't justify cutting himself any slack, not with what he was demanding from the others. "All right," he said. "I'll talk to him. But it'll have to wait. We need to talk—all of us. I've been having dreams."

Lucien eyed him questioningly. "There's no time like the present."

He pushed the door open, and Julian followed him into Aanu's room.

"William," Lucien said in English. "Desist for a bit. We need to pow-wow." Then, to Aanu, he added, "The three of us need to talk. There are things you need to know."

Aanu sighed, obviously relieved. "This language of yours is very difficult. I need to rest, anyway."

William laughed. "I have to say, I'm getting something of a headache, as well. You're not the easiest student." He touched Aanu's hand. "I'll come back later."

Julian noted that, as William slid past him and out of the room, he avoided his gaze.

When the door closed behind William, Lucien gave him a wink. In English, he said, "I thought he and Aanu might hit it off."

"What are you saying?" Aanu said, his voice edgy. He'd seemed more at ease in William's presence.

"Nothing," said Lucien. "I was just being rude." He settled into a chair. "Now—we need to talk about Ialdaboth."

Aanu nodded. "Tell me what I need to know."

Julian spun out the story as best he could, fighting through the second-hand memories that allowed him to speak Aanu's language. Lucien stepped in from time to time, correcting his word choice or phrasing. Aanu listened attentively, becoming more and more grim as the story unfolded.

"Do we even know for sure what we'll be facing?" he asked finally. "Ialdaboth has been in hiding. Do we know why?"

Lucien steepled his fingers under his chin. "I killed him in Romania. It will have left him weak. He's regathering his strength."

"I've seen it in my dreams," Julian added. "I can feel the power he's gathering. Dark power. Death power."

"You should have killed him, Lucien, when the opportunity was there," said Aanu. "He was weak after you attacked him—the two of you together might have been able to destroy him."

Julian shook his head. "We didn't know where he was. Eventually, I realized he'd gone underground. But even with the connection he and I seem to have developed, I don't know exactly where he is."

"You should have hunted him down."

Aanu seemed to know an awful lot about what should have been done, Julian thought, especially for someone who had been dead for the last four thousand years of plot development. Biting back his irritation, he said, "That would have left this place too vulnerable. It was not an acceptable risk."

"We did everything we reasonably could," Lucien put in. "We took the information we gathered in Romania, gathered additional information from Rafael and Lilith. I believe that if we wanted to, we could invade Ialdaboth's stronghold directly and expect a high degree of success."

Aanu shrugged. "Then we should do it."

"No, we shouldn't." Julian's voice was firm and grim. "'A high degree of success' isn't enough. We have to eradicate him completely, before he destroys everything."

A moment of silence passed, during which Julian endured Aanu's judgmental regard.

Finally, slowly, Aanu said, "The Dark Children have existed longer than there have been vampires. Ialdaboth has existed as long as Belial and myself. Why is it so important now that he be eliminated?"

"The power Ialdaboth wields is different than it was in the past," said Julian. "It's stronger and much darker. This argument—this war—has become more than a mere philosophical conflict. It's good against evil. What he grows inside him could destroy everything good that ever existed. And he intends to do exactly that. We have to stop him."

"He feeds off evil," Lucien added. "The same way you and I feed off positive emotions, he feeds from negative ones. From hatred, war, pain. He foments it and teaches his children to foment it. So not only do they feed and kill without remorse, they cause as much pain as possible, and when they see an opportunity to cause mass chaos, they take it."

Aanu nodded. "He was sliding even four thousand years ago. I should have known something like this would be the result." He mulled a moment, then looked at Lucien. "Is it even possible to kill him?"

Lucien nodded. "I believe so, yes."

"Ialdaboth and Ruha conquered me, but I wasn't destroyed. As you see."

"Maybe if they had cut you into pieces instead of leaving your skeleton intact?" Julian offered. It was a quandary, he had to admit, but there had to be some way to kill these creatures, these First Demons. Otherwise what had been the point of his own transformation?

"There has to be more to it than that," said Lucien. He regarded Julian narrowly. "It has to do with you, with what you've become. It has to."

"Him?" Aanu protested. "He's just a vampire. And only eight centuries old."

Lucien shook his head. "No, Julian is more than a vampire. He drinks no blood, hasn't for over two hundred years. He eats solid food and can live in the sunlight. And his lover is pregnant with twins. His biological children."

Clearly astonished, Aanu looked at Julian. "But how—"

Julian started to reply, but Lucien waved him off.

"We'll tell you all about it later, when we have time. What's important now is that Julian can do one more thing vampires can't do. He can restore life to the mortally wounded. And we have yet to see the extent of his powers."

Comprehension washed over Aanu's features. "The one who feeds from life without diminishing it," he murmured.

"Yes," Lucien replied. "We wrote it in the *Book*. And the *Book* has the other answers we need, as well, I'm certain. But so much of it has been lost."

"The *Book*," Aanu repeated. He frowned, thoughtful. "There is something. I know what it is, what we need to know."

"Please tell us," said Julian.

Aanu shook his head. "I can't. Not yet. But I will." He stood. "I have it here, somewhere in my head. I have to go think until I find it." He went to the door. "Give me time."

Julian watched him go, then looked at Lucien. "That's something, then."

Lucien nodded. "Let's hope so." He slapped Julian's shoulder lightly, encouraging. "I'll talk to William. He'll be by to see you in a couple of hours. Then I think we'll be well on the way to getting this thing done."

Julian paced his living room, waiting for William, nervous to the point of nausea.

It was his own fault, of course, that he was so distraught over what was about to transpire. He'd put it off far too long. He should have dealt with it right up front. But he'd had other things on his mind, and it had been easier to shove the hard things aside, hoping they would remain irrelevant.

He should have known better. After eight-hundred-plus years of living, he at least should have learned that things he tried to ignore eventually came back to bite him in the ass.

Briefly, he wondered how much Lucien had told William—if William had some idea what was coming, or if this was all going to be a horrible revelation for him. Julian wasn't sure which would be worse.

He nearly jumped out of his skin when the knock finally came. Opening the door, he found William on the other side, looking even more nervous than he was.

"May I come in?" William asked.

Julian stepped aside. "Of course."

William eyed him warily as he entered. "Lucien told me. Some of it, anyway." He stopped, swung around to face him. "Why the hell didn't you talk to me about this a long time ago?"

Julian gave a short laugh. "Good question. I was just asking myself the same thing." He gathered himself, studying William. William frowned. The light caught the lenses of his glasses, making it difficult for a moment to see his eyes. "Have a seat," Julian said.

William sat, still watching him with obvious discomfort. "How much?" he asked cautiously. "How much do you know?"

With a sigh, Julian settled into another chair. "Everything. He gave me his memories with his blood."

William's eyes widened, then his expression hardened, his face closing on a myriad of emotions Julian was hard-put to read. Anger, shock, pain, embarrassment.

Julian looked away, feeling many of the same emotions, himself. "I'm sorry," he ventured. "This has been difficult for me, too."

"Why bring it up now?"

"I have to get to Ruha. He and the Senior were lovers several centuries ago. For some reason that I don't understand, I have to go through you to get to him."

William laughed a little, the expression on his face more wry than amused. "All the lovers filed in the same mental cabinet?"

"Something like that, apparently," Julian replied.

The room reeked with awkwardness. Suddenly Julian had no idea what he should do with his hands. Strange. He so rarely thought about his hands.

"How much of it have you . . . seen?" William said finally.

"Glimpses. I've shied away from it. It's too strange, seeing you and seeing . . . what he remembers." He dared a sideways glance, but William wasn't looking at him. "I'm sorry, William."

Now William did look at him, and something flared in his eyes. "Are you?"

"Yes. I am."

"For what, exactly?"

Taken slightly aback, Julian paused to consider. "For being . . . the way I was."

"And why were you that way?" William's voice had become tight and brittle. "Was there a real reason, or just plain old-fashioned homophobia?"

His tone made Julian inexplicably angry. But was he really angry, or did his reaction come from the Senior within him? That the question even occurred to him fueled his anger—and made him afraid. It was the thing that scared him the most—feeling as if someone else were living inside his body, affecting his thoughts, guiding his emotions.

Regardless of whose anger he felt, though, William didn't deserve it.

Carefully, Julian said, "When he died . . . you were so cold. Like you didn't give a shit. Then I found out what he was to you. What was that about?" The anger grew as he spoke, becoming harder to control.

William's taut expression had given way to surprise. He blinked a few times, and when he spoke his voice was soft. "He knew he was going to die. He told me to do whatever I had to do to protect myself. For all I knew, you were going to kill us all."

Julian frowned in thought as he began to understand. "Like when you tried to protect me with his bones, all over my desk, right after he died. I thought you were just being a suck-up."

"I was. It seemed expedient."

Julian swallowed and looked at the wall. "After that, when the rest of the memories started coming, the emotions—when I found out what you meant to him—" He stopped, swallowed again. "It was hard to like you. I felt like you had betrayed him. And he was me—sort of."

"I assure you," William said in strained tones, "I loved him."

It struck Julian suddenly that this was as hard for William as it was for him. Stupid—incredibly stupid—not to have realized that from the outset. He'd been so wrapped up in his own problems, and the problems of the enclave in general, that he hadn't even considered William's loss. His pain.

Julian dragged his gaze away from the wall and looked at William.

He was staring at a spot on the opposite wall. "But I was the one left behind, and that was harder," he said.

Yes, it would be, Julian thought. "I should have talked to you before," he said. It was just . . . so strange to me."

Silence settled for a moment, less strained than it had been.

Finally William said, "You have to go through the memories. You have to find what Ruha knew. Otherwise we die. Am I right?"

"Yes." And, at last, Julian understood what he needed to hear. "I need your permission."

William laughed dryly. "My permission? You need my permission to rummage through your own mind?"

When William finally looked in his direction, Julian caught and held his gaze. It was easier, now. "Those memories don't belong to me. They're his. Yours. When I go there, it's a violation."

William's jaw clenched, but he didn't look away. "Do what you have to do. You should have done it already, instead of wasting time with me."

"If we live, I still have to be able to look you in the eye. That's important to me."

"You need to learn to be more ruthless. We're not going to get through this if you act like a pushover."

Julian smiled a little. "I know. I'll try."

William's eyes were flinty. "Don't try," he said. "Just get it done."

They'd reached an understanding, Julian realized, but forgiveness for the months of evasion and awkwardness between them—and for killing his lover, however necessary it may have been—would likely be a long time coming.

"William, I'm sorry," he said.

William's face softened, but only a little. "I know."

There was little left to do, then, but watch William leave. When the door closed behind him, Julian leaned back in his chair and stared at the ceiling.

Four

He was ready. He was sure of it. With Lorelei holding his hand, Julian leaned back in their bed, closed his eyes, and once again dove deep into the vast sea of inherited memories.

His first discovery surprised him. The Senior's relationship with William had spanned nearly a century. That pool of memories hadn't appeared that deep the last time he'd tried to get past them. But maybe that was because a hundred years was nothing in the great expanse the Senior's lifetime.

Just go.

Lorelei's voice echoed in his head. She sounded impatient. Lorelei often sounded impatient these days. He couldn't really blame her. She was concerned about the babies. If he didn't clear the way for their safe future, nothing would be safe for any of them again.

So he went. Went through the whispered conversations with William, private moments in the dark, things he had no right to see, skirting around them as best he could, because in spite of William's admonition to "just do it," it felt wrong to be here.

Soon he was back fifty years, seventy-five. . . . He heard Ruha's name drift by in a bubble and followed it.

You loved him, didn't you—Ruha? William's voice.

Until he changed, came the Senior's answer.

What changed him?

He changed himself. Chose a different path.

What happened to him?

I don't know. If you believe the legends, he's dead, or as close to dead as we can become, and has been for a long time.

He followed that thread, and it led him deeper. He fell all the way through, to a hundred and twelve years past, when the Senior found William feeding on drunks and criminals in Manhattan alleyways, and had taken him in. Somehow, that event was connected directly to Ruha, the memories of the earlier relationship being revisited and strengthened in the memories of William.

That explained the connection, then, and the reason he hadn't been able to find Ruha without dealing with William. The Senior's mind had set up the two relationships in a continuum, one blending a little into the other in spite of the space of several centuries between them.

Doesn't he have a name?

Lorelei again, though fainter than before.

A name?

It's the Senior. Always just the Senior. He must have had a name at some point. Probably several.

A strange question, he thought. It hadn't occurred to him to wonder. She was right, but whatever names the Senior had carried over his ten thousand years were buried deep. There were more important things to look for at the moment.

As he gently pushed Lorelei's question aside, he felt her mild amusement. *Just wondering.*

I love you. He wasn't sure why he felt the need to tell her that, but it seemed necessary. He made sure she'd heard him.

Then he jumped. With faith and Lorelei's reassuring presence shadowing him, he plunged through millennia, all the way from the beginning of the Senior's relationship with William to the end of his relationship with Ruha.

I can't stay with you if you take this path, and I will not follow you. The last thing the Senior had said to Ruha, before Ruha had left to join Ialdaboth.

And Ruha's reply—*You are a fool.*

The pain in that moment was so intense he thought he would weep with it. He pulled himself away, pushed deeper—and found yet another barrier.

More pain. The agony of Ruha's leaving had colored every other moment of their centuries-long union. Even the pleasant memories hurt.

It wasn't you. This isn't your pain.

Floundering in the depths of that anguish, he'd nearly forgotten Lorelei was with him. *But I can feel it. It's like knives,* he told her.

I can help. Let me take some of it.

No . . . the babies . . .

He plunged in alone, sadness a murky shroud around him. It was like trudging through a bog, thick and noxious. It reminded him of Ialdaboth's black, swarming insect power. The dense wretchedness of the Senior's grief, the crackling, crawling, overwhelming miasma of Ialdaboth's power—they seemed complementary in some way. But he didn't know if that meant there was a connection between the ancient vampire and the Demon, or if his mind was taking things it didn't understand and constructing interpretations based on similar metaphors.

Either way, it hurt.

Hold on to me.

Lorelei. His anchor. But he wasn't sure she would be enough.

Of course I'm enough. Just find what you need and get the hell out.

Trust her to boil the situation down to the essentials. And she was right. He didn't have to go through every single memory. He just had to find what he needed, take it, and leave.

Centuries. Over a millennia, they had been together, and no sort of order to the memories of those years. Then, abruptly the earliest memories bobbed to the top, and a strong truth leaped out, vivid with sensation and emotion.

Ruha had made the Senior. Ten thousand years ago, perhaps before any other blood-child had ever been created, Ruha had made the Senior.

He was the first vampire? Lorelei's presence radiated perplexity.

He told me he was. The other brothers, though, they would have made Children, as well. No way to know who did it first.

What made them think of it?

She had drifted into irrelevance again, he realized.

I mean, when do you think, "Hey, if I sucked his blood and then he sucked mine, what would happen?"

It's an instinct. He passed the thought to her, then brushed the rest of that line of questioning aside. He needed to concentrate.

Is it there? Can you see it?

If you'd shut up a minute, maybe.

She subsided, unoffended. Mentally, he caressed her, assured himself once again of her presence. Oddly, he suddenly felt the babies, small bundles of random emotion, some of which was fear, as Lorelei had told him. That more than anything else made him gather himself for another dive.

The end of Ruha's presence in the Senior's life was tied to the beginning, like the snake that ate its own tail, and all the bits in the middle seemed to be strung randomly along that continuum. He found moments of William there, as well, as if the two relationships had become inextricably linked.

So how was he to find what he needed? The language here was old, older even than the one he'd used to communicate with Aanu, and that made it even more difficult to find his way. Panic rushed through him. Surely, he would lose himself here, in the net of language and memory, lost in grammar as thoroughly as he was lost in this alien personality. . . .

I'm still here. Get yourself together.

The blast of English and irritation grounded him again.

Just look harder, find what you need, and get out. I have to pee.

And there it was. All at once, written in bright letters like fire across his interior vision. Then in words, whispered in the darkness of a tent or some small house that smelled of goat-leather.

There were visions. I think all of us had them, all of the four brothers. Belial and Aanu have gone missing, but wherever they are, they must have felt this, too.

That's it! Lorelei broke in.

I know. Just a minute. Let me get it all.

She subsided apologetically, and he continued to pick his way carefully through the gaps of personality, language, and sheer time.

I saw things. Heard words. Most of it made no sense, but somehow I knew it was important. It woke me out of sleep, then forced me into it again, over and over, night after night.

He felt the Senior's concern, his curiosity. He felt male skin under his fingers, a soft caress to Ruha's arm. Ruha's face looked into his, pained. Craggy features, blue eyes, like Lucien. Like Aanu and Ialdaboth.

Tell me. Was that the Senior, speaking to Ruha all those centuries before, or was it him, demanding what he needed from the memories inside his own skull?

There is power in the light, but also in the dark. Either power may shatter the other. The light, however, is more willing to die. The light, then is the stronger. The power of light, layered and joined, melded in the willingness to lose itself, can conquer anything.

There was more, but he knew the rest was irrelevant. He'd read the other bits before, in the reconstruction of the *Book* the Senior had worked on before he himself had taken over. That piece, though, those few lines, those he had never seen before. It fit into the puzzle started by Lucien.

We have it.

Lorelei spoke softly, the impatience mostly gone. *That's it. We're almost there. We've nearly won.*

Not quite. There will be tears before it's over. Slowly, he swam upward, through the ocean of alien memories, until he crossed the border into his own and he was, once again, himself.

And Julian opened his eyes and looked at Lorelei, sitting next to him, and he saw in her face that she understood.

He slept for a time, exhausted from his efforts. Some hours later, though, he woke abruptly to find Lorelei asleep next to him and Lucien bent over his bed.

"Wake up," Lucien murmured.

Julian swung out of the bed and followed Lucien into the living room. "What is it?" he asked, then realized they weren't alone. Aanu sat hunched in a chair, looking nearly as worn out as he had felt awhile ago, when he'd come up from the depths of the Senior's memories.

"You found it," he stated flatly in the language Aanu understood.

Aanu gave a single nod. "As did you."

"Yes."

"Let's share," said Lucien dryly.

Aanu shook his head slowly. "The dreams. They were so broken— You and I both had them, Lucien, you remember."

"I remember."

Julian was tempted to tell him to get on with it, but he cautioned himself to patience and let Aanu work through the story. Like his own search for answers, it had to be a process.

Aanu went on, haltingly. "The Black Sea flood—it was massive, deadly. It's no surprise they still write about it. Lucien and I were there. We tried to save some of the people, but it was too late. And the mud took us. Layers and layers of it, thick and black, and it killed us. And we dreamed."

"You dreamed the *Book.*"

"Yes. And we wrote down what we could remember, what we could make sense of. The dreams were—"

When he broke off, Lucien said, in English. "Freaky. Weirdest thing I've ever experienced." Then to Aanu, "Strange. Disturbing."

"Yes," Aanu agreed. "Some of it was lost simply in the writing of it. More was lost when the Dark Children destroyed what we had done. But I found the piece I was looking for."

Julian's impatience spiked again, but he kept his voice level. "What is it?"

"The power . . ." Aanu trailed off, then gathered the words again.

"The power in the life. The power in the life can defeat any power forged in death. The one who takes his life without diminishing the lives of others may channel the life of those who drink life from the air. The giving of the life that cannot end can end the life that feeds from death."

Lucien frowned. Julian nodded. "It fits."

"Does it?" said Lucien.

"It does." He recited what he'd found in the depths of his inherited memories, and Lucien nodded.

"We have an answer, then." His voice was grim.

"We do," said Aanu. He stood, walked toward the door. "I need to tell William."

Five

"It's time, Jarod," Julian said gently, conscious that, in using the doctor's name, he was breaking down yet another barrier. And about time, too, under the circumstances. He knew Jarod understood the gravity of the situation, and what would have to happen now, but he didn't know how the other man could face it. He didn't think he could. "We need to draw him out."

Jarod nodded. "We've been preparing."

"But are *you* prepared?" Lucien put in.

Jarod looked at the floor, studiously avoiding eye contact with anyone else in the room. "No, I'm not," he said quietly. "But I think she is."

Julian nodded. "Then let's do it."

He had left this part of the larger plan in Jarod's hands, and he wasn't surprised at how efficiently the doctor had dealt with it. Still, the thoroughness of the preparations came as a bit of a shock.

Uncomfortable with the possibility of confronting Ialdaboth in the hospital wing, Jarod had fortified a cave-like room several levels below the currently inhabited areas of the Underground. The magic was thick and dark down here, enough to make Julian's scalp prickle, and the place smelled of damp rock and vampires. Now that he'd broken some of the barriers, the Senior's memories were coming more easily to him, and he knew the place was one of the first the enclave had used—part of the original habitation the Senior had dug out and fortified, with Ruha's help.

Jarod had equipped the cave to contain Lilith when they re-opened her connection to Ialdaboth. A bed furnished with chains and cuffs, a tranquilizer gun leaning against the wall next to it—Julian could hardly bear to look at it, understanding what it must have cost Jarod to make these arrangements, knowing he might have to use them against his lover. But Lilith, following Jarod into the low-ceilinged, somewhat claustrophobic space, smiled at him and kissed his cheek.

"Nice work," she told him. "This should do it."

"How long has she been off the juice?" Lucien asked.

Lilith's consumption of Jarod's blood was, they had realized, the only thing keeping Ialdaboth from using the bond he established with his blood Children, of which Lilith was one.

Jarod looked at his watch. "Not quite an hour. It won't have worked out of her system yet."

Lilith settled onto the bed, examining the manacles attached to the headboard. "Better safe than sorry." She slanted a look at the doctor. "Tie me up, baby."

"Do you two need to be alone?" asked Lucien with a grin.

Julian laughed a little, glad somebody could handle the situation with some humor. He certainly couldn't, not knowing what he was going to have to do to win this war.

"Not really," Lilith answered. "I'm kind of an exhibitionist at heart." But then she looked at Jarod, and a little shimmer of fear, meant for her lover's eyes only, appeared in her gaze.

Julian looked away. He heard the manacles click as Jarod fastened them. When he looked back, Lilith was securely restrained, metal around her wrists and ankles, leather straps across her body.

"You okay?" Jarod asked her.

"I'm good."

"Anything else?" Lucien said. "Anything we've forgotten?"

"No, that's it." Julian supplied the answer. "Now we wait."

He arranged for alternating shifts, so that at least one of the three strongest of them—Lucien, Aanu, or himself—would be on hand at all times. He took the first watch, until daylight came and Lilith slipped into the Sleep.

Lucien arrived just as she faded into complete unconsciousness.

"Do you think we need to watch during the day?" Julian asked him.

"I think we need to take every precaution," Lucien answered and took his place in the chair next to the bed. "When did Jarod leave?"

"About an hour ago. He'll be back." Julian bent backwards, feeling his spine crack. "I'm going to see Lorelei. Call me if you need me."

He used the time with Lorelei to resettle himself. He was edgy, agitated, to the point where his skin felt like it no longer belonged to him. A cigarette would have been heaven right then, he thought. Or sex. Too bad he'd had to give up both of them. But stretching out next to Lorelei on the bed, spooning against her, helped.

Lorelei had questions, though, which didn't help at all. "Your power, then, allows you to channel their power? So you can kill Ialdaboth?"

"That appears to be the case, yes." She deserved honest answers. He just didn't want to think about what he knew was coming.

"Will it kill them?"

And that, of course, was the biggest of the questions he didn't want to consider.

"I don't know."

She nestled into him, seeming to understand his reticence, and took his hands, folded them together over her stomach. Over their children.

Several hours later, feeling more at peace, Julian returned to Lilith's cave. Lucien still sat watching.

"Aanu's sitting next watch," Lucien said as Julian took a seat. "You're not due back for ages."

Julian shrugged. "I know." He looked at Lilith. She lay still and pale, her platinum hair spread over the pillow. The cuffs and straps held her securely to the bed. Julian couldn't help wondering if it was really necessary to confine her so securely, but he supposed they had to take every precaution, even if it seemed like overkill. Though he had a feeling that, when Ialdaboth finally showed himself, the straps and chains would be not an overreaction but, rather, inconsequential.

"Where's Aanu now?" he said after a moment.

"With William, I suppose." Lucien, too, studied Lilith's inert form.

"It's not fair for him to have to face this," Julian said, the words bursting from his mouth; they'd been hammering in his head for the past three hours. "It just isn't fair, dammit. Not so soon after waking up."

"Not fair for me, either," Lucien added flatly. "I just found Vivian."

He had thought of that, too. After centuries of separation had interrupted the beginnings of a love affair between Lucien and Vivian, they'd found each other again only a few months ago.

"I know," said Julian.

"We don't know for sure that's how it'll go, though." Lucien tore his gaze away from Lilith and looked at him. "You might be misreading it. I mean, I think you have the basics right, as far as channeling the power, concentrating it, using it as a weapon. But there's nothing there, not in any of those passages, to state exactly what happens to me or Aanu—or even to you."

"True." And maybe he could hold on to that, Julian supposed, make it into a lifeline. If he could hope that he didn't have to actually . . . Shit, he couldn't even think the words.

He'd better hope he could do the deed, though, or they were all dead.

"It's all right, you know." Lucien's voice was soft, sincere. "Twelve thousand years. It's enough."

"But Vivian—"

"I know. That's the only thing."

They were silent for a time. Outside, darkness had begun to fall. Julian could still sense it, even though it no longer forced him to sleep.

"But what about—" Julian began, then stopped.

Because Lilith had opened her eyes and her mouth, and into the silence he had left behind, she said in a voice that sounded not at all like her own, "He's coming."

Then she writhed, convulsed on the bed, her body twisting in spasms. Julian shot to his feet, headed for the door. "I'll get Jarod."

By the time Julian returned with Jarod, Lilith had stopped convulsing, but she lay stiff on the bed, open eyes staring blankly at the ceiling.

"What happened?" Jarod asked Lucien.

"The seizures stopped. She didn't say anything else."

Jarod bent over Lilith's rigid body, examining her. Julian couldn't believe his calm. He was the consummate professional, even though the patient was his lover. But then he straightened, took off his glasses, and wiped them on his sweater with hands that were less than steady.

"She seems to be coming out of it." Jarod's voice was even. "I don't want to touch her, though, until she seems to be more lucid."

Lilith's stiffened posture had softened a little already, and, suddenly, she went limp, falling back onto the bed. Startled, Julian watched her closely. She rolled her head to one side, grinning at the doctor, her fangs protruding sharp and white. Whatever personality lay in those eyes, it wasn't Lilith. Not totally, not yet.

"Maybe a few more minutes," said Jarod, with only the faintest shiver in his voice. He turned to Julian, visibly gathering himself. "You found the answers? You know what to do when he comes?"

"Yes." He looked at Lucien. He felt as if he should say more . . . but what more was there? Goodbye?

"We can do this," said Lucien. "We can kill Ialdaboth."

Jarod gave a terse nod. "And I'm sure there's a little more to it than that, but I don't think I want to hear it." He looked at Lilith. She had closed her eyes again, and when she spoke, the voice was her own.

"Jarod."

He went to her, sat on the bed. His hands, still trembling, traced over hers, tangling in her fingers. "It's okay. It's okay."

Julian exchanged a glance with Lucien, and, as one, they left the room.

Julian returned to Lorelei, afraid down to his bones that it would be the last time he ever saw her. So, of course, the first thing she did was force him to face that very fear.

"How do you think this will go?" she said. "When he comes . . . when they call you . . . will you come back to me?"

"I will." He said it firmly.

"If you can." Her voice shook, broke a little.

He looked deep into the wide blue of her eyes, acknowledging the truth with his silence. After a moment he pulled him to her, held her, let his hands memorize all the shapes of her.

"You should go back," she told him after a time.

"Yes." He pulled her closer, nestling her into him. Her lips moved softly against his face as she tasted his skin. Then, gently, she pushed him away.

"Go. I'll be here when it's over."

He looked at her a moment longer, taking her in. Then, with a strangled sound he couldn't contain, he dragged her to him and kissed her—hard, frantic. But when he let her go, he didn't linger for one last kiss or caress. Instead, he left her, and he went to stand guard with Lucien and Aanu.

He was thinking of Lorelei—was there really anything else to think about?—when it finally happened. They were all there by then—Lucien and Jarod sitting near him, and Aanu sitting on the floor against the far wall with William beside him. Julian had told Jarod and William to leave, but they both refused.

One instant, it was silent, even calm, all of them lost and quiet in their own thoughts. Then, on the bed where she had slept for nearly three hours unmoving, curled onto her left side, Lilith suddenly rolled onto her back. Her mouth opened first, then her eyes, blank and staring.

Julian rose slowly from his chair. The air in the room tingled with power, dark and noxious. He knew that power, had felt it in his dreams, sticky and clinging, black and full of vile, unnamable things that crawled and chewed. He felt his own power rise to meet it, but he reined it in. It wasn't time. Not quite.

And so Ialdaboth came, spilling out of Lilith, out of her mouth and eyes, black and broken, in bits like insects that swarmed through the air together in a mass. The bits built one upon the other, stacking and meshing, until a figure began to form.

Out of the corner of his eye, Julian saw Lucien move toward his right side, until they stood shoulder-to-shoulder. Aanu joined them, clearly reluctant, glancing at William. Finally, he squared his shoulders, then came to stand at his left side.

They were ready. Or so Julian hoped. He flexed his fingers, trying to understand the nuances of the power he felt swarming and eddying around him.

Six feet in front of them, the black power coalesced. Ialdaboth had found his purchase on reality and was bringing all his parts together. Julian had never imagined such magic, though he'd felt hints of it in his dreams. So this was what one could learn, he thought, if one was willing to feed on death. Not an un-useful skill, but not one he envied. He had his own power, and he felt it shiver along his skin, growing, readying itself, so dense it felt like a second skin. Before this was over, when he'd done what he had to do, it would be even stronger. Strong enough to counter the black, shattered, insectile power uniting before him.

The weaving together of pieces picked up speed, until, at last, Ialdaboth's form appeared whole. They were of a height, the three half-brothers, with similarly craggy features and blue eyes. Julian looked from one to the other, seeing the similarities, the differences. Lucien's and Aanu's calm, placid faces seemed bland and useless next to the ferocity of Ialdaboth. But Julian knew what lay behind their outward tranquility, and he readied himself for it.

Ialdaboth flung out his arms, flexing his newly re-formed body. "Three against one," he said, his voice airy at first, then gaining strength as his throat knitted fully. "You don't believe in fair odds, do you?"

"Right now we pretty much believe in just kicking your ass," Julian said. He reached toward Lucien, toward Aanu, clasping their hands. And as he did, for the first time, he believed this could work. This could be the end of it, once and for all.

Except, perhaps, not for all.

But if he thought now about the likely cost of victory, he wouldn't be able to function. And Ialdaboth would win.

Not an option.

He tightened his grip on the large, warm hands he held in his own and felt the power move toward him. Down through the First Demons' bodies, surging from their hearts, down their arms and out of their hands—and into him.

His vision blurred as it hit him. Gold from Lucien, silver from Aanu, the power came from the depths of them, the power that allowed them to feed from the life force of a human being. Soul-power, the source of it the primal energy of their own lives.

He focused. Leveled his vision and his attention on Ialdaboth, at the same time he let his own power uncoil inside him and draw in the power Aanu and Lucien were feeding him. It was instinctive, all coming together without his conscious control, the three power masses joining, coiling into a single entity inside him. It was huge. It was alive, swirling and pulsing in his chest.

It was too much.

He couldn't hold it, certainly couldn't control it. But neither could he stop it. It worked itself deep into the middle of his body, beating there. It wanted to burst out of him, but it wasn't time. Not yet. It coiled inside, waiting.

He drew himself straight, barely aware of his surroundings, a dimness in his vision making it hard to tell where he was. Or who he was. There was no "self." No "Julian." There was only power. Ready. Light and heat and purity.

Ialdaboth struck. His power flew out of his eyes and his mouth in a black column, viscous and thick, spinning away from Ialdaboth. Julian watched it come, slamming straight toward him like a battering ram. It hit him hard in the chest. The impact jolted him, making his body shudder in uncontrollable spasms. But it didn't break him.

Ialdaboth was giving his all. Vaguely, Julian realized the power inside him, the life force that had come from Lucien and Aanu, seemed to know instinctively what Ialdaboth could and would do, seemed able to judge their brother's power on a deeper level than he could have judged it. Ialdaboth's life force, the miasma of evil he had allowed his soul to become, all of it flowed out of him in a last-ditch effort to conquer. But as it struck him, Julian felt the mass of power inside him rise, so huge, so primal, so bright and intense he could barely contain it, much less control it.

Repelled.

And then absorbed.

Ialdaboth's eyes widened in surprise as his black column began to disappear into his enemy's body.

Julian shuddered, his body wracked with something so far beyond pain that his nerves could only interpret it as ecstasy. This would be his death. It had to be.

But he wasn't dying. And all of the evil First Demon's twisted power was inside of him, there with his own power, born of his reconstituted blood; and Lucien's, born of twelve thousand years of life and all he had learned in that time; and Aanu's, born as was Lucien's but given four thousand years to sleep. And as Ialdaboth's power, black and sickened, touched the purity of the others, it cleared, joined with them. And was healed. Thus transformed and melded, the power soared inside him until it filled him so completely, he had no knowledge or awareness of anything else.

He hung on with everything he had, clinging to his last shred of self-awareness. Only in that did he have any control over the raw force that he had become.

Suddenly, he felt Aanu, then Lucien, drop to their knees on either side of him, as the greedy demands of his own power wrung them dry. Aanu's hand slid from his, then Lucien's. They both gasped as they hit the floor.

He had killed them. He'd known it would happen, as had they. They had given him everything they had, because they knew he would have to use it; and he had taken it, because he had known there was no other way. He had simply bled them to death. And now . . . now he would do the same to himself.

He raised his hands, turned his palms toward Ialdaboth.

"You made a very big mistake," he said. His voice echoed in his own head, the words seeming to come from everywhere at once. "If you had read the *Book*, instead of destroying it, you would have seen this coming."

He curled his fingers and turned his palms toward the ceiling, and the last smoky black tendrils of Ialdaboth's soul came to him as if summoned, snagged on his fingers, roped up his arms, moved downward to join the already incomprehensible force boiling in his chest.

He harvested, gathered, and spun as Ialdaboth writhed, helpless. And the part that was still him thought, *This isn't possible.* One creature couldn't hold and control this much energy. But the part that was no longer him knew differently, knew that whatever he had become, he could do this. It terrified him, but at the same time he exulted in it. The power moving inside him brought ecstasy more intense than anything he had ever experienced.

Suddenly Ialdaboth jerked backward as the last wispy thread tore loose and snapped across the room to its new owner. He was empty and broken, powerless. He caught himself, straightened, and stared at his nemesis through blank eyes. For the first time in his twelve thousand years, the first-born of the First Demons was only a man.

"You're aware this is over now," Julian said, and this time his voice felt more like his own. "You may speak if you like. I'll give you the time." He pressed his hands to his chest, waiting. . . .

Ialdaboth's face went lax, and there was fear in his eyes. "You want me to beg for forgiveness? Or for my life?"

"I don't care what you do," Julian said. "I just thought it would be the right thing to do, to give you time to speak."

Ialdaboth spat. "Fuck you."

"All right, then," said Julian, and lifted his hands away from his chest, and let the power go.

It burst out of him, a huge, violent wall of shining, brilliant light. *Now I'm dead,* he thought. *A body can't explode and still live.*

But he could hear his heart beating, and the hand that grabbed the chair behind him for support was his own. And it was through his own eyes that he watched the monstrous, dazzling mountain of energy he'd unleashed slam into Ialdaboth. It crashed into his face and chest, covering him in a shimmer of gold-white light. It encased him, head to foot, and he convulsed helplessly within it. His skin turned gold, then shattered, until his skeleton hung suspended in the aura of light. Finally that shuddered, as well, broke into a man-shaped form of glittering dust, and the luminous mountain of power contracted, gathering the shimmery remains into itself.

Then it turned. Julian stood rooted as it rushed toward him. He heard himself howl when it hit him, and he staggered as it flooded back into him. But it felt smaller now, no larger than his own soul, and he was able to accept it with a deep, gasping breath and a single convulsion of something that was not quite pain. He regained his balance, swallowed, breathed.

He was alive. More than alive. He was himself again.

Quickly, he dropped to his knees beside Lucien and Aanu. Had he left them anything? Anything at all? He only needed half a heartbeat.

Gently, he touched Lucien's chest. He had known him longer, was more familiar with the patterns and rhythms of his energies. He felt nothing. But had he drained Lucien, or was he himself too drained to be of any use? He couldn't tell. Channeling that massive power had taken more from him than he'd ever dreamed he could give. It would regenerate—somehow he knew that—but he didn't know how long it would take. And he needed something *now*. Otherwise neither Lucien nor Aanu would ever breathe again.

He pressed his hand harder into Lucien's chest, seeking a heartbeat. But also seeking something else, something he wasn't completely sure of. A new instinct had taken over. It made him lean closer, until finally his face lay against his hand, then he moved his hand away, pressing his ear against the place where Lucien's heartbeat should have been. He laid his palms flat on Lucien's chest, closed his eyes.

There. Faint, almost beyond his ability to sense it. A spark of something.

He reached for it, wrapped his own energies around it.

He had no idea how or why this worked, but he knew it did. And he knew it was his power, unlike any power any creature on earth had ever wielded. Later, when he could afford the time, he'd let himself marvel at it. Maybe even be humbled by it. Right now, he could only rejoice in his ability to sense that spark of life left inside this man, his friend, whom he'd been so certain he'd lost.

That spark, that tiny ember of near-life, seemed to grow even as he touched it. It sought him, reached for him, and he let his power enfold it.

Nestled in that light, the spark grew. He nurtured it as best he could—he hadn't quite gotten the feel for this new energy of his yet, all its permutations and possibilities. He could only ride with it, let it carry him where it needed to go. Until, finally, he felt something stir under his ear, heard the vague and trembling beginnings of a heartbeat.

And suddenly he knew. Understood what had happened, what had changed. Lucien was alive, but he had been changed. He had power that could restore Lucien's life, but not his immortality. There just hadn't been enough of him left.

Julian forced away the surge of regret that threatened his concentration. He nursed the growing spark of life carefully for a few more moments, until he was certain it would not go out if he left it. Then he shifted his attention to Aanu.

Again, the tiny flame, the barely distinguishable spark. It was enough to find, to nurture, to feed from and carefully augment, layer by glittering layer, until Aanu, too, breathed again.

The effort should have drained him, but it didn't. Instead, he realized as he leaned away from Aanu, he felt stronger, more focused. Full of light and power, as if nothing had been taken from him, but only absorbed.

Drawing a deep breath, he sat back and scanned the room to see Lilith, Jarod, and William all huddled on Lilith's bed, all looking at him, expectant.

"Are they . . ." Jarod ventured.

"They're alive," Julian answered. He touched Lucien's chest again, assessing the life force pulsing there. It was more than just the heartbeat—it was everything that made Lucien alive. It had grown, strengthened, even since he had finished his careful tending. "They're alive," he said again, reminding himself. Now that he could think again, all he could summon was sadness. Why would they have to pay such a price, when he had paid nothing? Indeed, had become stronger because of their sacrifice? It wasn't right.

They could chose to be Turned, to become vampires—but Julian didn't think either of them would. But even if they did choose that path, they would never again be what they had been. That power, that near-limitless indestructibility, was gone forever. The First Demons were gone.

"He's gone," said Lilith suddenly. "Ialdaboth. He's gone. He's dead." She smiled, laughed, then abruptly began to cry. "He's not in my head anymore. He's dead. Really, truly dead."

Jarod put his arm around her.

Lucien moved a little on the floor, and Julian leaned toward him. Slowly, Lucien opened his eyes.

"Hey," he said, and smiled a little. "I'm alive." He sat up, and Julian moved to help him. Lucien lifted his hands and looked at them. "I'm alive. That's so cool."

And, finally, Julian felt a wash of peace, of accomplishment, come over him. It was over.

* * *

It seemed too mundane to Julian, meeting in their usual configuration in his office only hours after he had torn the souls out of the last two First Demons. But that was what they did, because it was what they had always done. It was familiar.

Aanu sat with his head bent, his hand against his chest. "My heart beats differently," he said, his tone more than a little perplexed. He looked up at Lucien. "Does yours?"

Lucien put his hand against his chest. "Yes. Faster. A little louder, I think." He shook his head a little, smiled. "It's interesting, don't you think?"

"We're going to die," said Aanu. "We're actually going to die."
Lucien shrugged. "Well, not this afternoon."

Aanu grinned. "No, I suspect not."

Jarod took off his glasses and wiped the lenses on his shirttail. "What about you, Julian? Have there been any changes?"

He had examined both Aanu and Lucien, pronouncing them both fit and healthy, but quite mortal. Julian wasn't certain how the doctor had made that determination—something in their blood, perhaps—but it had only been confirmation of what all three of them already knew.

"I feel stronger," he said reluctantly. Lorelei laid a hand on his shoulder, but he found no comfort in her touch. "It shouldn't be this way," he said. "I should have lost something, too."

"It's your power," said Lucien gently. "That's what it says in the *Book*, though not very clearly or explicitly. Your gift is to give life back."

"But when—and to whom?" That was the hardest part, he thought. A gift it was, a profoundly powerful gift, but who the hell was he to decide who was worthy of it? Though he had yet to explore the limits and depths of the power, he might conceivably be able to raise the dead, make vampires mortal, make mortals immortal. Just who was he to be given that kind of strength—or responsibility?

"You start with the vampires," Lucien said. "The power came to a vampire. Therefore, it's meant for the vampire community. Others can follow your lead, become something other than bloodsuckers. We live on life—all of us do—but your way doesn't demand death. There are options now, different paths we can take. Mortality for the Children, courtesy of the good doctor, here. Possibly mortality even for the adults, by using some aspect of your powers." He shook his head. "Everything's going to change. I hope I'm here to see at least some of it."

"I'm sorry," said Julian.

"Don't be." Lucien shook his head again, his expression a mix of wonder and bewilderment. "Everything's going to change. Even the Dark Children will have a chance to be saved. And I get to stay with Vivian for a while. It really couldn't get much better than that."

Julian looked at Aanu, who had sat quietly through the exchange. Julian had no idea how much of the conversation Lucien's brother had been able to understand. In Sumerian, he said, "What about you? Are you all right?"

"Yes." Aanu pressed his hand more firmly against his chest.

246 *Vampire Apocalypse Book Two: Apotheosis*

"It's a different sound but a lovely one. And I, too, may live the rest of my life in happiness."

"Old age," said Lucien, then lapsed into English. "I don't care what Vivian says. I think it's gonna be cool."

Epilogue

Lorelei's hand clenched hard on Julian's, until he thought his fingers would snap. His other hand pressed against the huge, round mound of her belly as she strained with the burden her body carried. "Okay, stop at the end of this contraction." Jarod's voice was steady.

He sounded almost as if he'd specialized in the delivery of babies, Julian thought, rather than in the study of blood. They'd discussed the idea of having Lorelei deliver in a hospital, with a regular obstetrician, but she had balked, afraid they might see something untoward about the babies and try to take them away.

"I'm not stopping," Lorelei snarled between clenched teeth. "I want these things out of me."

"Just wait for the next contraction," said the doctor gently. "I want to be sure the babies are situated right."

As he checked the position of the first baby's head, Julian watched, caught up in the wonder of seeing even this small portion of his child. Lorelei's belly tensed again, and Jarod pressed his fingers against the baby's crown.

"Go ahead. Push. I'll keep it from going too fast."

The baby had other ideas, though, and in spite of the doctor's guiding hand, it slithered out after two more gargantuan efforts from its mother. *His* mother, Julian noted as the doctor passed the slimy, blood-streaked form into his hands.

"Now, wait just a minute for me, Lorelei. Breathe through the next contraction." The doctor quickly clipped the first baby's umbilical cord and clamped it off. "Get him on a towel over there, Julian. Wrap him up and dry him off a little. We'll give him to Lorelei as soon as she's done."

Lorelei's silence worried Julian. She should have been swearing profusely by now. He hoped she was just tired. He wrapped the baby in a soft towel and held him where she could see him, while Jarod coached her through the second delivery. She looked all right—in fact, she was swearing quite eloquently with her eyes.

"It's a girl!" the doctor announced finally. He handed the second baby to Lorelei, who, Julian noticed with some surprise, was crying.

"She's beautiful," she said. "Don't just stand there, Julian. Get her a blanket."

He did. When he came back to wrap the baby, Lorelei already had her at her breast, and the little girl was suckling happily.

"Give me the other one," said Lorelei. "Two boobs, two babies—it comes out even."

It took her a matter of moments to settle them both into position, one at each breast, both content and drifting off to sleep. Julian settled onto the edge of the bed and touched his daughter's head, then his son's. Eight hundred years of life, and he'd never before seen such a miracle.

"Do you have names?" the doctor asked.

"Michaela," said Lorelei. "Michaela, my little girl, and Gabriel my sweet little boy."

"Angel names," said Julian. "We thought it made a nice change from all the demon ones."

"Good call." Jarod rubbed at his eyes.

Some tears there, too, Julian believed. "So . . ." he ventured. "Did you notice anything unusual?"

Jarod shook his head. "Just babies, Julian. Just gorgeous, healthy babies."

Lorelei peered closely into Michaela's eyes. "Lucien said they weren't human."

Does it matter?" Julian asked, tracing a finger over Gabriel's shoulder.

Lorelei gave him with a watery smile. "No," she said. "We got exactly what we wanted."

Smiling in return, Julian kissed her forehead. "Yes, I think we did."

Printed in the United States
R317700001B/R3177PG15566X00007B/67